# The Last Rendezvous

# The Last Rendezvous

A NOVEL

## Anne Plantagenet

TRANSLATED FROM THE FRENCH
BY WILLARD WOOD

OTHER PRESS · NEW YORK

*Ouvrage publié avec le concours du Ministère français chargé de la Culture—Centre national du livre.*

This work has been published with the support of the Centre National du Livre of the French Ministry of Culture.

Production Editor: Yvonne E. Cárdenas

Book design: Simon M. Sullivan

This book was set in 10.75 pt Janson by Alpha Design & Composition of Pittsfield, NH.

10 9 8 7 6 5 4 3 2 1

LIBRARY OF CONGRESS CATALOGING-IN-PUBLICATION PATA

Plantagenet, Anne, 1972-
[Seule au rendez-vous. English]
The last rendezvous / by Anne Plantagenet ; translated from the French by Willard Wood.
p. cm.
ISBN 978-1-59051-278-4 (pbk.) —ISBN 978-1-59051-372-9 (e-book)
1. Desbordes-Valmore, Marceline, 1786–1859—Fiction.   I. Wood, Willard.   II. Title.
PQ2676.L268S4813   2009
843'.914—dc22   2009023472

*To Paris, Pont de la Tournelle*

*The Last Rendezvous*

SPENT THE AFTERNOON with Henri. Again the same vertigo, as though walking an exposed ridge and not knowing which side to fall on, a wild commotion in my chest. On the rue des Saints-Pères I teeter along the sidewalk. Whatever choice I make will be the wrong one anyway, and the options terrify me. Shall I jump feetfirst into the abyss? Shall I launch myself into the wide tomorrow with all the little caskets stacked up in me? Not surprising that I should feel such a tumult inside, a continuous uproar that addles my sleep and churns my stomach. I can bear it no longer. Even breathing hurts. The air, or is it just our love, is heavy beyond belief for the month of March in Paris.

Henri burrows into himself to get away from me, while I can find no avenue of flight. Nor am I certain of wanting to escape. How helpless I feel, how humiliated, to love a man who has renounced everything, who forbids himself the slightest emotion, and who takes refuge in his pain! Less than a year has passed, and already the mystery that bound us together has come undone. Henri barricades himself against me. His ardor has given way to fear. Or else he has grown weary. Worse yet, perhaps he was never sincere. Did I trample on what was once sacred to me for the sake of a lie? (A lie I am responsible for, one I consented to, and whose accomplice I am.) This is the question, finally, my haunting fear. Can I doubt our moments together, question the magnificence of a gesture or of a moment of abandon, the permanence of a vow? I can. If Henri absconds at this stage, he will nullify our whole love. I am prisoner to a man who no longer gives me anything, who has made my desire into a tomb. Night has come. Time for it to be over. I've lost faith in us. At each new laceration, my resistance grows less, and dejection gains on me. Yet still I hold on, though to what I'm not sure, and without knowing how, to this time stolen from death, to this man through whom I've known a love unlike any other—devastating, irreversible. It has cost me my home, my husband. How can I go back now?

In Henri's arms, my pleasure becomes painful. A way of condemning my bliss, no doubt, or expiating it. Also of regretting its briefness. Naked and disconcerted moments ago, hidden behind my hair, hunched over my body's shame, I concentrated on the silence behind me of the man to whom I'd wholly given myself, feeling his absence. The minutes that had gone before, the stripping, the saliva, the grasping, the fusing, the grace, that dazzling time when we cannot be other than ourselves already belonged to us no longer. The horror of the real assailed us once again.

"I've reached the end," I breathed.

In the bachelor's rooms where I join Henri at the cost of a thousand evasions and deceptions that chafe at my skin, there is always a moment when I feel the urge to run away, to escape, by noble means or base, from this scabby love. By what mystery am I here, playing with the abyss and defeat, exposed to the blows of a man whose entrance into my life destroyed my quiet peace? I don't understand. What bent of mine, previously unknown, draws me back despite myself between the sheets of this lover with a missing eye, this man spent before his time, whose sad flabby body, reddened with excess, can offer me only a disappointing embrace? What remorseful impulse? It is certainly not the flesh, unstable, alien, that sacrifices me implacably to Henri, but rather the search for a rapture and ravishment that only he has ever awakened in me. Or an irresistible desire to fall. But I don't let myself, I multiply my efforts to pull myself from the void, search feverishly for a branch to cling to, haul myself up onto the stable ground above, where fire crackles and children laugh. I know I must quickly disentangle myself from the lianas Henri has deftly wrapped around my neck, from his hands that mark me, hands like a vise, a harness, from his bronze, his divine fingers. I must. A question of life and death. But can I do it? And do I want to be delivered? For this feeling that bruises me will never again be mine to experience! Frantic, possessed, I am as afraid of the pain as of its cessation, its memory. One doesn't reach such heights of pleasure twice. To break off, what a horrid sound that has.

After crying for three days, terrified by the awful silence of life without him, I fly once again to my assignation with Henri, all the fractures in my being exposed by this great and tragic love—starving, thirsting, intensely alive.

For a year it has been this way.

IN THIS EARLY spring of 1821, the weather is heavy, lowering. Brought up in the town of Douai and inured to the severe climate of Flanders, I react uneasily to this unaccustomed warmth. The strange heat weighing down on Paris oppresses me. The temperatures we have experienced these last days in our little rooms under the eaves of the Hôtel du Paon have become unbearable to me, as I announced yesterday to my husband and my mother-in-law. And I wasn't lying. Or not entirely. My spells of nausea have grown stronger and more frequent. I break out in cold sweats. I would rather be on the rue Childebert, I told them, in the studio of my uncle Constant, where, thanks to the windows on three sides, it is cooler and I am better able to write. Not far from the church of Saint-Germain-des-Prés, the Childeberte is a big five-story structure inhabited by artists of every shade. Tucked in a corner behind the canvases and hardly bothered by the turpentine fumes, I am able to turn all my attention to my poems. Or so I pretend. But the truth is that for months I have been stopping at my uncle Constant's studio only briefly on my way to the rue des Saints-Pères.

"My son, your husband, is very obliging. To think that he wears himself out on the stage of the Odéon day after day, poor boy, so that we may live, while you traipse about the streets without the slightest concern for his reputation!" says Anne-Justine.

Her voice holds exasperation as well as hatred.

"When a person has a past such as yours," she goes on, "and has managed by a miracle—or by trickery—to marry the foremost actor of the day, one might expect some attempt at discretion. But you are mistaken if you think that I am like Prosper! I hear what people are saying . . ."

I sigh. There are rumors, I am well aware of it, prompted as much by my poetry as by my former career as an actress. My mother-in-law takes them in greedily. She has never accepted that her only son should marry a woman seven years older than himself. And one who, at least while I was still performing, received greater acclaim on the stage. I am untroubled by her words. In the early days of our marriage, Anne-Justine's attacks hit home and wounded me and Valmore both. Now they barely graze me. Shallow scratches that are quickly erased by Henri's claw marks.

"You know perfectly well that I am going to see my uncle."

"That's what you say. And even if it were true. A painter. In an atelier, a nest of rogues, all more intent on debauchery than art. My husband would never have allowed me to circulate in such company!"

Well, he'd have had his reasons. Was she not married at the time he seduced her? But I must at all costs avoid the argument that Anne-Justine is trying to kindle in an effort to keep me at home and stave off her loneliness. I swallow my sarcasms. My meekness nonetheless has all the marks of im-pertinence, which Anne-Justine senses perfectly well. Only her fear of ridicule keeps her from dragging out the scene. Her jealousy of me has its sources in her single-minded love for Prosper, the passions she has stifled, and the ambitions she has vested in him, while her own life has been nothing but frustration. I am no fool. And I would very much have liked her to love me. I expected it. I even called her "Mother" in the early days. The loss is all hers. I go out leaving her of-fended, to stew in her ill feelings.

I am bound elsewhere, and it is elsewhere that my feelings are engaged. I can see nothing. I advance blindly, dazzled and relieved, refusing to believe that it could end, that the situation might not last indefinitely. Valmore spends his days in re-hearsals, and our little Hippolyte, born in January of last year, is growing up in good health at the home of a wet nurse on the outskirts of Dreux, near the house of my sister Eugénie. Thanks to Henri, I published a book of poems a few months ago and a collection of Antillean stories, whose critical success momentarily gave me the illusion of at last breaking free from the theater that I so detest. What would I not do if it meant never having to perform monkey tricks on the stage again and living properly from my writing! That satisfaction, alas, has not been granted me. I must quiet my ambitions, for I have just learned (though my mother-in-law does not yet know it) that Prosper's contract with the Odéon will not be renewed next year. Valmore dislikes the capital in any case; he claims it is a center of malice, of ruthless ambition, and of worldliness. Tired of the duplicity and scheming, which he has resolutely steered away from, he has engaged us both at the Grand Théâtre in Lyon. Once the present season is over, we will again have to pack up our belongings. The wandering life I had hoped to be done with will resume. My endless vagabond existence.

THE PROSPECT OF leaving, of being torn from Henri and forced to return to the stage, afflicts me doubly. The fatal date, which I find myself alternately calling for and cursing, depending on whether I am queen or slave, whether Henri rebels or surrenders, is barely a month away. I sometimes feel he is rejoicing, finding my departure an easy solution to the problem of our love. His baseness repels me. I would like to slash his face with my nails. But then a tender word drops unexpectedly from him and fills me with pride. The joy, the importance I feel, at being loved by him makes me forget for a few hours the attendant debasement.

That is why, in this month of March 1821, ignoring the reprimands directed at me by Anne-Justine, the sacraments bind-ing me to Prosper, the vows I spoke over the grave where my mother molders alone in the Caribbean, shutting my eyes on my stolen youth, my violated happiness, passing over the remains of my three dead children, I fly to the rue des Saints-Pères, my stomach in knots, my throat constricted. I fly, yes, laughably free, like a novice to whom a last public outing is granted before the cloister, savoring the particularity of every second that carries me toward Henri, its fragility as well, while everything around me is subsumed by a great and triumphal purity.

HENRI'S NAME IS in fact Hyacinthe Thabaud de Latouche, but he has always hated it. A one-eyed man named after a flower is just too grotesque, he says. Early on he started to sign his articles with a pseudonym—a different one each time—and to initial his letters with an *H*, which everyone took to stand for Henri. He never objected, and he only told me the secret in the wake of many other disclosures, reluctantly and as if by mistake, at the same time asking me to continue calling him by a name that is not his. My lover is immoderately given to imposture. He goes masked.

Since separating from his wife, Latouche has lived in a small two-room apartment on the rue des Saints-Pères, near the banks of the Seine. I like to look out onto the river through the panes of his tall windows. In its waters I see other tragedies go by, onto which I sometimes manage to graft my words. Henri's apartment is a sort of bachelor's lair in an artfully studied state of neglect. "A Carthusian monk's cell," he claims. When I entered his apartment for the first time, after a moment of confusion, I quickly perceived behind the apparent disorder of the drawing room, filled as it was with books, rather ugly knickknacks, and exotic fabrics and hangings that bow to the current fashion for the Oriental style, an exacting logic. In this arrangement, which is at once pleasing and undeferential, Henri de Latouche is in his element. Or at least so he would have one believe, even as he suggests the opposite.

"I don't like these rooms," he told me that day. "I never invite anyone here."

"Then you do me a great honor."

"A great wrong, more like."

It didn't matter, really, as it was I and I alone who had decided to come to his rooms, and I who had chosen to give myself to him.

Always turned out with exacting elegance, a sign of the importance he gave to appearances, and of his confident, slightly contemptuous attitude toward the outside world, Henri had buckled before me, revealing his weaknesses. Behind his costume, a horrible drama was in progress. This great cynic in fact had a very low opinion of his own worth. His apartment, like a ship in a heavy swell, with its objects placed here and there in a moment of pique, or laziness, seemed vainly and obsessively to defy the storm and was the very image of his shipwreck.

"I've never managed to settle into this place. Can you understand that, Marceline? I put up with its noxious ambience. It was months before I could actually fall asleep here."

"Are you quite sure, Henri, that your discomfort comes from the place?"

His lips twitched slightly.

"What I mean," I went on, "is that perhaps your own company—"

"Silence, witch."

"As you like," I said, smiling. "For my part, I've moved so often that I make a point whenever I arrive in a new place of taking it in hand and bending it to my will. Within a few hours, I feel as though I've always lived there."

"I'm sure I believe you. But as for me, dear Marceline, I am a recluse and a misanthrope. I have tried the company of men, don't think I haven't. But now I am done with lies. Let others join in the masquerade . . ."

Such an exile, I told myself, such dire pronouncements! Why should this man, more loving of heart than he allowed, inflict this absurd penance on himself? With the greatest renunciation, Henri was secretly watching his life go down to defeat. But I would know how to bring him around!

I was convinced of it. Filled with wonderment at our having met, thankful at every hour of the day for the bond that held us together, and recognizing in Henri the man I might have been, the man I was, moved by our true selves as they collided continually in the general motion of the world, I was persuaded of victory. My certainty, my fervor, were absolutely unshakable. We were so strong, each of us, and so strong together, that nothing could harm us.

Nothing, that is, except Henri.


A YEAR LATER, as evening descends, I am rushing from the apartment on the rue des Saints-Pères, fleeing the dark shadows of the Seine, the scene of the pillage, spitting my tears, swallowing my anger, my hurt, my inability to save Henri from himself. I make a solemn vow always to love Valmore, his peace, his sunlit, fertile plains. From now on (but how many times in the last months have I promised myself the same thing) I will refuse my dark side its right to live and wreak havoc—by Christ I'll wring its atavistic neck. A few years ago, when I was at a low point and becoming, like my mother, a lost woman, did I not dream tearfully of the safe haven of married life, of the crowded table at Sunday dinners, of jams, nursery rhymes, and sprigs of thyme? More than anything, I wanted to get away from the theater, to feel myself protected, under a man's cover! I imagined myself in the arms of the handsomest husband, someone I might never dare hope for, whose magnificent and vigorous body would unfailingly awaken a thrill in mine. Then, surrounded by my little ones, I would fade quietly away one night in wise old age. This husband has by miracle been granted me. As for fading away, am I not doing so already? Each day that passes without noise, without writing, are they not each of them burying me a little deeper?

But yesterday, yesterday! Blessed Tuesday on the stern of the île Saint-Louis, Henri offered me eternity.

"Do you not see how frightened I am by my love for you?" his voice trembled in my ear.

And he interposed his hand between us, but too late, to keep me from hearing.

Veiled dampness of the quais along the Seine. And the house across the river, Henri had told me, was the home of Abelard and Héloïse. At that unhesitating moment, I would have severed all moorings to sail with him, to float down the river of our love to its mouth and meet the sea. "*Ma chérie*," he'd said. I left him in the mystic shadows of Notre-Dame, our love like an unbreakable shell, and Paris sanctified where my love pierced through into broad daylight.

There would probably never have been a better moment to separate forever.

. . .

TODAY I AM all fury and distress, discovering that Henri has reversed himself, that in the early hours of the morning after a night of insomnia, overcome by his fears, he sought to lose himself in the arms of a girl.

"You who manage to love me," he told me just now, "don't. Take what's there for the taking, Marceline, and hope for nothing more. I'm not one of those side-whiskered young dandies, high-waisted and well favored, who warble their love like martlets and chirp about the future. The concept of children, of living as man and wife, belongs to a world I no longer inhabit. Don't insist, you'll destroy the last of your strength. Take the crumbs that are there to be gleaned. There's nothing more to expect, I warn you."

"Then I'll have passed through your life without changing a thing . . . when I was ready to turn my own topsy-turvy for you. I'd have offered myself to you in a church, in my marriage bed, even, with my son asleep in the next room. I'd have gone to those lengths of depravity. I believed the feeling that held us in its grip would sweep everything before it."

"I did warn you."

"Yes, and you wrote me too. The exact opposite."

"I don't want to take this any farther. I wouldn't make you happy."

Implacable reasoning, from which he won't be swayed. Latouche has taken everything away from me, even the pleasure of waiting. Yesterday, I experienced a moment of grace, which the events of today have left blasted. I collapse, shaken by the oscillations of this passion that Henri is constantly betraying. And yet I can read the desire in his eyes, the fright, the feelings that even under torture he would make every effort to deny. Or I think I can read them. Perhaps I am my own worst enemy. I couldn't stand to be proven wrong. To discover that Latouche is making a fool of me, that our love is purely a literary game for him, an amusing fantasy. This man is my downfall. For a sou I come running on my knees, putting at risk the entire edifice of my life. I must break it off, I must absolutely break it off.

In tears, I walk along the banks of the hostile Seine in the direction of the rue du Paon-Saint-Germain. A feeling of nausea gradually overcomes me. Will writing keep me from losing my mind? In a month, yes, only a month, I will be leaving! Then everything will be over, the blows and the tears. In my memory, Henri will no longer wound me. Soon, comfortably aboard the marital ship beyond sight of land, I'll once more let my body wed the motion of the water, the indomitable current. But where is it leading me? Into what trough, onto what shoals?

I am wracked with vomiting. What have I walked into? I am lost. My love, spat out as yellowish bile, runs off over the sidewalk, splashing my bootees and the Flemish lace of my dress.

TONIGHT, WHILE VALMORE is appearing onstage and my mother-in-law is busy with her sewing, I shut myself in my room, wrung out. My thoughts are mournful, my heart empty and bruised. Exhausted, I think of death. A fallen woman is what I've become, and my only thought is to be with that man, who is probably thinking only of how to get rid of me. No. That's not possible. How can I impute such thoughts to Henri, doubt his sincerity, his very real suffering? I am ashamed of myself. Grief floods through me, sucks me down into the well where my demons wade, the beings I have loved and who are dead. My absent ones. Are they not calling me to them? I seem to see their veiled smiles. But then there is Hippolyte, my sturdy little boy, so handsome and alive, for whom all the others died. Despite all the blows it has dealt me, still, at the age of almost thirty-five, I love life. Angrily. Thanks to Latouche, I've reached one of its key moments. Beneath the seeming quiet of my existence since marrying Valmore, there lingered a troubled woman, thirsting for eternity, who was constantly paying for faults she hadn't committed and who hadn't yet had the courage to strangle once and for all the ghost of her past.

Filled with my desire for peace, my thirst for war, I must force my body not to run through Paris to be with Henri. The city weaves its fabric, interlacing our separate hearts.

For several days now, I have known that I am pregnant.

## 2

Y CHILDHOOD IS A SMELL, the smell of the *loées* my mother used to make after Sunday lunch which permeated the whole house from cellar to attic. A kind of armor. A veil that would never tear. Or so I thought. But like the cocoa that replaced coffee around 1790 when coffee grew too dear, everything in the Dutch genre painting of my early years has disappeared. Nothing is left of the family scene, frozen and false, portraying a beautiful blond-haired woman with her four children gathered around her. At her side sits her silent husband. In the background is her aged mother, her head nodding with the uncontrollable shake of those who live only through memory.

My grandmother spent most of her life, perhaps the best part of it, or the least false, waiting for her husband. Calling himself a watchmaker, he would visit towns collecting watches to repair and then abscond with them. He was a thorough crook. Usually he would slink off for a few months. Then he would return without warning before disappearing once again. My grandmother cursed him, but she always found herself pregnant after his unexpected reappearances. Then she would return to her waiting, as to a loathed but necessary piece of work. One day my grandfather left for good. He lived out the rest of his life, probably drunk, as a prompter in a Brussels theater. Lost, my grandmother came to sit by our stove in the dining-room rocking chair, its movement slowly becoming her own. She spent the greater part of the day knitting mutely into her blue apron, lost to the world around her. White strands of hair poked out from her fluted white bonnet. Her tiny feet grazed the sand on the red tile floor. She was no longer waiting.

After a stroke that paralyzed half of her body, she had to take to her bed, her handsome face resolutely turned to the side. Her eyes, focused on an invisible point, were intense, frightening, accusatory. Was she conscious? We preferred to think that she was not. From time to time she would come back to us, her pupils full of ooze and mud. Snippets of her youth broke over her thin-drawn lips, which smelled of age, of rot. Then she would retreat into her chasm. Her agony went on and on. I found her absurd, useless. For the first time in my short life, I wished for the death of a person I loved. Anything to stop this everlasting end, this inexorable decomposition.

"Like life beforehand, death is taking its time with her," my mother said.

She gave her a peck on the cheek three times a day and changed her without a murmur.

For my part, I could see that an era was coming to an end with my grandmother and that her death would bury it forever. A moribund part of me—my childhood—was drifting away, trying doggedly to hold on with unimaginable strength and desperate energy, fearful of what would come after.

"UP YOU GET, girl! Come see!" called my father to wake me up. "Gayant is going by with his whole family!"

The festival of Gayant, the biggest celebration of the year, commemorates the breaking of the siege of Douai in 1479 and the entrance of the French into the city. It lasts a week at the start of July.

"Here are the crossbowmen from Tournai!" said Cécile, my eldest sister.

"And the archers from Arras!" said Eugénie, the next oldest.

The whole town tagged along through the streets behind the procession of enormous wickerwork figures. My mother made us dress in our best clothes.

"No gingerbread men if you don't," she said, "and no beer or liqueurs."

We were happy. Fragmented images from this period come back to haunt me often. I see my mother at her spinning wheel, surrounded by pewter and tapestries, engravings and leatherwork. Muslin, lace, and guipure. At night I would listen to my sisters read, do their sums, I watched them sew and wind balls of wool. How impatiently I kept a lookout in the evening for their return from school, for the thick skirts of Cécile and Eugénie, their hair floating on the breeze above the sturdy cape of the Ursuline order! And Félix, my brother, so proud to recite his seminary Latin . . .

Then we would join together to sing from the old romances:

> *Our Lady, visit us in our sorrow,*
> *With all your angels at hand,*
> *And may the war depart tomorrow*
> *For a distant land.*

I would fall asleep on the primer that Cécile was using to teach me my letters. I drifted off smiling, surrounded by my toys, my porcelain shepherdesses, my sheep carved from wood and smelling of resin, my wax angels with their wings of cardboard and gauze.

WE LIVED IN the Notre-Dame neighborhood, at the foot of the abandoned ramparts I loved so much. With the other children, I would run off and play among the harebells along the old sentry path. A mass of rubble, really, but the pillar of my enchanted world. We lived beside the church and the cemetery, which was so neglected that it ran to ruin. Behind us were the narrow, dingy streets where the populace sheltered. Better off, we lived among a group of houses where our neighbors were a baker, a man who rented coaches, a lace weaver, and the proprietor of the inn on the corner. Ours was the fifth house. One of those gabled, red-brick, Dutch structures. On the ground floor, a long hallway led through to the yard in the back.

I was not yet old enough for school. Waiting for my brother and sisters, I played in the main room under an enormous umbrella with my doll, near my grandmother's feet, beside the great tiled stove.

"A hotroom," the old woman would say, "requires constant attention."

My mother and a group of neighbors—sometimes as many as twenty—spun linen in this room, whose floor was strewn with sand, while my grandmother, at least before her first stroke, tended the stove and prepared meals.

The bedrooms were on the floor above. As was common at the time, we had a lodger on the second floor, while a pauper family lived in the cellar. Before the Revolution, a small clay Virgin gazed out of the niche above the main door. But after falling into disgrace in 1789, she was removed to my mother's room with all the crosses and rosaries. The niche was left vacant, like an empty eye socket, disfiguring our house.

THEN CAME THE Terror.

Convents were torched, churches pillaged, priests assassinated. Gayant and the rest were gone. The reign of fear took hold. Fear and mistrust.

"Go out and fetch some water, girl," said my grandmother.

"Me?"

"Aren't you my sturdy little girl? You're not afraid of going out into the courtyard, now, are you?"

The same scene would be repeated every day. We shared the well and a rain barrel we used for doing laundry with our neighbors. There was a saint there. Or rather, the mutilated statue of a saint that my atheist father had picked up after the sack of the church next door. In a corner of the courtyard, near the stairs. This hideously wounded, violated figure terrorized me. I preferred playing knucklebones on the abandoned graves of the old cemetery, which I had turned into my private garden. But at home, in order to get water, you had to pass in front of the profaned idol. I had no choice. Each time, I made the sign of the cross, even though I wore the tricolor ribbons of the Revolution and a Phrygian cap. My grandmother sensed my fear and chided me gently for it.

"That child needs to shake herself," she would say to my mother. "She is as timid as a mouse."

"Marceline, give your grandmother a hand," my mother would say, never lifting her head from her work.

Under their mocking glance, I would set off valiantly. It was not cruelty on their part. Inured adults, they had forgotten the wounds of their childhood. Each of these women was struggling to hold her position and keep her own nightmares quiet, even at the cost of showing fierceness toward me. There was war on all sides.

Around this time my grandmother started to decline. In some ways it was for the best.

In our neighborhood, the priest of Notre-Dame celebrated the Catholic rites clandestinely. When he went to administer the last sacraments to a dying person, he used so much makeup for his disguise that he was frightful to look at.

"The dying mistake him for Death and expire at the sight of him!" my father said.

My mother would frown.

"Religion is nothing to joke about. Show a little respect! And bear in mind that this priest performed our marriage. And baptized all our children."

My mother, Catherine Lucas, and my father, Antoine-Félix Desbordes, were married in 1776. It was an arranged marriage, almost certainly. There was never any love between them, I'm afraid, or so little, and so fragile, that it dropped to the ground like a fruit that rots too soon. My mother was from a humble family, and her marriage brought her up in the world. She was just a girl, younger than her husband by seven years, very pretty, forthright, serious. Her handiwork was prized for its quality throughout the region. She kept an impeccable house, working maniacally at it. Our pewter always gleamed and nothing was left lying around, because my mother hated disorder. Her obsession with putting things away was a subject for ridicule among us. No one guessed at the great emptiness inside her that was masked by this apparent taste for organization, cleanliness, and regularity. My mother's probity contrasted strongly with my father's character, which was scattershot and always ready for a gamble. Despite their difference in age, he was in reality the first of her children. And for us, he was more a big brother than a father.

On her wedding day, my mother could neither read nor write, which was not at all unusual. My father didn't care, and if my mother decided to learn her letters, alone in the evenings by candlelight, it was not at her husband's urging. She took to it, and started devouring novels with a gravity that she transmitted to each of her four children. Reading was serious business. Before dinner, when my father was late getting home, my mother would sit us down and read aloud to us several chapters from a book. Though we were hungry, we would listen to her devoutly. Thus it was, on an empty stomach, that I discovered books. It was also thus that my mother, lured by the other world she glimpsed cutting open the pages of her books, succumbed in the end to madness.

MY FATHER'S DREAMS were also beyond the reach of his ambitions. He tried his hand at several trades: ceiling molder, master painter, gilder of cabinetry. But his naïveté and incompetence proved incurable, and his businesses failed every time. He papered over his successive disasters with stories that my mother and we children pretended to believe. Then the Revolution swept away all the carriages and all the coats of arms with them. There was nothing left to paint or to gild. Next my father bought a bailiff's practice and partnered with a grocery business that was in fact a den of swindlers. After that he claimed to be the confidential secretary and proxy for an important high cleric in Douai, as well as his provost, lawyer, and counselor. My family's decline proceeded inexorably.

In the end, some business about an unpaid debt brought the curtain down on his adventures. He started to drink and lie inveterately. He grew evasive. I still adored him, unaware of the approaching catastrophe. I liked the stories he told, the broad gestures he made with his arms, his eyes that sparkled with energy. My mother, by contrast, seemed to me an austere and untouchable goddess. The spark of madness, of fantasy, was my father's realm. But in this I was gravely mistaken. I never thought my mother could have another life. My separation from him was to be brutal.

CÉCILE WAS BORN a year after my parents married. Then there was another girl, a little Sophie, who died at almost twenty-four months. I very likely owe my life to her death, to my mother's silent crisis, to the fathomless pit opened in her heart by that death. The tragedy was ordinary enough. Out of a litter, not all can survive. The wet nurse, a cold spell, a passing epidemic—there are always reasons at hand, like so many nails to drive into the little coffins. A shovelful of dirt, then you move on. Another birth follows. People forget that a mother's pain is the same whether in a manor house or a hovel, that it pierces walls of brick as well as wattle.

We were not yet destitute, however. Life is more resilient in bourgeois homes, and my mother kept us to a high standard of cleanliness. Never did I hear her speak of this little girl. It was Cécile who told me about her one day. Surprised, I realized I had never thought about my mother's life. Everything in it just seemed to happen. I had denied her the potential for inner torments, zones of shadow. Or a capacity for devotion to anything besides her children. She, too, could cry, then. Know sorrows that were unrelated to us. It was almost a betrayal.

BUT A WOMAN'S womb is inexhaustible. Eugénie was born in 1780 and Félix in 1782. Childbirth at a regular cadence, the cycle reassuring if fragile, subject to inclemencies. In the familial home on the rue Notre-Dame in Douai, the family was growing. The fifth and last Desbordes child, I came into the world on June 20, 1786. My mother had not given birth in four years. My father chose the name Marceline as a tribute to the wife of a local magistrate whom he wanted to flatter and who accordingly became my godmother. I never knew her.

At the time I was born, my father had been a *mulquinier* for a year, which is to say a linen salesman, a common and honorable trade in our parts. The respite was a short one. All too soon, his debts to the innkeeper began to mount, his rent went unpaid, some swindles into which he had been drawn were uncovered, and he was declared bankrupt. We were left with nothing. At night, our boarder would noisily swallow his soup, while our bowls sat empty in the barren larder.

One terrible day, men came to place seals on three rooms in our house. My mother shrieked, we cried, my father gesticulated in vain. We had only three rooms left to live in. One of them was for my grandmother, who was dying interminably. It was like being in a house of death. My father sold the handsome furniture that had passed down through several generations of Desbordes and that my mother had maintained with fierce devotion for years. I could see her raging inside, barely mastering her hatred, her contempt for him. Our inner upheavals found an echo in the tumult of the world around us. There was a scaffold, unused, on the place d'Armes in Douai, and there might as well have been one in the middle of our house.

FOR THE SAKE of appearances and to hide his true sympathies, my father began to associate with the new political regime.

"It's a good idea to attend the revolutionary meetings," he said.

"But you are against them!" My mother was shocked.

"Yes but someone could turn us in!"

"And what about the girl? Aren't you ashamed to take her to that den of unbelievers?"

"She declaims prettily, she recites speeches against tyranny. It makes for a change."

My mother, who went to confession on the sly and continued secretly bringing provisions to the priest of Notre-Dame, was furious. For my part, I was already starting to detest the playacting.

Thanks to his machinations, my father managed for a time to wrangle from the revolutionary authorities a succession of largely fictitious positions. But in 1795, the curtain came down once and for all. He was by then a night watchman and moved us from our beautiful house on the rue Notre-Dame to look after a wineshop near the town hall where we had rooms on the floor above.

For my grandmother, it was the last straw. She passed away. My father, meanwhile, was still searching for excuses. Accepting no responsibility for our misfortunes, he invented harebrained stories, spun outrageous nonsense.

"You may not know it," he told us one day, "but in the fifteenth century, the 'De Bordes' were rich bourgeois, famous for the opulence of their weddings. People talked about them throughout the region. They were respected, envied, looked on with jealousy. And sometimes they were hated! Their women were beautiful and their children plump. But they had ties to the secret Calvinist community. Certain noblemen took a dislike to them and publicly accused them of heresy. At that point, one of the Desbordes fled to Antwerp. His son announced himself a Protestant and established trade posts abroad, becoming captain of the Dutch East Indian fleet. He received a title of nobility and grew tremendously rich!"

Rich! Rich! The word hovered, sparkling, over our heads.

"They all disappeared gradually," my father went on. "The only ones left today are two great-uncles, grandsons of the navy captain."

"That's impossible," Félix objected. "They would be more than a hundred years old!"

My father shrugged. The facts were irrelevant. We were simply meant to believe him.

"As they have no direct descendants and have heard of our little setbacks, the crisis in the textile industry, and our financial embarrassment, they offered to leave us their fortune. Quite a considerable fortune!"

"And?"

We hung on his every word.

"There was a condition attached to it," said my father, drawing on his pipe and growing heated at his own eloquence. "They wanted us to convert. Can you imagine? Us, Protestants? I turned them down. That's why we're in the fix we're in now. Otherwise, we'd be the richest family in Flanders!"

In a corner of the room, my mother glared at him, quiet as a stone. I did my best to ignore her. I actually liked my father's stories. Even as a small child, I understood the docile warmth of a falsehood, and how a beautiful lie could be more companionable than a nasty truth. We were living a perpetual imposture. I still didn't want to admit it. And yet I'd seen my parents attack each other with the ferocity of raptors. Even after the Terror was over and the Directoire had been declared, when the saints were resettled on their pedestals and religion had been restored. But I closed my eyes, holding fast to my years of innocence, to the Lenten flowers that I picked between gravestones and pressed between pages of a sketchbook. Like dried slices of time.

BELLS AT THE town hall replaced the carillon in the belfry of Notre-Dame. My mother's endurance had apparently come to an end. Seven years after me, she gave birth to a tiny creature that died after three weeks. My father did not even attend the funeral. After twenty years of marriage and six live births, here was my mother living shamefacedly on a noisy, gloomy street over a wineshop, keeping a boarder, terrified that the bailiffs would appear at any moment. I, a child of ten, was her only companion. Divorce, a recent institution, had found favor among a number of her friends, most of whom had left Douai. My mother was alone, neglected by her husband, who drank as much wine as he sold and probably supported mistresses, perhaps even natural children. In twenty years, the unfeeling gears of daily life had ground down her girlhood dreams. The exemplary wife had seen her spinning wheel develop a multitude of cracks. A pauper now, her trunk no longer had room for the painting of the Dutch interior from the days of the *loées*, when she reigned as queen. Its paint flaking, it had been worn away by disillusion, by sacrifice, and by resignation.

Between stagnation and indignity, as between the rope and the dagger, my mother resolved to make a choice, and she took a lover.

IT WAS THUS that, one morning in November 1796, my mother left Douai, her husband, and three of her children forever, dragging me along, a terrified girl ripped from her native soil, where one last time I shed uncomprehending tears.

## 3

UR DEPARTURE FOR LYON is almost upon us. Already
I hear the coach rattling, the horses neighing. I
must at all costs arrange with Valmore for a delay. Separations
have always had for me the bitter taste of soil, of a soil left
behind forever with its burden of graves to be tended, their
surface gradually sagging, a vast garden from the past overrun
with ruins, rubble, and opprobrium, the trees uprooted where
I climbed, as a child, toward unattainable crests. Leaving is always leaving my father again, being exiled a little farther from
my childhood. Every year I find it harder to get used to.

"I'm not ready," I tell Prosper by way of excuse. "I need to
see my uncle about Hippolyte and talk to my editor about my
next book of poems. I still have much to do. I could join you
later, your mother and you. Pauline has offered to take me in
for a few days."

"Pauline? All right. If you like."

Valmore is so happy to leave Paris it is indecent. Or so it is
to me at any rate. His good humor affects me like a bright sun
at a funeral. He blithely agrees to set off first, alone with Anne-
Justine. A lesser evil. I knew all along he would. Prosper generally bows willingly enough to my suggestions, my wishes. He will
think I am at Pauline's for these three days, during which I will
betray his trust for the last time. My husband doesn't especially

like Pauline. She is far too extravagant a woman for him. But he respects our friendship, which began several months ago at my uncle Constant's studio, where the explosive Mme Pauline Duchambge arrived in her voluminous silks, with her trinkets and perfume, enchanted by the poems I had just published and which she wished to set to music. Ten years my elder, Pauline is sinfully beautiful. At our first meeting, I could only stammer from emotion. With the sensuality of a Creole Madonna, she is dark in a way that attracts me. She is everything that I am not. But we share the pain of having lost children. In every other respect—divorced, aristocratic, an excellent musician and singer—Pauline Duchambge is the free woman that I will never be. She writes romances that have created as much stir in the capital as her supposed Antillean origins and her stormy relations with the musician Auber.

Given my awkward ways and provincial garb, I couldn't understand her interest in me. A friend of the beautiful Mme Tallien, countess of Caraman-Chimay! I blushed with pride. I still blush when I think of her. She knows a great deal about me. She is the only person to whom I have described my adventure with Henri.

But I won't go to Pauline's.


VALMORE REALLY DOES not like her very much. He generally mistrusts women of the world. And he thinks I open my heart too freely. Pauline Duchambge's feelings are perhaps not as noble as you imagine, he tells me. He warns me that any confidences I make to her will soon be flying all over Paris in altered form. Prosper is obviously right. But his good sense and advice, intended to protect me from being duped, run counter to my thirst for passion. I need to fuse with another being, man, woman, or child. At the risk of burning my wings and despite several disappointments, I choose flight each time. It doesn't escape me that my husband tries always to be standing with outstretched arms near where I am likely to fall. A net. He is the best of men, thoughtful, solid as a rock. I owe him so much. Could I live without him? I wonder. Marked as with a red-hot iron by Henri's body, I am still filled with inexplicable tenderness for Prosper and drawn to his striking presence, his Olympian fineness, his athlete's figure. Valmore onstage in belted costumes. A marvel. I tell myself this over and over as I accompany Anne-Justine and my husband to the mail coach.

From the window of the carriage they have climbed into, he sweetly extends his hand to me. Adorable Prosper. He is just a child. Perhaps I want to mother him too much. My loves have always been childish loves. Until Henri. Will we regain, Prosper and I, the peace and serenity, the gentle waters of our earlier years? Right now, standing in his loving gaze, I hate the furious wave that has caught me and is carrying me away from him! This isn't me anymore. Is it me? I so want to bask on that peaceful plain, but part of me, stubborn and inexplicable, sets a different course, takes up arms, cries havoc. I have struggled so hard to become a respectable woman, a wife, the mother of a happy family. How could it come to this? Have the simple ambitions of a provincial girl been overtaken with fever in the capital? When, where did I go astray?

We have agreed that I will rejoin them in three days. Three paltry little days of eternity in which to embrace the ardent body of my other life, to smother the impossible bed of coals it has so selfishly and irresponsibly set alight. Three seedy days to shrug off my fantasies and put on once more the tight overcoat of reality, made to my measure and buttoned to the neck. I still have three days of dust and music before shutting myself away in the cloister of silence.

I BURST IMPATIENTLY into Constant's studio to discuss with him the subject of Hippolyte's nanny. My beautiful little boy has inherited his father's features. He is just starting, with little burbles of satisfaction, to take his first steps. I have made up my mind that he is not going to stay with a nurse somewhere far off. I lost a baby that way. But before I bring him to be with me, before I manage to prepare our life somewhat in Lyon, for convenience I have decided to leave him for a short time with my uncle. This is a painful decision for me, because I take poorly to being separated from my boy.

"Now you won't forget to give him his sedative solution, will you, Uncle? Oh, and especially his borage tea. These were the particular recommendations of Dr. Alibert himself."

"Yes, yes," says Constant. "But I can't help thinking, my precious *tiote*, that all these doctors . . . but I'll do just as you say."

From time to time, my uncle drops a word of patois into his speech, the sound of our lost village bells. Of my church of Notre-Dame. The old painter doesn't see it, but each time I am deeply moved by his unintended gift. My uncle is so distracted, though, that for a moment I am afraid to place the life of my only son in his paint-stained hands, in the chaos of his lair. The two of us have traveled an arduous road together. Long estranged, we have recently been reconciled. To put Hippolyte in his care is to prove my undying love for him. No woman is more a mother than I am. I live and breathe for my child, having lost two babies and a little boy of five, my light-haired angel buried one morning in Brussels, whom I have often come to mourn for in secret at the Childeberte studio.

Yet as this April 1821 draws to a close, each minute brings me toward another bereavement. I find myself hurrying to settle the last details. My uncle, whose life has bound him to his easel without ever granting him a child, is delighted to be temporarily in charge of Hippolyte. Rushed and effusive, I take leave of my curly-headed baby. The moment I am out the studio door my scruples are gone. All I can think of now is seeing Latouche. Though I could scarcely have imagined it, I am to be for another three days more a woman than a mother.

Resolute, willful, with quick steps and a light body, I walk toward my lover, cherishing every pebble, every centimeter of the way that leads me to him. It is the hour when everything is still possible. I believe in us. Why would we sack the kingdom that was given us? My accomplice, my pride and joy—I never knew the meaning of love until I met him. I am confident. There along the Seine, between the rue Childebert and the rue des Saints-Pères, words are being engraved in my heavy womb. The sun is reflected in the river, seeming to open it from end to end, and the vast gash of water unashamedly reveals its true carmine color. I am no longer that extinguished woman, dull, already faded, whose stolen childhood has barred her from being beautiful. I am no longer that huddled shadow of maternal deference, that hated wrong helplessly repeated in memory of a dead woman, that soul that goes to earth, contracts into itself because afraid of loving and being left, because afraid of enduring further pain, preferring to shrivel into its own fears. I am a loosed head of hair, a goddess of mythology, touched by grace and transfigured by the sureness of the feeling that buoys me. Nothing can stop me, not blame, not questions, not shame at betraying the unsullied faith of my husband, whom I would leave at a word, a whisper, without a backward glance. I know myself to be free.


Rue des Saints-Pères. Climbing the final set of stairs to Henri's apartment, I have lost all my certainty. I sense what little connection our story has to reality, how much it owes to its nonactuality and how much it feeds to the point of nausea on its own truth. Our passion navigates the rim of the absolute, which it can abandon only at the cost of losing its raison d'être. Latouche's love is fated to remain a vow, a sacred vocation. Only Prosper's, which sometimes fails, is real. In point of fact, I have no choice to make between them.

Henri is waiting for me with extended claws. I know he is going to hurt me. All is lost, even now. He is livid with pain, and only admits to it angrily. After sparring with himself, he has most likely rejected once and for all the temptation to grant our love a different outcome. So as not to be dissuaded, he is prepared to parry my every thrust. He will be hateful, most certainly, keep himself hidden, and strip our leave-taking of any regret. He looks like an opera singer ready to belt out a song of freedom. He greets me with the satiated air of a man who has spent the night in a strange bed and congratulates himself on it with impudence. I cannot help but notice.

"How elegant you are," I tell him. "That color green suits you remarkably well."

"Last night, if you can believe it, I wound up in Sophie Gay's salon," Henri answers, a smile playing at the corners of his mouth. "Deschamps dragged me there as usual, despite my protests. But it turned out to be rather an entertaining evening. I enjoyed myself thoroughly."

"I'm sure of it."

Hurt, I cast about for something to say. Paris society is closed to me, and I do not yet have access to literary circles. I am just an actress who writes poems, romances. Within me, like a stubborn vine, mortification is growing. I find Latouche's false lightheartedness unbearable.

"On the way up, did you happen to meet a young man with a high forehead, thin, but rather well built?"

"I think so, yes. I didn't really notice."

"That is young Hugo, I've mentioned him to you before. Vigny introduced us. He lives nearby, rue du Dragon. He is so poor, so scrimping, that I gave him a leftover dish of boiled potatoes with salt lard, you know, that specialty of my native Berry. The poor boy strikes me as rather sympathetic, I confess. He too admires Chénier, and doesn't turn up his nose at that thin little wine from La Châtre that I keep on hand . . ."

"Henri . . ."

"Can I offer you a cup of tea? You seem overwrought . . ."

For all of a season, Latouche loved me. That is enough to establish, during the life that remains to me, a cult in his name. Nothing must be touched. I'll write for him, my poetry will be his, it will be him. Our love will stay as it was during the long spring that has just passed and that now belongs to me. In the flesh, Henri dispossesses me of everything, even my emotions. Far away, absent, lost, he will no longer affect me, he will be obliged to give me back my memories, pristine and unalterable. They will be beyond his power to soil, to negate. After today, we will have all eternity.

But now for our last hours together! I would like to read suffering in his face. Could I be alone in hurting? Such a waste, this rout of the emotions. He hasn't much love for me, apparently.

Did he ever love me? I'll never know. Everything has already been said. The time has come for mourning. Latouche already stinks of carrion. I must forget the suppleness of his skin, all that has made an imprint on my body, what I have felt in my flesh. How could I still stand for Prosper to touch me? I have hollowed out an abyss in the marital bed. But it will be erased. With time, everything is erased, even aversion. I will never have slept all night with Henri, his face in my hair and his hands on my waist. Yet that is true possession. Not the clattering gallop of breathless bodies. How I hurt! Who is crushing me so cruelly? How do I exit this nightmare?

Henri tries to ignore it, but he is too astute not to notice that I am foundering by the minute. Ordinarily, I am more voluble, talking with him for hours at a time about political or literary feuds, the theater, the country and property, childhood, crops, the sowing of seeds, wheat fields, and all sorts of idle chatter. But since entering his apartment, I have not moved from the orange-colored bergère where I normally sit, beside the piano in the window recess. The truth is that my nausea has returned and my legs will no longer carry me. The Seine below ferries floods of dramas and deceptions past me tauntingly.

"There was a splendid crowd at the Arsenal the other night," says Latouche.

His captivating voice has come down a note.

"Observe the hypocrisy of these people, Marceline. If I hadn't written that article on *Adèle*, which Nodier commissioned for *Le Constitutionnel*, the man would spend part of every day blackening my name. Instead of which, I have become an indispensable part of his literary clique. You probably think I have given a portion of myself away in the process, no? That I have betrayed myself? But then you are pure. And I beg you to stay that way and not let yourself become sullied . . ."

Pure. What did it mean? Provincial? Plebeian? I am overcome with bitterness. I am jealous of the impure women that
Henri holds in his arms at night, with their smell of fox and
darkness. Why does he not keep some of my sweat on his skin?
He wants to protect me from himself, not to hurt me, he often
says. These warnings exasperate me. I want to be hurt.

"Henri . . ."

"What is it, darling?" he asks, anxious, exasperated. "You're
pale. Do you feel unwell?"

"No—or rather, I've never felt so dejected in all my life . . ."

At that moment, I have forgotten my whole past, my tears,
my dead ones. I am the most sincere of women. Before the
man I love helplessly, I find myself facing the void. Never has
life seemed so desperately absurd to me. Two people with such
a wealth of words between them! I feel deceived, humiliated
by the very man who made me beautiful beyond compare, in
a world that revolved around me, a world from which his absence was inconceivable, and where I awoke each day to the
wondering realization of his existence. Today, useless, I no longer belong to that world.

"No—please, Marceline, don't cry. I don't like it—I can't
bear to see you suffer."

His face has shattered. The affectations, the grimaces are
gone, he has become again the man I love. It is once more the
face of my one-eyed lover, in which anguish and avowal are
joined. I will pack it away in my heart's jolted travel trunks,
along with the little furrows at the corners of his pond-colored
eyes, and his smile that he holds down the way a prude tugs on
her dress so as not to show her ankles. Latouche's eyes are two
marshes, one salt, the other dry.

"What upsets me, Henri, is the falseness. Your indifference,
if only a pretense, is torturing me. If real, it is killing me. In

either case, I no longer recognize you. Henri—please—we have so little time left . . ."

Irrationally, I go on waiting. By pressuring him behind his defenses, I am hoping for a last burst of passion. Perhaps he won't allow me to leave. Perhaps he won't consent to lose me. How I should like him to seize me, rain blows on me, detain me!

"You're reading me wrong," he says finally. "Do I not have the right to act a part plainly, to say one thing and then its opposite, to play the buffoon when everything is cracking, fissuring, and collapsing around me? Dear angel, who sees through all my crude masks so well, I've lost my taste for defeat. You are well aware of my distress, of the power you have had over me. I deny no part of what has happened between us. There are hours, sculpted in the bronze of time, that nothing can dismantle, hours in which I wait for you, in which you come to me, Paris is full of them, is it not? But another force drives me, Marceline, which refuses happiness and forbids me to love you. Will you forgive me one day? Can you see us as staid lovers? Come, think what it took us to find each other, how easily we could have brushed past each other again and again, in the boxes of the theaters where you acted and where I happened by, without ever connecting. Only poetry could bring us face to face. You have affected me far more forcibly than I could confess, and you know it. I believe I have freed you from a certain number of shackles. You, who are enlarged by emotion, possess words far more than do I, whom emotion chokes. We have loved each other, we do love each other, and you are leaving. I will not prevent you from going. I have nothing to offer you. It's stupid, I realize, pitiful. I'll probably never entirely recover. The idea that your womb might some day carry a child is such a beautiful one . . ."

"Henri—"

Shall I tell him? My God, shall I reveal everything, now, here, before another moment passes?

"No. Save your tears for tomorrow. I am saying nothing you don't already know, and you are far too sharp not to have seen, even before I did, that I could not be, and will not be, the architect of your future. I am too given to sulfur, and the kisses with which I vow to love you always reek of debauchery. Would you really want, Marceline, for me to ask you to choose between Prosper and me, between bound days and loose sheets? No, that isn't what you want. You made your mind up at the start. What holds you back is the fear of growing old. After him, you think in a panic, there is nothing and no one. But I who love even your developing wrinkles and your tired breasts, I have no elixir of youth in my cupboards. All the better, all the better, dear shadow, dear tightrope walker, whose future beauty I divine. That lip I see tremble! If you knew, Marceline, just how much this loss is mine above all. I am not sacrificing you, I am sacrificing myself . . . I still have your portrait, the fine pencil sketch your uncle drew, your proud and conquering beauty barely hidden by a modest profile. I have your portrait, yes, a precious gift from you, and it will perhaps hold me in the world of the living for yet a time. You will be reborn, make loss and absence your familiars, soften the trench henceforth gouged into the soil of our hearts. You'll write, my queen. It is an order I charge you with, a prayer I address to you, and the only sacrament that binds us, independent of man, in the eyes of art alone. Come, my love, lean against me for now. Listen to the storm roar outside and swell the Seine with the sobs that I am stifling. Because I too am crying quietly."

It is raining over Paris, Marceline, it is raining.

## 4

*I* WAS TEN and I had just celebrated the feast of Saint Nicholas for the last time. In the coach that was carrying us away, I nestled against my silent mother, my eyes empty, staring at the mist-fringed fields and their sudden, skeletal trees. A nestling miraculously still alive after the death of all its nestmates. My hair, a nondescript brown, fell shapelessly to my shoulders. My nose, straight and severe, was too long. My pinched lips were too small. My skin was pale, giving my face a sad look and accentuating my eyes, which were ringed with a nasty red. My features reflected the cares of the wide world, and I carried my body like a heavy burden. My mother, tall, blond, and beautiful, squelched any gossip among those around us. I was but a poor copy of her splendor.

An honest woman did not travel unaccompanied. The other passengers glared at us disapprovingly, to which my mother gave no more notice than to the ruts in the road. Suddenly remembering me as, shivering with fear and incomprehension, I tried to disappear against her bosom, she gently gathered me in her arms, pinning us together, every rattle of the coach bringing us closer, blending us. Up to that point, I had been more afraid than sad. I'd never left Douai before. Poor Father, poor Félix, Cécile, and Eugénie ... Where were we going? What was happening? We had brought nothing with us. Not even my doll! I was alone in the world, bumping along toward a destination that could only hold disaster.

Roubaix, an hour from Douai, was our goal. A sinister, forlorn town where my mother and I took shelter in a set of dark rooms. I was afraid. I could make no sense of this Nicolas Saintenoy whom we were going to meet. Drafted into the administration of the Directoire, where he held more or less made-up posts, my mother's lover neglected us most of the time to pursue idle women, a habit he was unable to rid himself of, the way others pick their noses or crack their joints. He hardly knew he was doing it. Unlike my father, who was rather squat and nondescript, Saintenoy was tall, with a strong face and piercing blue eyes. The ladies were apparently drawn to him. My mother, now that she was his for the taking, had lost all appeal for him. The poor woman, stifling her grief at losing her children, sensed his lack of interest clearly and saw herself once again playing the role of the neglected wife. She was a long way from having gained anything in the bargain, but she could no longer turn back.

"Why not just go home?" I asked her timidly one day.

"It would be impossible," she said. "Never, do you hear, never!"

She paid a high price for her pitiful freedom. An anonymous Medea condemned to a life of wandering, she had forgone all dignity and all remorse. Where could she go now except forward, ever forward, to die poor and alone at the far end of the world?

My mother. While she read to me from a book, I would brush her long golden hair. We went to the market together, and she taught me to cook. To kill the remaining hours, we knitted and embroidered with Roubaix's abundant and inexpensive woolen yarn. Sometimes, I noticed tears forming at the edges of her eyelids, which by an extreme effort she would manage to resorb. How I would have loved for her to confide her unhappiness to me! But an ocean of emotional modesty lay between us. We never talked about the past.

"From now on, we'll live here with Citizen Saintenoy," she announced on our arrival in Roubaix.

And that was all. When did they meet? How long had they been lovers? I was taken entirely by surprise. Later I learned that they had met through my father's younger brother, Constant, who wanted to be a painter. That was as much as I was to know. Questions were unwelcome. I should try to forget our wrenching departure and my father's curse. Roubaix, the whereabouts of which I understood hazily, struck me as lying beyond any imaginable territory.

GRADUALLY I CAME to know the man for whom my mother had left my father. He was the son of a famous drunkard from Douai. Divorced and debt-ridden, the younger Saintenoy had fled to Roubaix to lie low. I wondered to what depths of need my mother had fallen to believe that this man, false, arrogant, and pretentious as he was, could make her happy. But her quest was not for happiness. Confined to the Roubaisian hovel where we had fetched up, she worked hard not to see Saintenoy's faults. His amorous intrigues and political conniving brought him new enemies every day. A letter publicly revealing his brazen affair with my mother cost him his administrative position. He was stripped of his office in October 1797. At the same time, a child widely believed to have been fathered by

Saintenoy was born in the lower depths of the town. This time, there was no way to hush up the scandal.

Toward the end of that year, in appalling circumstances, we left Roubaix for the town of Lille, once more slipping away at dawn like criminals in the first coach traveling our way.

For a year, longing to return to my father's house, to my sisters and Félix, I had tried to escape the world around me, denied plain evidence, and rejected our new circumstances. Roubaix never existed. Roubaix did not exist. I experienced the same resentment every morning at seeing the town still standing. I called for an earthquake, a fire. When we arrived in Lille, I gradually understood with tears and sighs that all hope was truly gone. I would never see Douai again, and nothing would ever be the same. I had to admit it and confront the world. My childhood was over.


WE LIKED LILLE. The town was so big that the three of us could pass unnoticed. In the neighborhood around the place du Marché-au-Fil-de-Lin where we lived, my mother had found some old friends of hers, mostly women who had been divorced. No longer so completely alone, she could talk with other women of her age and situation in life. This was probably the only time in her years of unhappy exile when she did not privately regret her decision. But everything was more expensive than in Roubaix, and Saintenoy, dodging both the law and his creditors, had stopped doing anything at all. He no longer even went outdoors. It was my mother who kept our household going by taking in sewing and embroidery. As soon as I returned from school, where my mother had enrolled me immediately on reaching Lille, I would help her as much as possible.

. . .

"WHAT HAVE WE here, dear Catherine? Is this your daughter? Look at those big eyes, in that delicate little face! What an expression! This one has stories to tell, clearly. What is your name, Citizeness of the Big Eyes?"

It was mid-morning. I was accompanying my mother to the office of a pharmacist friend when a lady with the air of a faded cocotte accosted us in the street.

"Marceline Desbordes, Citizeness."

"I've heard that you like to recite poetry, is it true?"

"Yes, Citizeness."

"Well, I'm listening, O Marceline of the overflowing eyes. What can you improvise for me?"

Without giving it much thought, I obediently began to recite a poem that Saintenoy had taught me, while making me promise to keep it secret.

> *As a last ray of sun, a last flutter of wings,*
> *May enliven the last hours of the day,*
> *At the foot of the scaffold I touch my lyre's strings.*
> *Perhaps my turn is next to climb that way,*
> *Perhaps before the hour has—*

"Marceline, what are you saying!" my mother interrupted, her face suddenly pale.

Saintenoy's injunction, the reasons for which I didn't understand, came suddenly back to me. I blushed to the roots of my hair.

"No, no, it's wonderful, how very pleasant!"said the delighted lady. "What a pretty voice you have, Citizeness Marceline! Do you know, Catherine, you should put her in the theater, seriously. There has been a great vogue for it these last few years in Lille. They are always looking for new faces. I'm quite earnest. You must think about it, dear."

"We are grateful for your advice," said my mother quickly. "Good-bye."

Holding tightly to my arm, she pulled me away. Behind us, I heard the slightly mocking voice of the perfumed lady:

"Tell me, young Marceline, who was the author of that . . . *pointed* . . . verse?"

"I cannot tell you," I mumbled, before melting into the crowd.

Thus did André Chénier, guillotined barely three years before, enter my life.

"As you like poetry, we shall get along well," said Saintenoy that night, after hearing of the incident.

Since being ousted from office, the strange man had returned to his royalist allegiance and now started teaching me counterrevolutionary texts that he found God knows where and that it was wisest not to recite out loud. My mother dared say nothing. Saintenoy's interest in Chénier, whose poems were circulating clandestinely, owed more to the poet's politics than to his art. I, on the contrary, heard only their music. Each line wore a groove in my memory like an obsessively repeated melody.

BUT POETRY PROVIDED no nourishment for our thin bodies.

"We haven't enough. We'll never get by this way!" my mother wailed angrily every day. "I can't do any more."

"Then the girl will just have to work."

"I so want her to get an education."

"She'll pick things up in the school of life, which has the most practical curriculum."

My mother cried. Saintenoy shrugged. His power over her disgusted me. I didn't know whether she was still in love with him, but she was passionately dependent on him, and terrified at the idea that he might leave her for another. She would have done anything to keep him. So she gave in. Remembering what the lady on the street had told her, she came to see the theater as our only hope and assigned me the responsibility of providing for all three of us. I was not yet twelve. I didn't argue. Life, as I understood it, consisted of following and obeying.

In April 1798 I left the school in Lille that I had only recently entered, never to go back. My studies, though barely begun, were over forever. They had lasted four months.

On the very same day, I joined the chorus of the Théâtre de Lille. I was happy for a time. Church was the only performance hall I had ever set foot in before then. The fairy-tale enchantment of this new world exhilarated me. My daydreams were full of eccentric props, exotic costumes, and magical scenery, in which I seemed to discover fragments of my childhood. But I quickly learned the rules of this ship of the line. Once on board, discipline was essential, and danger was often present. A true war vessel, with twelve-pound guns. The stagehands who raised and lowered the flats, and who maintained the system of pulleys, weights, and counterweights, were in fact often former sailors, familiar with the intricacies of a ship's rigging and inured to vertigo.

I was soon cast in bit parts with only a line or two to say. I memorized my parts quickly. Like my mother, I had a thirst for knowledge. I carefully copied out page after page from printed books, Fénelon in particular, in order to improve my spelling. It was in this laborious school, of feathers and froufrous, of rolling and pitching, that I learned to write. The stage, on which I would have been ashamed to exhibit the drama of my life, paradoxically freed me from it by allowing me to become someone else. When my double felt pain, I groaned with her, the way one might do to support a friend. Without being aware of it, I was maturing and growing stronger. I was developing endurance.

AT THE TIME, theater was going through an odd period. Since the Revolution, any play that reflected royalist sentiments—or could somehow be thought to reflect them—had been forbidden. Only the most patriotic plays were permitted. The public, of course, had a definite preference for the old repertory. Even with all the forbidden words removed—"Duke," "Marquis," and "Count," for instance—people were more interested in hearing Molière than tales of Citizen This and Citizeness That. Fed up, audiences stayed away. The theaters grew emptier and emptier. To rescue their ticket sales, directors started to ignore the regulations and stage plays that were forbidden or considered frivolous, on the grounds that the newly commissioned republican dramas were not yet ready. When a director stepped too far beyond the bounds and tried the patience of the municipal council too severely, he would resign from his post, naming the troupe's leading actor to replace him, while he assumed the role of stage manager. And when it happened again, the two would simply switch back to their initial functions. Thus by small insubordinations and illegal maneuvers, theaters managed to get around the idiotic laws regulating the arts.

Despite his subterfuges, though, in April 1799 the director of the Théâtre de Lille found himself on the brink of bankruptcy. My mother didn't hesitate for a minute. She and Saintenoy lived entirely from the meager wages I earned on the stage, and she had heard some actors talk about Rochefort as a welcoming town. Quickly, she repacked our trunks. Saintenoy, who had sold all his belongings, was a ruined man and lived entirely from my charity.

WE WERE LEAVING again, but on what quest? What mirage were we pursuing now? To me, leaving Lille and going to Rochefort meant tearing myself even more radically from Douai, annihilating all hope of returning home, seeing my brother, my sisters, and my father, whom my obliging memory had endowed solely with virtues. It meant starting on a long descent toward a destination never to be reached, always dancing ahead, shining like a false light.

Or like love.

## 5

SSENTIAL," was what he'd whispered. A splendid finale, truly. I could not ask for a better nor find cause to complain. The epithet remains on me for several seconds, on this April dawn in 1821, clinging, like Henri's smell, which I would like to keep on my skin for a while longer. But already my arms close around empty space. Already my hands search in vain for a body to caress. Teeth marks, bruises, everything passes. I see again the downcast figure of the man I have just left forever, who stands motionless as the coach carries me away. Frozen on the threshold of our separation. Gradually only his outline remains, as though all flesh had been rubbed out between us, then just the rough sketch of his suit, an uncertain spot of color, a dot, and finally nothing. It's over. Latouche has disappeared from my dismal horizon. Love has capitulated, abdicated in the face of fear. I am destroyed. How will I go on living without him? My fate is bound to another man, and it is with another man that I will have to do battle on a daily basis. I am going to spend my life with someone who is not Henri. By what absurdity, what catastrophe? I will have to relearn the gestures of love all over again with Prosper. I have been amputated, rained with blows. Will I walk again someday?

Shaken by the potholes in the road, I feel nothing as my head strikes the sides of the coach. I did not tell Latouche that I am expecting a child.

. . .

Two DAYS FROM now, I will arrive in Lyon and be reunited
with my husband. How I hate Valmore at present! His placid
adoration, his rectitude, his unswerving honesty! But leaving
such a man is unthinkable. We married almost four years ago,
and for life. To think that nothing seemed more magnificent
to me, more indestructible than our union! At the time, Prosper's joyful love had swept away the black crepe that was strung
around me. Choked with mourning after all I had undergone,
I thought I had seen the last of happiness. As to marriage, I
had stopped believing in it long before. My life was a desert,
and Valmore's appearance there was miraculous. I could have
kissed his feet every day. And yet during the very reign of my
husband, despite his youth and sculpted body, one-eyed Henri
has subjugated me to his laws. Throughout this past year I have
barely managed to breathe, pulled on the one side by a man
who has taken everything from me and on the other by a man
who has given me too much. I have made a mockery of honor,
then cursed myself for my misdeeds, ever uncertain, incom-
plete, incapable of deciding where my heart should lead me. I
came even to wish that both men would disappear. Could it be
that I love neither?

"Essential, you have become essential to me!" Latouche finally sighed at our parting.

Too late, and only a temporary weakening. He corrected
himself immediately:

"I would have ruined everything, Marceline. I would never
have forgiven myself."

The look in Henri's eyes is now just an unspoken and tra-
duced lament. I absorb its melody and turn my head away.

Already Latouche is advancing on his side of the mountain. Already I am hurtling down the other. We have made our choice.

Lyon, for which I have been torn from Paris, seems detestable at first sight. Putting on a good face for Prosper and hiding my disarray, I arrive there, sore and battered, at the end of April. I must henceforth come to terms with my life, suffer a thousand small irritations, a thousand punishments day in and day out. The apartment we have rented on the place Terreaux has nothing to recommend it except for its location a few steps from the Grand Théâtre in the center of town. But it is tucked under the roof of an unsavory building so run-down, so forlorn, with its beams half eaten by termites and its walls coated with ineradicable grime, that I hardly dare to breathe there during the first days, so foul-smelling is the air. Lyon is a furnace, which doesn't help the stubborn infection of our wretched dwelling place.

Like a ribbon tied too tightly around my neck, this spring is definitely choking me. Nothing can untie it, seemingly. I suffer from the heat and feel as though I'm caged behind invisible bars. For all the hustle and bustle of moving, the furniture to deal with, the arrangements to see to, and despite this new city whose peel, whose bitter husk, needs to be scraped away to get at the flesh, I can attach no meaning to my days. Hardly had we opened our luggage than we found ourselves onstage desperately rehearsing the opening plays of the season. I am unconcerned: I recognize the roll and heave, having been harnessed to a ship's mast in mid-ocean before. I feel practically nothing. I walk like an automaton, performing my tasks mechanically. I seem to be sleeping on my feet.

. . .

"An attic! That's where your Marceline has brought us! If you had listened to me, if you had waited before making such a bad match, we wouldn't be here, in this miserable barn! Look, the only thing missing is hay, oats!"

"You're exaggerating, Mother."

"A hayloft! Ending my days in a hayloft, me!"

Ill and every day growing more sour, Anne-Justine is slowly dying, her rancorous outbursts stabbing Valmore incessantly. The constant presence of my detested mother-in-law prevents Prosper and me from ever being alone. In a sense, this is not for the worst. Everything about Valmore strikes me as loathsome: his voice, his way of talking, his gestures, his confidence, his good looks, his whole self. Even his breathing at night is a torture to me. But I accept my punishment in silence. With time, I tell myself doubtfully, I'll again find the man I married for love. At the moment, he is just the one who is not Henri. He can't help it, but I hold it against him.

My silent hatred does not keep me from attending the Grand Théâtre for his first performance. But Prosper is troubled by his mother and appears before the public of Lyon in less than his best form.

"Did you hear? Nothing. No hooting, no heckling. There was silence—total, humiliating, sarcastic silence—the worst of all insults."

"Come, you know that actors from Paris are not allowed to show the slightest fault. And Dorante is a role that takes time to prepare. Don't worry about it, dear heart, you'll win them over in Corneille's *Le Menteur.* They are always resistant to anything new in the provinces."

Prosper was bitter, hurt. My return to the boards, by contrast, despite all expectations and despite the calumnies that circulated about me following the publication of my verse, was rapturous, puzzlingly so. For my part, I approached the theater as though it were the slaughterhouse. My lack of enthusiasm for acting was flagrant. At thirty-five, worn in appearance, I was given the part of the artless Agnès in *The School for Wives*. Truly punished, I found myself onstage reading out "the maxims of marriage or the duties of the married woman":

> *She who in fulfillment of an honest vow*
> *Enters another's bed*
> *Must in despite of how things are done now*
> *Keep one thought in her head:*
> *That a man reserves sole claim to the woman he has wed . . .*

It was grotesque. And the critics adored me. But the public's favor, as I'm well aware, lasts only so long. Soon, as my condition becomes increasingly visible, the ridicule will grow beyond all bounds, and I will find myself playing ingenues with a great swollen belly.

WHEN HE LEARNED that I was expecting, Prosper danced with joy. It has made me find him more detestable than ever, though I can't quite say why. At least it gives me a pretext for putting off his advances. I have a few months' peace. Latouche's embraces, though not particularly memorable, have walled my body in. Blows could rain down on me, I am of stone. Valmore is in such transports that he readily accepts the distance I impose and, blaming my apathy on my delicate condition, hardly notices my failure to share in his joy. The loss of our first baby, my frail health, and my age have probably made him believe his mother's prattling, and she predicted from the outset that we would never have children. At Hippolyte's birth, the cinch that that woman kept around Valmore was loosened. The announcement of my new pregnancy has taken the bridle off my husband for good. It was high time.

Again with this pregnancy finding myself exhausted, nauseous, and alternating between despondency and rapture, I painfully endure my body's changes. I pass through all the seasons in a day. For no apparent reason I am gray or summery. Carrying this child in my womb, I feel as though I have been charged with murder, only the corpse has not been found yet. With the threat always hanging over me, I go on pretending to live as a free woman, sometimes euphoric at having gotten the better of human justice, sometimes terrified that my sins will catch up to me. I am like a criminal on the run.

And yet the guilty life sending out roots inside me is helping me cope with the devastating emptiness I feel, with the temptation to surrender, to wail, and with the endless wait for letters from Paris that never come. Silence is the deadliest weapon that could be aimed at me. In the capital, where I published a few poems, where new friends swore eternal friendship to me, and where many places carry the memory of Henri, I am already being forgotten. Caught up in the bustle around her, Pauline writes infrequently. As for Latouche, his accomplished letters, which I await with bated breath, give me a mixed, an atrocious pleasure. Some afford me moments of respite that bring color and hope back to my life. Others scratch a barbarous scrawl across the sky. A sentence, a single word can alter the tone of my days. There is nothing left to expect, yet I still believe. In what? I dread Henri's letters as much as his silence. Then, when everything seems lost, I think of this child that he will never be able to take back from me, that he will know nothing of. A little creature of rage and foam that I will have to care for in false climes, but whom I want with all my heart.

I AM RETURNING to my poetry. People say that women shouldn't write. But I write. Henri has unlaced the girdle around my heart. It is the only freedom left me, but it is a considerable one. It also keeps me on the side of normality, adding to my daily life its needed quotient of unreason, a connection to my other lives. I no longer make an attempt to seem, to resemble, to appear to be somebody else. Rid of all influences, I am finally me, sculpting my words in my own image.

Just as I foresaw, the Lyon public's craze for me comes to an end as extravagantly as it began.

"There, what did I tell you, Prosper? They will never like us anywhere but in Paris."

"The theater audience is being manipulated. The Chaprons, who have ruled the Grand Théâtre for many years, were against our coming here. And they own all the critics."

"The Chaprons or someone else, it makes no difference. There will always be jealousies, rivalries. Let's leave."

"And go where? Who would hire us in your present condition?"

The last months of my pregnancy are a painful trial. Exhausted, sick, I arrive onstage to whistles and low laughter. In the back of our attic apartment, curled up like a porcupine, I lose myself in writing, while my mother-in-law, for whom I care not a fig, glares at me balefully. I miss Hippolyte's gaiety, the creative peace of Constant's studio, Pauline, Latouche, Paris. Paris, where I could be loved, cherished, celebrated—me, orphaned and ignorant, the poor little girl from the provinces. Paris, from which Valmore has abducted me, though he cannot offer me a life. Resentment toward him builds up quietly in me.

It is in these circumstances that my daughter is born. I name her Hyacinthe.

"In Greek mythology," I tell Prosper, "it was a character who was changed into a flower. Look at all those blond curls. Just like a bouquet."

Hyacinthe. It's pure madness, but no one knows Henri's real name. Other than he. I was weak and couldn't resist, though I may come to regret it later. We'll see, at any rate. For the moment, with my life in a state of drought, my daughter is like a bulb that has flowered out of season. I am enamored of her. She smells like the île Saint-Louis, the pont de la Tournelle, the poplar behind Notre-Dame, the Seine, the rue des Saints-Pères. Yet when the month of rest that I was granted by the director of the Grand Théâtre comes to an end, I am obliged, though barely recovered from my confinement, to tread the boards again, putting my baby out to be nursed by a vigorous peasant woman on the outskirts of Lyon.

"How much longer must we endure the buckets of tears wept by Mme Valmore, whose excess of sensibility is as tiresome as her worn face? Only her voice and her impeccable diction justify her presence on the stage. And yet . . ." Egged on by the Chapron clan, the critics have been so insulting at my expense, so hurtful, that I am coming to an end of my endurance. At dawn, after a night of insomnia and tears, I find myself balling up my fists to keep from packing my bags and running away, leaving behind my marriage and the theater, which are similar lies. I am past the point of being able to dissemble any longer. Then suddenly, at the end of December, Anne-Justine dies. Prosper is relieved, inevitably, but so undone by his mother's demise that I have no choice but to put aside, as one carefully folds away clean sheets in the household linen closet, my desire to go elsewhere. The man needs me. Who else calls on me in this way? No one. Latouche is clearly living his life perfectly well without me.

And so, little by little, not realizing it, not wanting to realize it, I lose track of the key to the old wooden chest in which my dreams lie folded away.

I have finally convinced Valmore that we should leave the harmful atmosphere of Lyon, where Hippolyte—at my request—has rejoined us. My son's joyful presence, in concert with the visits I make to my little Hyacinthe, has proved such a balm after the bitterness of Anne-Justine that I have started to regain strength. Rapturous, I bestir myself on Prosper's behalf, firing off queries and entreaties to get him another engagement in Paris. Nothing comes of it. Our exile is to last a bit longer. Pauline writes me sporadic letters with the latest news of the capital and her views on Henri's literary hackwork: "By satirizing the literary world and scattering his efforts in many directions—think of it, he is publishing a novel, a travel book on Montmorency, and a translation of Goethe's *Alder King* all at the same time, while living an utterly dissolute life—he has earned a fair number of enemies . . ."

In the end, Henri de Latouche amounts to little. Henri, my great love, my treasure. My head is spinning. At times, I lose control. I fall into a trance, find myself writing letters to dead friends, talking to myself, composing immodest and dangerous poems about my mad and obsessive passion. I address Latouche directly, cast doubt on him and his sincerity, live all over again the hours of splendor and pain, imagine a new day, then bring it all crashing down. As though committing suicide, I finally ask him to stop writing me: "Don't write. For me to learn in the depths of your absence that you love me is to glimpse heaven without ever being allowed to reach it." Yet if I am to be reborn, I have no choice. Hoping secretly to be disobeyed, I request that Henri break the last bond uniting us. He complies. Accepts defeat.

I still have poetry.

AT THE END of April 1823 we are in Bordeaux, where Valmore has signed on for a season's engagement. I was so happy to leave Lyon that I forgot how much I had suffered in Bordeaux some twenty years before with my mother. An era now long vanished. Paris too is fading. All the better. The capital now makes me shudder. After two years in purgatory, Bordeaux's blue sky, its white walls, its fountains, its sun, and its soft breezes bring me back with an abrupt swerve toward the world of the living. Here I am seen as an honorable wife and the mother of a young family. To my considerable surprise, I am welcomed as a woman of letters. The little poems that I published in Paris have reached more readers than I thought. Henri has not done me harm only. He is also acting to my benefit, I'm sure of it, in the salons of Paris. What a sweet revenge on society! I who have remained so long hidden am eager to be recognized. The large and airy apartment we occupy on the rue de la Grande-Taupe quickly fills with all the literary world of Bordeaux. Prosper's success at the Grand Théâtre puts us in a more comfortable situation. His earnings have increased considerably. It is settled: I will quit the stage and withdraw from the theater. No regrets. Finally I will be able to devote myself to my two children and to writing. I am now in regular attendance at the Nairacs' on the rue du Palais-Gallien, the most fashionable and prestigious salon in the whole region. At peace with myself and Valmore, I have plunged into the pleasures of society. In Paris, where I was ashamed of my origins and afraid of saying the wrong thing, I was always retiring. Here it is different. On some nights, by general request, I rise and sing ballads to the assembled guests while accompanying myself on the guitar. Or I tell old Flemish legends, or myths from the Antilles. I want to be loved.

ACCLAIMED ON ALL sides, Valmore renews his contract for three more years, which allows us to move into even larger quarters on the rue Montesquieu. I have stopped asking myself questions. Provincial life lends itself to stillness and peace. Time's breeze wafts around me. I sink into this sleepy life, savoring all its fecundity, our bodies in harmony again, tasting the simple joy of sharing with another the flatness of daily life, its occasional mindlessness, its silences—but sharing, yes, separating ourselves from the animals. It's not all that bad. The pain I felt is almost gone. I refuse to indulge it. No sign at all from Henri. Pauline is right, the man is too scattered. He coolly takes the sacrament at every altar and forswears his old idols without the least compunction. How he betrayed me! How wrong I was about him! Sometimes as I compose a poem, his face appears before me, remorseful and unsure. I take up my pen, my cutlass, to disfigure him. I avoid giving my thoughts too much license.

At the Nairacs' house, which I frequent as a star of the Parisian firmament, I have met the very young Vigny and Goya, the painter, stooped with age, who is painting my portrait. In my spare time I study English, prudently filling even the slightest void in my day. Active, very active. Entreated on all sides, I finally publish a new collection of poems in December 1824. I am unaware of my notoriety in Paris. I simply don't realize it. Pauline says that everyone is talking about me. It is difficult for me to believe this, and I put it out of my mind. Strengthened by the stability of my life in Bordeaux, the adulation of my little circle, the incomparable happiness of having living children (despite the fragility of Hyacinthe's health) and a loving husband, and believing myself freed from the jail of my lost passion, I feel myself to be invulnerable. One hundred fifty leagues from Henri, unthinking and naive, I no longer fear him. I am afraid only of myself, and only intermittently. Of my desire to backslide, to fail. The flatness of the plain.

The boredom of the plain.

## 6.

*I*T WAS IN ROCHEFORT that I wrote my first poem and gave my first kiss. As if poetry was to be entwined from the outset with love. I was almost thirteen and had seen only the darker side of the emotions: weariness between man and wife, betrayal between lovers. The imprint was a negative one, embedded in me unawares. Yet my mistrust gave way under the first assault. In the battle of love I would follow the path of defeat, as my mother's model daughter.

It started in Charente.

WE CAME TO Rochefort in late April 1799. The season was just starting. Our lodgings were a few steps off the place d'Armes, a short distance from the Théâtre de la Coupe d'Or, whose charming hall held three hundred seats, all of them filled night after night by the navy officers laying over in town. I was cast in nearly all the productions set before this rowdy audience. Eager for new faces, they attended with rapt and dreamy expressions. I was expected to learn dozens of speeches by heart and to change out of one role immediately into the next. There was so much to do that I easily found work for my mother as a seamstress, taking in costumes, letting them out, rearranging or repairing them. It was a very different experience from the theater in Lille. The stage was much smaller and much closer to the spectators, which placed me immodestly among all those young men. In the light of the candles, I sometimes saw them looking at me awkwardly. Naively, I laughed at their shyness. The nuance between clumsiness and confusion escaped me utterly.

Rochefort was tiny, and oddly laid out. It was a port, or more accurately a shipyard, differing markedly from the three towns I had previously known, casting all my points of reference to the winds. The sight of masts suddenly rising at the end of a street astonished me. I could never get used to seeing a ship between two houses. I was intrigued, charmed, and vaguely frightened.

Everything was related to the sea. A rope manufactory sprawled along one bank of the Charente River. The foundry, whose royal fleur-de-lis had been pried from the facade during the Revolution, employed two hundred workers and had four furnaces, placed so as to catch the wind, for casting cannons, mortars, and bells. The naval academy, even the prison ship where the convicts languished, reiterated that Rochefort's sole reason for being was the ocean.

Among the actors in our troupe, there was a great fascination with the ships that had been built along the Charente.

"I saw Lafayette sail for America with my own two eyes."

"The *Hermione*, now there was a ship! They don't build frigates like that anymore," said another.

"Brave men who went out to defend the cause of liberty—"

"And thumb their noses at the English!"

Yet something about the geometrical streets at right angles struck a false, an artificial note. The town was conceived top to bottom by Louis XIV and Colbert, who designed the plan for it. Charming as it was, it had the aspect of an abandoned toy, a forgotten whim—soulless. After the Revolution its main church was turned into a fencing hall.

It was raining, the wind blowing, but gently so that the stays and halyards chattered. We had a day off at the end of the summer. I was strolling in the shipyard with my mother and several friends.

"Have you noticed these oaks?" one of the women said. "Some have an anchor and a fleur-de-lis carved into the trunk."

"Why would the trees be marked in that way?" another asked.

"Because they're reserved for the navy," said a bantering voice behind us. "First they pick them out, then they cut them down in the fall or winter when the sap stops running."

He was young and handsomely proportioned, wearing the uniform of a student at the naval academy. His face was as delicate as a woman's, his nose aquiline. Chestnut locks tumbled onto his forehead. Tall, and with a ruddy glow suffusing his cheeks, he cut a fine figure.

"If I may introduce myself, Citizeness Saintenoy, my name is Louis Lacour and I am studying mathematics with your husband. My compliments to you," he said, addressing my mother, whose eyes shone with unspoken gratitude.

She felt for a moment that she had entered fashionable society. The cadet's manners were refined and his ways flattering. He had managed more or less by ruse to score a point in his favor.

"And to your gracious daughter," he went on, turning toward me.

Awkward in the extreme and little used to compliments, I blushed to the roots of my hair.

"You are very kind, sir," said my mother, who could never bring herself to use the term "Citizen."

Her keeping to the old usage had in fact nothing to do with politics. It was just a question of habit.

"Do you expect to be shipping out presently?"

It was all the cadets ever thought of, their raison d'être, their only subject of discussion. Shipping out, shipping out! The words were always on their lips.

"I hope to, ma'am," he confided. "A bright future awaits me there, a long way off, beyond the seas . . ."

"Where would that be?" asked my mother, whose voice trembled slightly.

"In Saint Domingue . . ."

It was thus that the dream of the Antilles began its gradual, mad conquest of my mother's mind and that Louis Lacour entered my life.



HE HAD FOLLOWED us along the banks of the Charente, he confessed to me later, in order to accost us. Having gained our acquaintance, the handsome cadet was invited to our lodgings. My mother thought him nice.

"Agreeable, he's very agreeable," she would say.

She arranged to tender invitations to him through Saintenoy. Since our arrival in Rochefort, Saintenoy had regained some of his confidence, thanks to his reputation as a teacher, which for once he did not squander, and thanks also probably to the fire he so effortlessly ignited in the eyes of the easy women of this port town. For my part, I never understood whether Louis Lacour was more interested in my mother or myself. And what were her intentions toward him? Had she noticed the confusion that came over me at the sight of his dashing uniform? I was unsure. Most likely she thought that

I was still young and naive. Struggling with her own difficulties, she may have seen Louis only as a playmate for me. She did not notice that I was growing up. It would have meant that she was growing old. No doubt she also liked to think that the young naval man was courting her.

I on the other hand was quite desperate to detach myself from her skirts. Other things existed, I felt sure, than this rough and starchy fabric. For all my shyness, I made attachments easily and was given to friendship. I confided readily in others. After Roubaix, where I had coiled inwardly on myself, I opened up to the world outside. Yet there were subjects that I deliberately kept in shadow, or only exposed when I could control the lighting. My past, I was well aware, belonged to me alone.

My MOTHER SAW nothing to fear in a man of twenty-one being thrown into the company of her young daughter and must have had another reason for taking an interest in her lover's pupil. Louis Lacour, whose parents had died in the French islands, spoke of the Antilles without ever having set foot in them.

"There are such riches there, Citizeness Saintenoy. They even say the floors and walls of the houses are covered in plaques of pure gold!"

An inexhaustible storyteller, an excellent orator who loved to hear himself speak, he would launch for our benefit into endless, picturesque, and zany tales about the colonies. At first amused but skeptical, my mother gradually became besotted with Louis's fancies, which she appropriated for herself. The only book she still read was the romance *Paul et Virginie*. Crossing the ocean toward those exotic lands where all our yesterdays would be erased was an idea that soon grew from an idle distraction to a serious obsession. I saw the danger early on but was unsure how to counter it. I was terrified. Saintenoy made no effort to draw my mother away from her fantastic daydreams. Her somnambulism offered him no inconvenience. He took the opportunity to pay his full addresses to the *filles de joie*. The mulattas could wait. He was quite happy with the girls of Rochefort.

I felt Louis's frank and confident voice flow through my veins. I saw his fleshy lips form into savage pouts. Words emerged. Something to do with frigates, Bougainville, begonias, but I listened only to their music.

WE HAD NOT yet been in Rochefort a full season. In the early spring of 1800, despite all its success, the Coupe d'Or theater signed an agreement with the theaters of Bayonne, Dax, Pau, and Bordeaux to rotate the actors among the towns. Some members of the company decided to leave immediately for Bordeaux to arrange a more secure contract that would not require them to travel. Once again my mother made an abrupt decision. We, too, would move to Bordeaux.

I said nothing. I had been a child when we arrived in Rochefort but would leave it an adolescent, carrying my first poems and the memory of Louis's furtive kisses, planted when my mother's back was turned. Nothing more had passed between us. My first romance did not stray beyond the bounds of modesty. But I freed it in my poetry. Louis's clumsy hugs, his pretension, even his vanity were transformed by my pen. I secretly imagined that he married me. Humble and obedient, I would have waited for him at home while he traveled the seas. My ambitions reached no farther. I wished for no more vivid a fate. A boy had kissed me a little, run his hands through my hair, whispered a few sweet things in my ear, and already I saw myself sharing his household. I was in love. At least I thought so.

While we were packing our trunks for the trip to Bordeaux, Louis Lacour shipped for the Antilles without warning. Rochefort, a town I would never return to, had given me my first love wound and a furious need to write.


Louis had left. On the sly, not bothering to say good-bye, already absorbed in his own adventure, a stranger. My first love was an interrupted voyage. I had trouble admitting the thought. Why should I convince myself that I would never see Louis again, that he would never return, that the part he was to play in my life was over? The idea that Louis's path would never again cross mine was painful to me. I made up my mind simply to ignore it.

In front of the others, though, I had to hide my feelings. My mother joked cruelly about Louis, calling him "Marceline's sweetheart." Could she have known how her words lacerated me each time? Was she aware of it? I pretended indifference, kept to myself my tears and the emotions I had silenced, my secret hopes and the words of love destined never to be heard. By now we were in Bordeaux. Ever lower on the continent, ever farther from Flanders and my native town. How far would our flight take us? I didn't dare ask my mother any questions. I was afraid she would begin her delirium about the islands again, this litany that terrified me because I sensed its ineluctable force, fatefully driving us toward our port of embarkation. My own dreams were so much more modest! How difficult it was to recognize myself in my mother, who so longed for permanent change, and to trade her life for another! I didn't understand her. Had she been willing, she would not have lacked for suitors. She was beautiful, with a cold majesty that was slightly terrifying. But she had too elevated an opinion of love. My father had been imposed on her, and she had endured his mediocrity for twenty years. Then she had chosen Saintenoy. But even though she passed him off in Bordeaux as her second husband, I think it was all over between them. No one came to take his place. My mother politely held off all advances. To accept them would have been to fall from the role of sovereign lover to that of encumbered mistress, to exchange old chains for new. She had learned her lesson.

Bordeaux, spring 1800. It was growing to be, it had grown to be, an obsession: this accursed ocean crossing that my mother produced like a bogey at the slightest pretext. Realizing that it bought him a temporary respite, Saintenoy had started to fall in with her fantasies. The cad was even encouraging her. Whenever I heard them nattering on this subject, I would slip into the imaginary room where Louis was waiting for me, and I would hear the sand that had been strewn over the floor, as in every respectable Flemish house, crackle under my hurrying feet.

Bordeaux appealed to me. With its medieval aspect, its treeplanted alleys, its big, red-tiled, white-stone buildings, its high, clear windows, its sumptuous townhouses, its wrought-iron balconies, it looked something like the Spain that was so much talked of. The air was soft, the sun generous. As a girl from the north, I felt every morning as though I were entering a veil of light. This impression came to an end at the threshold of the Grand Théâtre, which, with its twelve columns to the nine muses and three goddesses, rose like a recently built cathedral. The first time I went to the place de la Comédie, it left me open-mouthed with astonishment. One of the most prestigious stages in all France. The hall, with its blue velvet seats, was magnificent.

By 1800, however, Bordeaux's theater had slipped considerably in reputation. It was no longer a theater but a brothel. In 1796, a woman named Suzanne Latrappy, a mediocre singer and a grasping, dishonest, and thoroughly unpleasant person, had somehow become its director. After the evening performance, about which she cared not a fig, La Latrappy organized clandestine balls, where women of loose morals danced with the more prominent members of Bordeaux society. Given the circumstances, most of the actors quickly took to their heels.

I, of course, was far from imagining the situation that awaited me and was readily hired in the role of "third ingenue."

I quickly caught on. Every day hell gaped a little wider at my feet. Small unpleasantnesses, repeated humiliations. The brutality of La Latrappy terrified me. As much as possible I avoided her. After a few months, she sought me out backstage.

"How young you are! Look at your slender waist, your air of innocence. Do you realize you could take home a lot more money than you do, my sweet?"

"Truly, ma'am? How, ma'am?"

"After this evening's performance, there is a—what should I call it—a second performance. Do you see what I'm saying?"

"No, ma'am."

"You stupid girl," she said. "Are you really such a ninny?"

"I don't understand. What do you mean?"

She was now holding me tightly by the arm and bending her gaze on me fiercely.

"Listen, my dear, either you come tonight after the performance and play on the laps of the consequential men of this town, or you can look elsewhere for work. Is that clear enough?"

I ran to the garret, where we lived packed together, my mother, Saintenoy, and I, and which the sun flooded with afternoon light. The building, set at the angle of rue Sainte-Catherine and rue de la Merci, was old and dilapidated, but it had the advantage of being only a few steps from the Grand Théâtre. Also, the landlady was not very particular and was generally disposed to believe her lodgers' stories. Caught up in the plans for her trip, my mother, who worked at the theater as an usher, had shut her eyes to the unsavory goings-on after hours. I, too, had pretended not to notice that when the music lovers and solid citizens filed out of their loges, they were replaced by ladies of light virtue.

"By all the saints," said my mother when she heard my story, "what an atrocity!"

She immediately dragged me into the church behind the place du Saint-Projet.

"Lord, show us the way," she implored.

As we emerged onto the square, she began to tremble. Her eyes grew round and staring. She pointed to a house not far from the church.

"Look, Marceline, look! That is where the comte de Tustal lived, the man who made his fortune in Saint Domingue."

Dejected, I said nothing. I thought of the rent to be paid, Saintenoy's increasingly flagrant betrayals, and the quiet madness of my mother, whom I was bound to follow to her journey's end. Where would that be? I preferred not to know. In the place du Saint-Projet, my eyes wandered over the sculpted flowers and seashells under the overhang of the fountain.

. . .

"Your wages?" said La Latrappy, after I screwed up my courage to ask for what was owed me. "Would you listen to that! The impertinent, disobedient little wretch! Why did you not come to the evening's entertainment when I asked you?"

"My—honor—"

I fumbled for words, from fear and hunger.

"Your honor?" she said, with so vicious an expression that I instinctively backed away. "Then let your honor be your payment!"

And she slapped me across the face.

I had never felt so miserable, so humiliated. I had not eaten a true meal for several days. On the way home, by the rue Porte-Dijeaux, I collapsed. A young woman who played walk-on parts recognized me and had me carried to our lodgings.

My story quickly made the rounds of Bordeaux. People felt sympathy for me. I was visited by two important actors who happened to be passing through town, André and Anne-Justine Lanchantin, who used the stage name "Valmore." Anne-Justine already at that point was hardly acting anymore. André Valmore, like me, had taken to the stage only because he was forced to.

"I had no choice: I didn't believe in God, and my father was doing everything he could to convert me. Once he even made me eat dirt that he had dug up from a cemetery on the pretext that it was sacred. Then he had me locked up with the Benedictines, from whom I managed to escape. So I changed my name and went into the theater to make a living."

I liked André Valmore immediately. Much more than his wife, who had been deceived in her first marriage and was still

bitter and unhappy. The love between her and André, condemned and illicit, had only become an accepted fact once the
divorce law was instituted. Late in their lives their marriage
produced an adorable little boy called Prosper. On the day of
their visit, buoyed by a gust of good humor, he kissed me passionately on the lips and disappeared at a run with his face a
flaming red. I was fifteen and he was barely eight.

The Valmores left Bordeaux soon afterward. I became the
leader of a dissident troupe of actors who were as disgusted as
I with the carryings-on of La Latrappy. We played in another
theater. The growing weight of scandal and the complaints
against her in the end ruined the horrible woman. But the
harm had been done. The Grand Théâtre would take years to
reclaim its place in the first rank of theaters. And I was forever
revolted by the stage.

My mother's hair was starting to turn white. In the spring of
1801, she decided to realize her Antillean dream. It was reportedly easier to find passage from Bayonne, and so for months
while we waited for our travel authorization, the three of us—
my mother, Saintenoy, and I—worked for the Bayonne Theater's traveling company, seeing a succession of new roads and
towns: Tarbes, Pau, Dax. Desperate, my mother also took up
acting. One more depravity hardly mattered. Saintenoy filled
the position of prompter. My mother, I hardly know how,
scraped together enough money for my passage and hers. But
Saintenoy didn't have the resources for a ticket of his own and
signed on with the ship as a steward.

The moment finally arrived. It was the month of November. On the morning of the twenty-eighth, tears streaming

helplessly down my face and certain I would never see France again, I boarded the brig *Le Mars* with my mother. Saintenoy was supposed to meet us there. My mother stood on the bridge and scanned the wharf in every direction. Silent, dignified. She waited several minutes, her whitening hair lifted by the breeze. Then her lips trembled a little, her shoulders sagged in a movement that lasted only a few seconds. Raising her head, she took a deep breath and said: "He isn't coming. Let's get on with our business. Come."

And so it was that the two of us, alone in the world, prepared to cross the ocean.

## 7

ECEMBER 1824. My new collection of verse, *Elegies and New Poems*, has just been published. It has abruptly plunged me into a sadness I did not expect to feel again. Writing, I realize, fills the voids in me and stills my urge to surrender. When I am not writing, I don't know what to do with my hands. What will people's reaction be? I am so far from Paris. The small glory I have won in Bordeaux has colored my vision. It is not hard to become a provincial queen. In the capital, though, nobody outside a tiny circle may know my name. What if my clumsy verse were merely to elicit indifference or contempt? Have I persuaded myself of something more to help me stand the pain of being only myself? And Henri, who knows everything and will read between the lines? Suddenly I am afraid. I made my entrance into literature in my own guise, presented myself with my flesh exposed. I am afraid now that I have shown too much, or not enough. It feels as though I am awaiting sentencing. At present I am alone, between moments, unable to find anything in my days to hold on to, everything once more smooth and slippery. My life in Bordeaux seems hollow, the town's conservatism unbearable, and the snobbery of its inhabitants ridiculous. Nothing of what first enchanted me retains any merit in my eyes, not even the Holy Week procession, whose poetry I praised on our arrival and which I now think is over-blown and hypocritical. The smell of incense disgusts me. I can't stand the sound of drums and bugles.

I should immediately get back to writing, but I can't bring myself to. The Nairacs have left Bordeaux for Paris. Their hurried departure has made it all the more evident that I am at loose ends. Empty, the hours ahead send back only the echo of what has been lost. Nostalgia for the capital has overtaken me again, boredom pulls me inward. At times when the children are asleep and I lean my forehead against the large windows of the drawing room, my gaze roams over the paving stones, the glistening and too clean walls of the building across the way, and I find that I almost miss the theater. What use is the freedom I fought so hard to obtain? My life has passed. I will soon be forty. The silence around me is the silence of a burial, my own, in plain style, in the miserable neglect of a provincial town.

ONE DAY UNCLE Constant sends me a newspaper article from Paris praising my new collection. Behind the writer's pseudonym I easily recognize Latouche's hand. I shiver uncontrollably. It is at once a delicious and a crushing sensation. I have waited so long for this moment. Did I not write for him, are not all my poems aimed at him, have they not replaced the letters I forbade myself to send him, is he not the only one who can read them? His reaction does not come as a surprise. Publishing this book was a way of holding out my hand to him. His compliments perturb me. His literary opinion means a great deal to me, but I sense that his criticism is not free of calculation and rage. And when I look around at Hippolyte leaping joyfully and Hyacinthe taking her first steps, his violence turns my blood cold. Distraught, acting on instinct, I rub myself in the dark against Prosper's rough bark, as though against an age-old tree.

But my uncle is insistent. Sending word through him, I thank Henri for his complimentary remarks. I am a polite courtesan, distant and humiliated, bending low as greatness sweeps past with a cursory nod of recognition. I blush at the indignity. More than three years on, I shudder at the state of dependency to which Henri could easily reduce me. I know his power over me. Recognizing this, my body wants to live one last spring before the inevitable decline. Fighting not to hear the wolf's call, I become aware that I am pregnant. Life seems to want to give me back the three babies she took from me earlier. It is only fair. For the time being, I stifle all other feelings and let nature blossom inside me.

DURING THIS SAME period, in the fat handwriting of a diligent farmwife, my sister Eugénie writes to say that Félix, who had been sinking a little deeper in drink every day, has fled from her home, where he was recently staying. Despite Valmore's express ban, she writes, he may be trying to wheedle his way into our house to sponge off me. The prospect is terrifying. Prosper would chase him off with his gun, and my tears would count for nothing. He thinks my brother is just a drunkard and a vagabond. I see it differently. The army, the war, and a prison sentence have destroyed him. Félix was sacrificed, just as I was. Under his tousled mop, he is still my old playmate. Will the poor wretch dare to knock at Constant's door, though my uncle is so poor now that he eats only once a day? Where will Félix go? Not to Rouen, to Cécile's house. Abandoned by her companion and her sons, my eldest sister lives

in a perpetual dream, her hair untended. She has started talking to her cats and to the flowers in her garden.

My family's decline often keeps me awake at night.

"Look on them more coldly, Marceline, put them out of
your mind," says Prosper. "You can't help everyone on earth."

"They are my family."

"You are not responsible for what they do," he says.

But I consider that I owe them something all the same, as
though it were my fault that I was extricated from the mud and
left them behind. As though I should pay the rest of my life for
having followed my mother when I was ten years old. As though
I were an accomplice in her desertion. It is a burden I bear with
bent back, unable to voice a complaint, a tacit agreement that
exists between my siblings and me. For years I have been bleed-
ing myself white so that they could get by. It's just the way it is,
and there's no changing it. I need their love. My heart flutters
when I open Eugénie's letters, eager to sniff the scent of Lenten
flowers again. And each time there is the same disappointment,
each time I feel the little girl from Douai, who used to run
laughing among the graves of the church of Notre-Dame, die a
further death. Only poetry still allows me to find that girl again.
But when I don't write, I only want to look straight in front of
me. Is it possible that I still have some good years ahead?

*I confess that I am puzzled, dear niece, at the contempt you
show Monsieur de Latouche, who has made such proofs of
kindness toward you and defended you like a tiger everywhere
in Paris. Since his near duel with Nodier last month, this
high-minded man had chosen the path of discretion and withdrawn from public view to help (though with no plans to make
a practice of it) a promising young writer, Balzac by name, or*

*something in that vein. Henri de Latouche has only emerged*
*from his retirement to champion your poems. Your silence,*
*about which he has complained to me several times, has driven*
*him back into hiding. Ingratitude was never like you. Have*
*the provinces changed you so utterly?*

So Uncle Constant wrote me in March. It's too much! Un-
knowingly, my uncle is delivering me into Henri's hands once
again. I can already see the slight movement of his head with
which he brushes away any trifling contrariety. Lost in his palettes and gouaches, he is far from imagining what Henri and
I lived through. And are still living through. So as not to displease my uncle, and because I need no other pretext to end my
vow of silence, I take up my pen again. Almost four years have
passed since I broke off contact with Latouche, since I asked
him not to write me. Today I am going back on the resolve that
has cost me more than any other in my life, and I want the tone
to be reserved, detached.

The postman soon arrives back at my door with a letter. Henri
did not wait long to reply. At first I refuse to take receipt of it,
an animal defense that surprises me. But it is beyond my powers.
Changing my mind, I run downstairs after the postal employee,
then climb back up to my room, winded, imagining that I am
still safe there. Yet I have once again invited my lover in.

GINGERLY AT FIRST, our correspondence picks up again. I am
practically immobilized by my pregnancy, which is more exhausting than the earlier ones. I have trouble keeping up with
my duties as a wife and mother, and now there is the added
burden of taking care of old Valmore. Prosper's father has fi-

nally retired from the stage and come to live with us. I abandon
myself to the pleasure of words, gradually letting go of all reserve. Hundreds of leagues from Henri, without the slightest
prospect of seeing him again, I dare to write him things that I
would never say, perhaps even that I do not think. I like love. I
like to hear it, give it, receive it, contemplate it, unfurl it in long
sentences that go beyond my timid feelings. At the receiving
end the gratitude is so lively, the understanding so penetrating,
that it sweeps away my better judgment. Never had I imagined such a ravine within myself. Never had anyone managed
to extract its ore. My head spins with my new wealth, and with
Latouche's celebration of it. In daily life, Prosper assuages my
profane needs. I should be perfectly satisfied.

Yet the more Henri writes me, the more I expect him to
write. Our letters have become the most important element
in my life. Hardly do I receive a letter of his than I run to
my writing desk to compose my reply—a flow that is stronger
every time. The danger excites and disconcerts me. I have the
impression that I am someone else. I hold my breath for a moment, caught in a quickening whirl that I am unaware of, convinced that I have achieved a perfect equilibrium between the
two lives I want to lead, but in the end I am probably rejecting
both. Henri inhabits me completely, a secret lodger whom I try
to keep out of sight as best as possible. An attentive observer,
though, would easily guess at his hiding place. And I sometimes
catch Prosper looking at me with suspicion and worry.

"I AM A great deal of trouble to you, aren't I, daughter?"

I have always loved old Valmore like a father, and his presence here anchors me to the family hearth. It also spares me

an awkward confrontation with Prosper, whose conversation these days strikes me as thin.

"Not in the least, father-in-law. The children adore you, and you know how much Prosper and I hold you in affection."

"All the same, dear Marceline, it's one more weight for you to carry."

"Don't be silly. In fact, you keep me company, tell me stories, listen when I tell mine, and you even like my cooking. Prosper is always off at rehearsals, so—without you, I'd be pacing back and forth like a lion in a cage."

I am also that woman, satisfied with little nothings, simple, wearing a coarse dress and resting her tired hands, who would sacrifice all art for a kiss from her son, a laugh from her daughter. Yes, and I am also that nurturing mother, who takes pleasure in comfortable habits, enjoys the company of ordinary people more than the great and the good, and relishes a quiet evening with nothing at venture or at risk beside her loving husband. I can flutter easily enough among titles and family crests, hold up my end of a pointed discussion, shine in the salons, and elicit perfect love. But perhaps in the end I am only truly myself in my life's backstage areas, where Prosper caresses my unpainted face.

And in the upholstered loges of my verse, where only Henri can find me.

Pauline and Latouche both write to tell me that all Paris is besotted with my poems, but I don't believe them and think they are exaggerating. The little girl from Douai whose misadventures, grossly distorted, are being talked of in the highest circles now has the wind at her back. People shake their heads over my father's mishap at becoming a victim of the Revolution.

They worship my mother, who sought her fortune beyond the seas for the sake of her children, as a saint of virtue and courage. And they applaud the rhymes of the orphan girl who was thrown into the theater, and who found salvation through love and poetry. Deep in the provinces, certain of having been forgotten by everyone, I never imagined that my poems would so catch people's fancy, or that my own person would elicit such a raft of questions and polemics. Some say I am debauched, others a martyr. My celebrity clearly derives from Latouche. Beyond defending my interests, he speaks actively in my favor. Thus he has managed to obtain for me, through the good graces of Madame Récamier, whom he met during her stay in Italy a few years ago, the offer of a royal grant. As he must have expected, for I have never hidden my Bonapartist sympathies, I refuse it. Henri kicks up a tremendous fuss. Prosper, on the other hand, approves my decision.


THIS TIME THE pain is horrendous. I am almost forty years old. On November 29, 1825, I give birth to my last child. A little girl as dark-haired as my earlier one was blond, and who is also not to be baptized. Valmore, a fierce atheist, is against it. For my part I give little weight to appearances, holding more to faith than to the faithful, and to the sacred than the sacraments. Enamored of all things Spanish since meeting Goya and having undertaken to learn the language, I decide to call my daughter Inès. It is also the name of the heroine in one of Latouche's novels, but who will ever notice? My obsession, as I believe, is invisible.

I am having trouble recovering. My body, which has endured six confinements, is devastated and surrenders to the enemy Time, keenly aware that this is a final capitulation. Though my heart rebels, I feel that I have suddenly migrated from one generation to another. I am no longer in the class of women but of old ladies. With a start, I realize that I have reached my mother's age at her death. The thought terrifies me. What about Prosper? So young still, so handsome! I look at him as if he were my son, his eyes bulging with pride and fear.

FOR MORE THAN a year, while gradually erasing the marks of my last pregnancy, I continue to put off the time when I shall have to assume my rightful age. Again I am coquettish. I run to town all of a sudden looking for a hat, or silk shawls, or elegant little boots, and try to mask the persistent graying of my hair by various artifices. Perhaps it is not too late? My thoughtless spending comes at a bad time. Since the birth of Inès I have had a maid constantly in attendance, and then there is old Valmore. No wonder our situation has again become precarious. Prosper's contract with the Grand Théâtre de Bordeaux ends in the spring of 1827 and will not be renewed. After four years, they have let Valmore know that it is time for him to find another theater in which to play the romantic lead. Once more I dream only of Paris. It is madness. I am terrified but also in a fever to see Henri, whose letters have me by the throat day and night. Yet our correspondence, I am well aware, places us in a space and a time that are not those of daily life, that do not truly exist. I cannot help but think that absence, distance, and separation are our terrain of choice.

But though I again make every effort and entreat all my acquaintance, not a single opening can be found for Valmore in Paris. Caught unawares and pressured by my uncle, by Latouche, and by others to drop my scruples toward the monarchy, I am forced to reverse my decision and accept the royal grant that was offered me earlier. To my great despair, Prosper signs a two-year contract with the Théâtre de Lyon. Though being in Lyon would bring me closer to Paris, I feel an unconquerable distaste for the city. The prospect of returning there makes me ill. I have a fever, a facial edema, sudden onslaughts of tears. It reaches a stage where one morning Valmore suggests that I spend three weeks in Paris in the spring before going to Lyon to join him.

"You can stay with Pauline and see your old friends. I'll take care of moving our household. You are overburdened as it is. Go, have a little fun. You've richly deserved it."

On March 29, 1827, heartbroken, I leave Prosper and Bordeaux, taking Hippolyte and Hyacinthe with me. Am I ever to see the town or my husband again? After six years of separation, I finally return to Paris. And Henri.

## 8

*S*INCE SETTING SAIL, my mother had wasted away to a shadow. She hardly spoke, ate unwillingly, and slept only with reluctance. Now that it was becoming a reality, her dream of the Antilles disappeared, no longer beckoning as the unreachable goal that had made her days short and her nights beautiful. She never spoke of Saintenoy's betrayal, and I felt how painful and unnecessary it would be to mention it. She was from this time on an old woman, abused and abandoned.

"I'm seasick, the humidity is suffocating me," she complained. "And this salt gets all over my skin."

She would scratch herself until she bled. Her flesh so delicate, so translucent.

"Look at how heavy and stiff our clothes are. Such a burden. I just can't go on."

Exhausted by life. She sensed, my quiet mother, that she was sailing toward her death. And every lurch of the ship seemed a further step toward this end.

Rats, cockroaches, lice, and fleas darted out to tickle our ankles and frighten us to death. As we were the only women on board, the captain allowed us to use the roundhouses, the privies on either side of the stern normally reserved for officers. The seven other passengers had to make do with the exposed latrines in the bow. This was the only special favor granted us.

In everything else, we received the same treatment as the crew. Everyone complained:

"Biscuits again! In a few days, just you watch, there will be more worms than flour."

"I wouldn't mind taking a peek at the food stores in the lazaret."

"It's locked and bolted. The menu is simple and you may as well get used to it. At midday: beef, lard, or cod. At night: beans, broad beans, or peas. That's the lot. It will be the same all the way to Basse-Terre."

Because of our diet, my mother lived in dread of scurvy. She was terrified in any case of the illnesses that one might get at sea and that would then grow horribly worse during the voyage. The specter of gangrene and amputation hung over the vessel night and day.


IN THE MIDDLE of the ocean, I on the other hand recovered my spirits and hopes. I felt perfectly at ease far from shore. The die had been cast, and I was at present enjoying the adventure with all a child's playfulness. No more dissembling, no more lies, no more nonsense. I tried to imagine our future, which my mother seemingly dismissed, and allowed myself to dream once more. For the first time, I even found myself thinking I might see my father again, and my brother and sisters. And there was the mirage of Louis. My mother was leaving a man behind her, whereas I was traveling toward one. Yet Louis Lacour was by report at Saint Domingue, while we were traveling to Guadeloupe, where my mother had a cousin she believed would help us. My sense of geography was vague enough that it made little difference to me.

With ample time on my hands, I scribbled down my impressions and whiled away the hours by writing verse.

> *As the ship, bounding one night under full sail,*
> *Laid down a shimmering star path in its trail,*
> *I searched the sea, knifed open at our bow:*
> *"Is it toward my happiness that I go now?"*

I had quickly learned the laws of life aboard a ship. I liked them, felt reassured by them. The hard-and-fast rules governing conduct found in my own rather unbridled nature a surprising eagerness to obey. Freedom is too heavy a burden for a child. I had been turned loose, without landmarks or boundaries. I needed structure around me.

EVERY DAY, THE bells rang out on the bridge to mark mealtimes and the call to mass. The cadence brought me comfort. How far we had come from our old life as actors! Nothing in the last five years had seemed as stable to me as the swaying deck of *Le Mars*. I was never seasick. My mother, on the other hand, was terrified by the racket of the wind in the hempen cloth of the sails. Storms were an agony to her, as to most of the passengers. But not to me. Nor was I unduly concerned about pirates. I had the deep conviction that my life would be a long one. Standing by the capstan, I followed the sailors' maneuvers, listened to the raucous shanties the captain allowed them to sing at the end of the day, or watched them play dice and cards when they were off watch. I loved hearing their talk.

"I'd give anything for a cheroot!"

"You know what you'll get if you're caught!"

I would join their company pretending to have seen and heard nothing. In fact I quickly picked up their language.

"What are you talking about?"

They would compete amongst themselves for the chance to answer me.

"About wanting to smoke—"

"Which is strictly prohibited, young lady."

"Strictly!"

"And can earn you a severe punishment."

"What punishment?"

"Having wicks put between the fingers of your hand and set alight to burn down slowly."

"How awful!"

"And don't you go blaspheming either, do you hear? They'll pierce your tongue for that."

Aside from describing tortures, the sailors also told stories. At night, the passengers gathered around in a close circle to hear their tales, doing their best to forget the slow passage of time, the country they had left, the heart they might have broken. The darkness encouraged the exchange of confidences.

Among the seven passengers was a strange young man. Sad and pale, he never spoke. No one dared to approach him. Was he mute? Dejected? Mad? Contagious? Rumors flew back and forth. As superstitious as actors, the sailors looked askance at this taciturn passenger.

"He has a crime weighing on his conscience—"

"Seduced some poor young thing—"

"Struck a bargain with the devil so as not to have to bargain with men—"

"And what if he has simply had his tongue cut out?"

From the gun decks to the bowsprit, the mizzenmast to the scuttle holes, unlikely stories circulated about this young man. But as we were to learn, the poor boy was struggling only with himself. Worried not to find him skulking as usual on the poop deck, several of the cabin boys set out looking for him, suspecting him of mischief. But it was I who found the note he had tacked to the mainmast before jumping overboard. "I cannot live without her" was all he had written.

There existed people, then, who put love before all else, before the fear of loss or suffering, even before breathing! Admirable creatures, enthralled by the ideal. The world looked different to me suddenly. I too wanted to lose my mind. To live was to love. To lock eyes, to steal a kiss. A total and life-taking gift. Nothing else, I decided, was worth the trouble.

The suicide of the bilious young man cast a pall over the ship. My mother collapsed on herself a little more. The sailors and the passengers both were impatient to make landfall.

FINALLY OUR SHIP reached the Canary Current and the Sargasso Sea, the realm of the bluefin tuna. There was the crossing of the line, with its traditional hazing rituals.

"At this point, all the sailors are thrown into a tub of water," one of the cabin boys told me. "It's the custom."

"The threshold into the Kingdom of the Tropics has been crossed," wrote Christopher Columbus. "The sky becomes friendlier, the nights are luminous. Unknown constellations swim into view, and shooting stars flare across the heavens." The water, not as deep here, had changed color. Kelp floated on the surface, and sticks of wood. Small birds came to rest on the spars. Flying fish leaped into the sails. The trade winds brought with them the scent of sugar and vanilla. Everyone took heart and felt life returning.

"Guadeloupe has closed its port," the captain informed us, cutting our illusions short. "The island is in quarantine, the slaves are in revolt. We are advised to make for the Les Saintes islands. I will let you know my decision."

What a disappointment. What should we do? Pass right on, as others were doing, or sail in a circle so as not to lose the value of the cargo? The ship's stores were at a minimum. Fresh water was starting to run low. I wandered over the ship from end to end. The ship's surgeon suggested that he inoculate me against yellow fever. The other passengers had all refused. Shrugging, I consented.

"Don't forget to drink camphor and rum every day," he recommended.

WE HAD BEEN gone from Bordeaux for forty days. Our provisions were exhausted. The captain finally decided to put in at the island of Saint-Barthélemy, a free port where he could land his cargo. It was high time to unload the raw sugar, salt meat, cured hams, cambric and linen, hardware, forged nails, haberdashery, porcelain, and barrels of sulfur that were packed away in the hold. The prospect of standing on solid ground again rejoiced both the passengers and the crew. It didn't matter that we would disembark at a different place than we'd planned. My mother, exhausted by the sea voyage and our various setbacks, was indifferent anyway and sank into a constant state of dull incomprehension.

Then, showing a surge of combative energy, she might mention Pointe-à-Pitre. I let her talk, knowing how important it was for her always to have a virgin destination on the horizon, a fallow territory, bearing a strange and dream-inducing name, an incantatory outlet.

On the island, where a family kindly took us in, my mother, with her graying golden hair, her eyes that gazed into the distance, and her errant soul, made a strong impression on the inhabitants. A species of foreign divinity. But as we sheltered in the shade of a flame tree, to which I made her retreat from the bite of the sun, I realized helplessly that she was already gone from this world. Her hand, which I grasped in a desperate attempt to bring her back to me, was ice-cold. The blood had drained from it. She seemed like a former sinner, repentant in the extreme, preparing herself for martyrdom. And it was my task to accompany her along her endless penitential road! Would I be strong enough?

"Come along, we'll tell you what the healers and kenbwaze say when they find a silk-cotton tree . . ."

With their long colorful skirts, their embroidered petticoats, their lace blouses, and their pointed madras head scarfs, the local girls showed a greedy attention toward me, as though I were an exotic fruit.

"And when it rains, don't stand under a manchineel tree. The water dripping from it is horribly acidic."

They talked about carambolas and breadfruits as they laughingly dragged me along through banana plantations and fields of tall, sculptural sugarcane.

We lived in a traditional Creole house. Set on one level and made entirely of wood, it had a wide porch all the way around it. For the first few nights the nocturnal chorus of frogs, blackbirds, and crickets frightened me. The slanting course of the moon kept me awake for hours. Within a few weeks I could follow a conversation in Creole and take part in activities around the hearth. A nomad for almost five years, I had learned to adapt quickly to new places and circumstances, even to new foods, which in the Antilles were highly spiced. My mother, though, was still sick and could not accustom herself to the cardamom, star anise, and coriander, to the meats grilled over sugarcane dust, or to the produce, the yams, guavas, and papayas.

I took to it all. During wakes they would tell stories about the deceased while drinking rum, of which they spilled a drop on the ground. For the dead person. Nothing surprised me.

Three months after we landed in Saint-Barthélemy, the port of Guadeloupe was reopened. When my mother learned this, she decided to go to Pointe-à-Pitre to find her putative cousin. She must have known how little strength she had left and wanted to put me among people who could care for me. I was sad to leave my Antillean sisters. My life was like that. Meet people, develop a friendship, grow attached, and say good-bye to them forever. All I had left were songs. I wrote them myself. "No, no, not sleep no more, come share big flame, you kisses be like honey picked from flowers. You heart sigh, call out me name. Me soul go from me lips, me die under da flowers." Poetry made my story over. It altered the course of events and lessened the pain.

Already I was learning to retell my life.

SAINT-BARTHÉLEMY HAD BEEN a small, green Eden. Guadeloupe, by contrast, in that month of May presented us a burnt landscape. Fire, murder, torture, and rape had ravaged the butterfly-shaped island. Rebel slaves had driven their masters away and taken possession of their homes. In the terrible reprisals that followed, the rebellion was crushed with inordinate savagery. Blacks were put on view like wild animals at different places in Pointe-à-Pitre, by way of example. Moaning and bestial, their naked bodies were pressed one against the other. Their outstretched arms implored us through the bars.

"How can anyone inflict such suffering on another?" my mother asked.

The governor, who greeted us in his house, was a large man swimming in sweat. He mopped his brow with a white handkerchief, from a large supply on his desk. He and his wife, who was small and mean as a snake, had eyes sunk deep in their sockets. Cold, cruel eyes, circled in black. They mistreated their slaves. We had barely arrived, still horrified by what we had seen outside, when the governor threw a young boy who had displeased him out the second floor window of his villa. My mother fainted immediately.

"It must be the climate. The heat is hard to bear when you aren't used to it," said the governor's wife, patting my mother on the cheeks to revive her.

"The boy . . ." said my mother when she came to.

"Who?" asked the horrid woman. "Oh, *that* boy," she said, suddenly understanding. "You have to make sure that they're afraid of you, don't you see. You'll soon catch on. It's obvious that you've just stepped off the boat."

As soon as she recovered, my mother dragged me out into the street with her.

"I want to find that boy," she said with sincere determination.

The black child was still where he had fallen, his father beside him.

"He is unhurt, God be praised!" said my mother.

"Leg broken, several pieces, finished," said the father of the young slave, his eyes fixed on the ground.

"How awful!" said my mother.

"One left. That leg will be free. Better one leg free than two in chains," he said, not looking at us.

And he walked away, straight and tall, his son in his arms.


IT WAS THE last straw for my mother. After that she walled herself off in silence and never came out. Everything grew worse. She vomited, shivered. The young widow who had taken us under her roof on a recommendation from the governor's wife spoke to me frankly: my mother had yellow fever. The end. The end of the journey for my poor mother, who was too weak to realize how absurd our crossing had been, how laughably useless. The cousin she had pinned her hopes on had left Basse-Terre two years before, returning to the continent to make a comfortable home for himself there. In Bordeaux, of all cities. The rich relative of my mother's dreams was quite possibly one of the gentlemen invited to La Latrappy's soirées, perhaps even one of the men who had condescendingly given us alms!

But it was too late to bewail a life that had been full of misunderstandings, frustrations, and setbacks. My mother was rendering her soul to God, too full of the happiness that had always eluded her. In atrocious pain, and with convulsions the horrific sight of which I will long remember, she expiated the sin of having followed her heart despite all reason and all duty, spitting out in blood her desire to be free, a desire she passed on to me, her one loyal companion for six years, as my sole inheritance.

Grief engulfed me. I saw her beautiful white body lowered into a large dark vault. The whole island, the world at that moment, was to me nothing more than an enormous mass grave.

. . .

I was about to be sixteen. Slavery had just been reinstituted, violating the governor's earlier promise of emancipation. Three hundred prisoners, in despair, blew themselves up at Fort Saint-Charles. Lost in the Caribbean, in a town that was on fire and awash in blood, afraid of everything and ill with fever, I became an orphan. I thought I too would die, and if I survived it was only because of the inoculation administered by the ship's surgeon. Everyone around me was dying. During those terrible days, some even died while sneezing. I wanted only one thing: to get out of this hell, this shaking death house, and return to Douai to find my father.

"At the moment, there is only a merchantman in the port of Pointe-à-Pitre," said the governor when I told him of my intention. "You know as well as I do the dangers that these ships run. And you're feverish and in frail condition."

"I want to leave."

"The cargo is likely to draw much attention along the way. Of course, no one is going to rob you, you haven't got anything. But the pirates will abduct you and sell you on the Barbary Coast! Besides, there's nothing on board resembling food: just salt beef and those biscuits you need a hatchet to split."

"I want to leave," I said again.

I was so determined that nothing could have stopped me, neither the specter of my mother's remains nor the dangers inherent in an ocean crossing for a young girl. Even less would I respond to threats or entreaties. I had fulfilled my task and accompanied my mother to the end. Now I wanted to be reunited with my family. Wearying of the matter, and at bottom indifferent, the governor and his wife decided to abandon me to my fate, which they expected to be short and nasty. It was the first time I had made a decision on my own, and I chose to trust in God, having no master now but Him. The young widow who had watched at my side as my mother's life ran out moved heaven and earth to get me taken aboard a warship at the last moment. Since the Treaty of Amiens, we had nothing to fear from the English. It was the surest way to travel. Many warships were at that time in the Antilles, transporting white families that had suffered recent losses in the colonies back to Europe.

I left at the beginning of July. The ship's captain was vain and violent, reeked of alcohol, tobacco, and tar, and brazenly pressed his assiduous and misplaced attentions on his female passengers, who faced enough afflictions already. After harassing the widow of the late governor of Saint-Domingue, who had succumbed in the epidemic, the vile man took a fancy to me. He pursued me with such effrontery that the crew rebelled and threatened to report him to the minister of the navy. The crossing was horrendous. Several people died every day, and all their personal effects had to be tossed overboard. The weather was foul. Storms struck us one after another, robbing the poor passengers of any last strength left to them by their illness.

One apocalyptic night of storm, while food was being haphazardly dispensed, I asked the sailors to bind me to the mainmast. I wanted to see the waves unleashed, the sea in rebellion, feel death embrace me and release me, die—if I had to—without a blindfold over my eyes. I was no longer afraid of anything, knew that henceforth I was indestructible. The sailors at first refused, then eventually gave in to my request. After all, as they admitted to me later, not one among them believed we would come through the storm alive. They saw my plea as a last wish before death. But against all expectations, the gallant vessel stayed afloat. I, for my part, had seen everything, heard everything, the sirens' song, the darkness. I saw my young life pass in review and made vows, defying the heavens to prevent me from living the life I chose.

I HAD LEFT Douai six years before. At the end of a murderous trip, I was coming back alone. All the passengers who had sailed out on *Le Mars* were now dead. Life clung to me. Why? Who still waited for me at my port of destination? How would my family welcome me? What had happened to it? I had lost everything, except my honor. But for how much longer? Returning to the continent, I was leaving my mother behind once and for all. Also Louis Lacour, who was somewhere in the Antilles. I hadn't seen him again.

As for my mother, no inoculation could have saved her. So I left her there, under the casuarinas. I would often travel back, I knew, to the shore where she rested, and silently mourn her fate and mine. She had gone to eternal peace, I toward sorrow. I would now have to pay for her crime, I felt it. She had chosen to leave. But I was truly in exile.

And it was to last a long time.

## 9

ON THIS APRIL NIGHT IN 1827, Auber's new opera *La Muette de Portici* is having its opening performance. Standing beside Pauline, who is still so ravishing although ten years my senior, I can hardly breathe. My new corset, which I bought this afternoon on a whim, constricts me almost to the point of suffocation. I have been in Paris for twelve days already and have not seen Latouche, who seems to be avoiding me. Stunned by his behavior, enervated, shattered, I spend hours inventing explanations. The first few days I don't dare leave Pauline's apartment on the rue Saint-Lazare and invent all sorts of excuses for him. I'm afraid he'll send word while I'm out, bidding me to a rendezvous that I'll then miss.

"It's ridiculous," says Pauline. "You're not going to stay indoors your entire visit. The people who love you want to see you."

"It's such a disappointment . . ."

"What did you think, Marceline? That he was going to come running like a puppy dog? Really, that's not his style!"

"I expected a little more eagerness. What does his silence mean? Fear? Perversity? Disdain? Indifference?"

"Hold him in contempt. If you pay no attention to him, he'll come back. It's always that way."

"Being cagey. Presenting myself to Henri as other than I am, as thinking what I don't think. Holding my peace when what I particularly want is to be ungagged. My time is short, Pauline. I return soon to Lyon. What a waste, again. So many opportunities to meet thrown away!"

"His last book, written under a pseudonym, took a great deal of effort," Pauline argues to comfort me. "*Clement XIV and Carlo Bertinazzi: The Unpublished Correspondence.* The book is already in its third printing."

"I had hoped that book was his. I even wrote to congratulate him on it. But it doesn't explain everything. I have traveled the entire breadth of France on the chance of seeing him. He won't even cross the Seine with the certainty of finding me."

"He is terrified. Time has passed. The picture you have of each other and that you keep alive in your letters doesn't correspond with what you both are today. Latouche is afraid of losing your esteem and the place he holds in your poems. Absence, as he knows, works to his advantage. It is a question of who is to have more power between the two of you. Don't give in."

"And why not? I'm here. I'm dying to see him. Why should I pretend the opposite? I don't care about these calculations . . ."

I am afraid neither of my wrinkles, nor of my graying hair, nor of the brownish spots that have appeared on my skin. Nothing would make me miss my rendezvous with Henri. Too bad if he is no longer waiting for me, if he lied to me, deceived me, imprisoned me for many years in a love that he stopped believing in long ago, or perhaps never believed in. A love that is for him only flattering, literary in nature, and troublesome now that the distance between us has closed. Passion consumes me and I feel ageless. Coming to life, I run through Paris, to the rue des Saints-Pères of my eternal spring, and slam into a closed door.

"Monsieur de Latouche is out of town," says the landlady.

It doesn't matter, I don't hear her. Only movement lessens my pain, seals off my sorrow. Had I really planned to wallow in Henri's embrace, like one of those girls that he takes fully dressed, standing, at night, under a doorway, in the terror and excitement of imminent discovery? Am I not condemned to remain a sample of purity preserved, a gem tucked away in his jewel case? I resume walking across Paris. For a long time. My legs hurt. This is good. Notre-Dame, the pont de la Tournelle, the île Saint-Louis. Henri, wherever he is, doesn't imagine my desire to be robbed, ravished in the nave of a cathedral where he would drag me, serve me, assuage me. Instead of presiding dust-covered in one of those high niches. I only want to be unbolted. But I myself have forged the pedestal on which I am worshipped. I am the prisoner of my own religion.

ALL OF PARIS society is gathering at the Opéra-Comique. Pauline and I, pale as ghosts, clinging to each other for moral support, arrive at the theater after a long day of trying on dresses and hats, disgruntled and dull. Spurned and aging mistresses, we both feel tonight that we are facing a public that knows of our disgrace. Auber no longer loves Pauline, and I have lost Latouche. People will laugh at us behind our backs. Yet we are both ready to accept the humiliation to catch a glimpse of our lovers in the crowd, she of her composer, I of my writer. We border on the grotesque. Among the alluring young, and despite our attempts at elegance, we look like two Spanish duennas, painted to no avail. That Pauline's affair with Auber has come to an end is an open secret. On my side, I don't know what to expect.

Pauline has warned me that I am adored. Hardly have we entered the lobby of the Opéra than I am surrounded by people. Young men, Hugo, Lamartine, pay their respects to me. The rising champion of Romanticism, Théophile Gautier, does everything in his power to be properly introduced. Others as well, publishers of newspapers and keepsake volumes, bookstore owners. Here is Scribe, who writes Auber's librettos and whose talents all the composers are vying for. Quite a mob. My head starts to spin. Is it really me they are welcoming in this fashion? How false and cruel they are, I tell myself, thinking ashamedly of Valmore with his frank and straightforward ways. What pleasure could I possibly find in this swirl of powdered faces? And this man tendering me compliments, will he not mock me in a few minutes, citing my dry skin, my country manners?

Anxious, pursued, I lean on Pauline, who sweeps a path for us through the crowd to our box. I scan the orchestra in search of Henri, flitting over headdresses, scrutinizing every silhouette. Dizzy, I eventually find myself sitting down. Pauline whispers into my ear the names of the figures who appear in the field of her opera glass.

"In the blue dress, over there, that's Sophie Gay. A tongue like a viper, and she spends her time saying terrible things about Latouche . . . Hello, there's your cousin Bra. Are the two of you still not speaking? In the front row, in white, wearing a little beret, is Mélanie Waldor, Dumas's old mistress. She's very eager to meet you."

I am hardly listening. I have always liked the stir before a performance, the rustling of dresses, the laughter pealing here

and there, as high-strung as violins being tuned, the great con-
flagration of sound that is abruptly doused when the first note
is struck. Then suddenly I see him. I see him, and Pauline and
the entire hall notice him at the same moment. Heads turn in
my direction. People whisper. But I don't hear a thing, unless it
is the sound of something shattering on the ground at my feet,
something like my heart.

Henri de Latouche has just made his entrance into the
packed orchestra with a resplendent creature on his arm.

"Madame Noblet, a singer," Pauline whispers to me during
the overture, which wins all hearts. "He is just having his fling,
you can be sure."

I can be sure. A lovely filly, from a stable by the gates of
Paris, round-rumped and full-chested. A real thoroughbred,
her complexion a slightly muddy brown, true, but unquestionably youthful, with the kind of youthfulness that puts itself on show and makes the groom holding the bridle puff
himself with pride, like an old peacock fanning his worn tail
feathers. Latouche wears his new conquest the way one wears
a new jabot, starched and stiff. In comparison I must look like
rumpled linen. Henri has always taken care to be irreproachable. His impeccable clothes, his beautiful women dangling
from his crisp shirtfront like so many war medals, like so
many snooks cocked at his childhood humiliations, offer
some restitution for his dead eye. The one-eyed runt takes
his revenge on a society that struck him full in the face when,
in the courtyard at school, as a promising boy, he ran toward
life with giant steps. Poor Henri! He likes a stinging victory.
He has to shout his paltry triumph in everyone's face, though
he himself is undeceived. Deep inside, the crushing failure of
his existence eats at him. While others mock him, the stone

that put his eye out pierces his retina again each day, and he falls to the ground crying out to his unloving mother.

I know all this, the dried snot of the barely tolerated child, his skinned knees, his torn clothes. I am the only one not to see Henri de Latouche in dress regalia surrounded by these angular jaws, these fashionable mouths, but as the child he was. His nose is running. I would like to push all these people away and wipe his face with my handkerchief. Tears run down my cheeks. What an insult to her, people must be thinking. Yet it is only love. Henri and I speak a language of our own, and the flesh no longer plays a part in it.

On this night, the five acts of *La Muette de Portici* kindle a fire in the hearts of the rebellious. A revolution is brewing. And I am done forever with being a woman.

HENCEFORTH BETWEEN LATOUCHE and me, it is a question of souls. The rest has no importance, or so I try to persuade myself. I spend the last days of my stay in Paris collecting pebbles, leaves, and every scrap, detail, and cast-off bit from the streets—stray pieces of Paris that will accompany me into the exile ahead. I latch onto the look, the expression on the faces of those I love, unashamedly gathering the material for my poetry. It is all that I have now. I find it a little difficult to admit that I am only a spirit. My body still feels, still shrinks from the wind and the wave of humanity in the boulevards. I pass in front of theaters where no one will hire Prosper, my fists clenched until my knuckles whiten. I stroll again along the places that we liked, Henri and I, now distant lands, both familiar and lost.

The fervor that follows me in literary circles leaves me cold as marble. I persist in believing it insincere, even mocking. Marie d'Agoult writes me a note. Liszt mentioned my name to her! The coteries open their doors to me. I am the toast of Paris.

"Marie Dorval has ordered me to bring you to her house," says Vigny, whom I know from Bordeaux.

I won't go. Actresses frighten me. Dressed as I am now, I don't feel comfortable in the salons. Also, I'm afraid of running into Latouche in flattering company.

"Different. You are different. That is precisely what constitutes your charm, your particularity," says Pauline. "What Henri loved about you. Your spirit wins everyone over, you shine, there is no one in the room but you."

This celebration, which I don't understand, brings me little pleasure. To these tiresome receptions, I still prefer my uncle Constant's studio, where, as in a family attic, I can dust off sketches and half-finished paintings of my life. I rediscover points of reference that are mine beyond any shift in fashion, a permanence inscribed on canvas in colors forever wet. I hear the footsteps of my little laughing boy, taken from me by death, and the voice of Henri the day our glances first crossed: "Madame Valmore?" "Yes . . . ?"


MY UNCLE HAS grown so old that for the first time in his life he is showing his years. He always looked the same to me, and now I have the impression of standing in front of his portrait, cracked by time, and feel swindled at the fragility of a work I had thought eternal. It's as if I were seeing my father die a second time, especially as Constant has assumed the hunched walk and trembling hands of his brother's last months. Nearly deaf, he looks at me with swollen, wet eyes and makes incoherent speeches in which scenes from the past, startlingly reborn among his paintbrushes, are mixed with fragments of a shaky present.

"If you like, Catherine, I'll come visit you next time with young Nicolas Saintenoy, for whom they are predicting a brilliant political future. They say he has connections . . . Anyway, his conversation is very lively, as you'll see, it will amuse you . . ."

"I'm not Catherine, Uncle. I'm Marceline, her daughter. Don't you recognize me?"

"Of course I do, who else would you be? My little Marceline, my little match girl. Didn't I introduce you in this very room to that well-mannered young man who was so fond of Canova?"

"Monsieur de Latouche . . ."

"The very one—you see? I haven't lost my wits yet. He turned out a queer old stick in the end, though. If I'd known, Catherine, what I was leading you toward . . ."

Constant sails on from era to era, forcing me to follow in his wake. Exhausted, I emerge from the Childeberte building as though I had just completed a long voyage.

"There's nothing to be done about it, Madame Valmore," says the servant who keeps him company. "His life is slowly going out, that's all. He still paints for an hour or two a day, no more, sitting in a chair because he is tired . . . It's sad to see Monsieur like this, when he was always so lively, so engaging— but that's life. What can you do?"

After my three-week pilgrimage in the footsteps of the woman I once was, this desperate incursion into the life of a woman who no longer waits for me, I return to Prosper and my little Inès in Lyon, a city I secretly hope to leave very soon.


"THE BOARD OF censors has refused to let us stage *Hernani*, dear Marceline. Despite all your efforts and mine. Our reception is no more favorable here than in the capital. We'll have to go back to the old repertoire . . ."

Desroches lowers his face into his hands. This old friend, who has become director of the Grand Théâtre de Lyon, had agreed to my request. Hugo had personally authorized and encouraged me to perform his most recent play, whose Paris run had been so scandalous.

"It was a foregone conclusion. And Hugo warned me. A shame. But we'll go on, Desroches, we'll go on."

EASTER 1829. I am far from the retirement in which I thought to live when I returned here from Paris two years ago. Lyon the rebellious has allowed me to penetrate its secrets, admitted me to its treasures. Better late than never. In the end I have become the queen of Lyon, an obligatory sight for travelers, a sort of local madonna and emblem to be brandished in aid of all lost causes. Within my own home, loved by my three children and Prosper, who acted that first season at the Grand Théâtre to considerable acclaim, I have snuffed out the last tendrils of my woman's passion for Henri, for Henri's body. I refine and transform it in my poetry, ignore the bitter taste in my mouth from my last stay in Paris. To admit my disappointment would be almost to sign a confession of error. I categorically reject that possibility. I have suffered too much in my life, seen too much ugliness not to entertain this flame that Latouche also keeps alive. We both of us need it. Our correspondence has resumed with even greater fervor. Like a circular race, constantly accelerating though it leads nowhere. After every lap, our story takes off anew, indifferent to the surrounding clamor. My letters slice through cities and revolts, the wax sealed with the vow: "Nothing before you, nothing after."

I thought to isolate myself, to live only in the past, secure from the shocks of the heart and the tremors of the flesh. But once more, the call of what lies elsewhere has won out over my instinct for self-preservation. While I marvel at Valmore's gentleness, his admiring tenderness, and while renewed out-pourings of shared affection wash over us, I concurrently write to Latouche how much I regret not having married him. Am I a monster of duplicity? It is a mystery even to me. The most gen-erous of men adores me with his whole being, devotes himself body and soul to my happiness, surrounds me with his protec-tive concern, his unshakable faith in me. Without him, I would collapse, be unable to live. But at night in our common bed, when he puts his hand on mine, I dream that I am married to another man, one who never promised me anything. And it all seems normal. This intoxication, so unreasonable now that the snows have settled on my head, will never leave me, I now know. Every day I see our child Hyacinthe. I have never said anything to Henri. Nor to anyone else. Even Pauline. Prosper adores her. She is a precocious child, lively in her intelligence, grave in her curiosity and maturity. Nothing like Hippolyte, who is lazy, and Inès, who is somber. Hyacinthe is Valmore's favorite, his pride, a fact he hardly disguises. One of fate's iro-nies. And I, faced with my husband's confident pride and walled in by a heavy secret, often find myself hating this glaring proof of my transgression, this crushing evidence of my guilt. Then, remembering Henri's kisses, remembering what we might have been had we both dared, I venerate my daughter as the only success in my life. I do not understand myself.

THE DEFEAT OF the Romantics' bid for the stage in Lyon has substantially diminished actors' earnings. The public is show-ing its distaste for the old repertoire. Valmore is not immune to the general rule. We are obliged to give up our quarters in the place Saint-Clair and move into three rooms on the rue de la Monnaie. It is at this point that I learn about my uncle's death. Constant! He was with me through so many trials, and his studio was at the intersection of so many of my lives! I refuse to accept his departure. I have always deflected the truths that disagree with me. I suppose I do not have much aptitude for reality. I continue writing Constant as though nothing has happened. I simply no longer put my letters in the mail. In the world outside, History has unexpectedly jerked at the traces. The rumor of rioting rises from the streets. In me this groundswell takes the form of poems, letters, dialogues with the dead, of ocean crossings, chaotic coach rides, anticipations, birthings. History constantly remakes itself, sometimes leaving me, in the shadow of the strangers who surround me, fallen to earth, drained and dazed.

Something is about to, must, explode.

## 10

B Y MARCH 1805, less than two years after my return from the Antilles, I had become the princi-
pal actress at the Opéra-Comique in Paris. I was about to be
nineteen. My name was on all lips, and fashionable authors
such as Jars and Grétry were writing parts especially for me.
Pampered and in demand, I went from one play to another,
barely surprised, though my face was not even pretty, to find
myself worshipped by the public on one of the most prestigious stages in France. And only two years earlier, after standing off and on the port of Brest in quarantine, I had landed
in Brittany an unwashed orphan, my rags gnawed by vermin.
Glossing over the weakness of my singing voice and reproaching me sometimes for an "excess of sensibility," the journalists
praised my acting and my diction. "Mademoiselle Desbordes
wonderfully embodies persecuted virtue, the eternal victim
of vice," they wrote. It was a time when theatergoers loved
tearful tragedies. A fortunate state of affairs. There was no
one to touch me for sobbing, supplicating, and whimpering.
I worked conscientiously. I knew music well enough and how
to dance the pas de deux. But at bottom I hated the theater. I
was ashamed of it. My mother had pushed me onto the stage
when I was only twelve. I had obeyed her. And to a certain
degree, I was continuing to do so. People thought I had tal-

ent and a certain poignant sincerity. It seemed to me that I was merely saying onstage what I was not allowed to express in life. Acting was a sort of fever, of exaggeration. I could cry out, fall to my knees, implore. The rest mattered little. Compliments rolled right off me, and criticisms only tore into me briefly. Theater was a rotten plank in an angry sea. I believed that I was battle-hardened. Among the vain and the debauched, I seemed an intruder, a usurper. And I was. But on my return from Guadeloupe two years before I had had no choice. What else could I do? I was in a pitiful state, a beggar waif with sores, scabs, and boils, as hungry as a she-wolf.

If my father recognized me when I stood before him in my rags unheralded, it was probably because my eyes, resembling those of the woman he had repudiated six years before, awakened a world within him he had thought forever lost.

MY FATHER AND two sisters lived in Lille. Or rather, they had gone into hiding there, having fled Douai because of debts and humiliations. My father's wineshop had eaten up whatever remained of his dignity and his savings. With an effort, he managed to get a municipal post in the new capital of the Nord. It proved another will-o'-the-wisp. My sister Cécile, seduced by a married man, had just given birth to a baby girl, whom I encountered only on the day of her funeral, for the child expired at the very moment I crossed the threshold of my father's house. My sister Eugénie, an occasional seamstress, was pregnant though she did not know by whom. Both had given up on the idea of ever getting married. Who would have wanted them? Out of weakness, out of mediocrity, they surrendered to the first person who gripped them with any

firmness around their fat necks. As for my brother Félix, my
old faithful playmate, my father had sold him into the army
to pay off a creditor. It was common for a poor man, in return
for compensation, to take the place of a rich man who had
been conscripted by the luck of the draw. Learning of my
dear brother's fate, I cried for weeks. Félix a soldier! He will
come back crushed and gutted, I told myself in horror. Nor
was I wrong.

What a slap in the face! A haven of peace? This family,
which in my exile I had called to and cried for with all my
strength, had become a sordid battlefield. A battle I had no
wish to fight, a cause I did not espouse. Wrongly, I had thought
my trials over. In fact, they were just beginning. Finding myself
with a drunk on my hands and two wayward women, I needed
to take the situation in hand quickly, find some gainful activity,
provide for my ailing lambs. "Mother is no more," I had told
them, without any intention—being the youngest—of assuming her role. The news made them sink deeper into the mud
they had been wallowing in since our departure. I could never
have imagined the stagnation that it had caused in the family.
Guilty through my mother, I felt called on to arrest their fall.
Thus it was that, a week after my return, I was already looking
for work. And the first door on which I knocked, naturally, was
the theater's.

TWO MONTHS LATER, in November 1803, I was making my
stage debut as Pauline in Beaumarchais's *Two Friends*. The Lille
theater company was facing difficulties and toured all through
the region. Eventually, working from stage to stage, we even
performed in Douai. My father leaped at the chance to ac-

company me. It was an opportunity for him to revisit his old acquaintances, claiming to be a painter now, though he was already living entirely at my expense and drinking away a large part of my meager pay. My native Douai had undergone considerable change. It had the effect on me of a town for the dead, a provincial burial ground still visited from time to time by carrion birds. This was not the Douai I loved and continued to venerate throughout my life. I thought it was gone forever, not knowing that I would find it again in my writing. Then it would belong to me completely. For the moment, I had no wish to remain in this pitiful copy of my childhood setting, where the stink of my father's breath, laced with wine and idiocy, had replaced the smell of my mother's Sunday afternoon *loées*.

When the director of the Théâtre de Lille, who liked me so much that he gave a benefit performance for me, offered to recommend me to the theater company in Rouen, I didn't hesitate for a second.

"You'll play romantic leads, strong supporting roles, comic ingenues, and second or third romantic parts in operas," he told me.

A challenge. But I would have accepted anything at all to break free of my family. At whatever cost.

I made my first appearance on the stage of Rouen's Théâtre des Arts in May 1804, with roles in two five-act plays. Within a few days, I was the toast of the public and the critics. The city struck me as beautiful and serene. I breathed easily there, found myself dreaming again, imagining that Louis Lacour was back and had come to lift me from my ignominy and make me his wife. A period of tranquillity and reflection that lasted only a short time. My father and two sisters, unable to get by in Lille despite what Félix and I independently sent them, were threatening to descend on me in Rouen at any moment. For a time, my uncle Constant shouldered part of the burden and allowed my father to stay in his Paris studio, remembering that many years before, when my grandfather, the watch thief, had disappeared without warning, his older brother had seen to his education. My father had in fact wasted and spent in drink a good part of their inheritance. But the remainder, it was true, he had allotted to Constant. My uncle consequently felt under obligation to him and held my father above any reasoned reproach. He adored him. He welcomed him with open arms, while I took in Eugénie and obtained work for her as a seamstress at the theater. I constantly needed dresses. Though not good at much of anything, my sister had in fact learned to patch and mend with the Ursuline sisters in Douai. At least it was something.

Cécile also came to Rouen, but later. Discovered in a house of sin with her lover, a certain Bigo, she ended up in prison, where she spent two weeks before I came and fetched her, promising that our father would never learn of her misadventure. The lesson was short-lived. In the spring of 1804, pregnant to her eyeballs, Cécile came to live not far from me, on the place Saint-Sever, accompanied by César Bigo, who had decided to desert his wife and four legitimate children. Earlier, in April, Eugénie had given birth to a child who soon died and whose father she never determined.

Into this atmosphere of diapers and death rattles, my father now entered, tired of the pleasures of the capital. Amenable but terrified at my responsibility, forced to sustain this crowd in my cramped lodgings, I was almost grateful to my sisters' progeny for exiting without much fuss a scene that was already overcrowded, and where no one much cared to see them linger.

IN THE FALL when the news arrived, I had trouble believing that it was true: I had received an "order to appear" from the Opéra-Comique in Paris, an official summons. For the first time in years, life had sprung a surprise on me that was not unpleasant. Without a second thought, I packed my few belongings and started alone on the road to the capital. No question of taking along my horde of hangers-on, like a sack of hopelessly soiled laundry. Paris was the whole world to me, the city of possibilities, meant for the anonymous, those intent on making good, where my past would be erased. Paris, city of intense encounters. My uncle had often enough described its enchanting splendor. I was more than ready to succumb to its bewitchments.

I arrived in the capital in November 1804 and a month later was on the stage. Parisian critics, less indulgent than those in the provinces, nonetheless received me favorably.

"I'll explain a few things to you," said Délia, an actress who took a liking to me. "The truth is that they brought you into this theater as an attack on the Saint-Aubin woman. To give her a rival. For years no one has managed to unseat her. So it's a compliment to you in one sense. But the problem is that she still has a lot of people on her side. Old actresses don't give up their places easily."

"But I don't want to be in the middle of a quarrel!"

"You're in the thick of it, my sweet. The critics who flatter you are trying to dislodge Saint-Aubin. The rest have an interest in holding their place in her entourage. They are all of them nasty pieces of work. Which doesn't mean you don't have talent. You do. But no one cares, and that's the truth."

"What should I do then?"

"Be cleverer than all the rest, and know your enemies. Be suspicious, especially when someone claims to be your friend. Have no scruples. None."

Délia's revelation astonished me and made me detest the theater and newspapers all the more. To get by in this world of double-dealing, one had to be extremely grasping or ambitious. I was neither. Fortunately, Madame de Saint-Aubin sensed this. To put an end to the false competition, she kept me by her on the stage until the month of July. When we took our bows, she held my hand. The incident was closed. Then the Opéra-Comique shut down for renovations.

That was the time when I should have worried about my situation. I had survived my first season on the Paris stage, a remorselessly fierce environment. But in the capital one's credit carried over to the next season even less than in the provinces. I would have been well advised to arm myself, sharpen my weapons. Or simply huddle out of sight behind my defenses. Instead I walked out into the open, just as when I ran laughing between the graves as a child. It is perhaps because my favorite playground had been a cemetery that the settings for my loves have been sepulchers.

I had fallen in love.

IN THE THICK of the Saint-Aubin business, the dramatist Jars created a play for me, *Julie or the Pot of Flowers*, in which I appeared to great acclaim every night. On leaving the stage after a performance, still glowing from the applause, I saw a handsome naval officer waiting staunchly at my dressing room door. A carnivorous smile twisted his face. His skin smelled of manioc and saffron. His eyes were the color of the land where I had left my mother. It was Louis Lacour. Every night, I had dreamed that he would arrive, and that his unlikely return would allow me to finish a story whose ups and downs I had till then weathered with very little say in the matter. It was high time for me to rewrite that story, I had decided. And my apprenticeship began at Louis Lacour's lips.

Touched at being found attractive, keen to love, I saw in him an opportunity to revenge myself on fate. At the same time, paradoxically, Louis's return itself seemed fateful, a resummoning of what my mother had been, what my sisters were, and all that I had sworn not to be. Nineteen years old. In the world of actresses I was surely the only one who still preserved her virtue. If I lost it in subsequent days, from believing in Creole kisses, in the young seaman's tales of a sparkling ocean, volcanoes and the cannibal Caribbean, at least I gave up my virtue without bargaining for anything in return, unlike my fellow actresses who sold theirs to the highest bidder. Louis brought my mother to life again and murdered her a second time. Perhaps I liked the confused emotion, the mix of guilt and freedom, the desire to be pure, to give myself solely for love, and the desire, burning in my blood and part of my heredity, to be tainted. I liked love that made me bow down and that knotted my stomach with a fright I didn't feel in the theater. Love that kept me awake, or roused me from sleep at dawn, my head stuffed with dreams and tunnels, that stole my appetite and my power of speech, that subjugated me even as it broke my chains. I liked love's lies, more poetic than the ugly truth of reality, the finitude of a kiss, and the infinitude of its memory.

Louis Lacour, little suspecting that he gave me all of that, reveled in finding an agreeable port of call on his journey toward glory, a career, and the fulfillment of his ambitions. But neither his great selfishness nor his cruel opportunism could ever take his gift away from me.

DURING THE SUMMER of 1805 I followed him everywhere. To Boulogne, and even to Lille, where I gave five special performances as a star of the Paris theater. I avoided Rouen, however, which had become peopled with my sisters' successive offspring and as quickly rid of them. Like my brother Félix, also prostituted to support the paternal fiasco, I went only so far as to send my family a portion of my wages. I felt no obligation to do more and easily went without my family's company.

In early September I was once again working at the Opéra-Comique, which had moved to the Salle Feydeau. The battle started up in the press again more virulently than ever. Now that Madame de Saint-Aubin was safe from harm, another rival was found for me. Convinced that it would again come to nothing, I paid no attention to it.

"You're wrong, Marceline," said Délia. "No one is above everything. They'll get you in the end."

She was right. Without my noticing it, these absurd attacks were damaging me. Although the playwrights Grétry and Jars gave me their protection, I would soon fall from public grace. Admittedly, the scales were further tipped toward my unpopularity by the fact that I was pregnant.

My first pregnancy was difficult, and I found myself constantly alternating between dizziness and euphoria. Exhausted, sick, I tried to ignore my condition and hide it, following the advice of my actress friends. My moment of favor, though, had passed. I was quietly dropped from the theater's performances. The public had seen enough of me. Fed up, I resigned in April citing "concern for my father's well-being." My thought was to return to the Théâtre de Lille, where, as I believed, I still had a few friends. In truth I was mortified, terrified at the prospect of giving birth unpartnered, in a state of poverty, to a tiny creature that would never know its father. Sated of his little actress with her waning reputation, Louis, who liked public honors, had in fact left me at the beginning of the year.

"I must join the Emperor," he told me. "I'll write to you. I'll come back afterward so we can marry. Just wait for me."

Naive, I had believed I could escape ancestral type, the rope to which one returns early or late to hang oneself. A fine inheritance my mother had left my sisters and me . . . While I had believed myself, willed myself, to be different, stronger, I too—made submissive by love and in rebellion because of it—was preparing to become a child-mother.


ON SEPTEMBER 9, 1806, in the apartment of Cécile and Bigo, who had just ushered a child into the world and out of it again, I gave birth to a little girl. Sick and abandoned, I had been taken in by my eldest sister in Rouen. My father, who lived with Eugénie and her pregnancies, had finally come to terms with the public dishonor of his two older daughters. But when he learned of my own he howled and cast me from him as an unclean woman. Was my father more attached to me than it appeared? I asked myself through my tears. Had he prayed that the family curse not strike his youngest daughter? Or was it simply that my fall would cause a source of revenue to dry up?

Gnawed by doubt, drunk with the pain of childbirth, worn out, I barely had time to hold my little Louisa in my arms before she went to a nursemaid on the outskirts of town. Three weeks later she was gone. I was still recovering from labor.

In vain I waited for a letter from the boy who had one day confusedly promised me marriage and was unaware that he had been a father.

Tʜᴇ ʏᴇᴀʀ 1806 ended in sadness. Eugénie had just buried her third infant. It seemed that we Desbordes girls only knew how to carry promises. Life, so quick to lodge in us, shattered at the first turn in the road. We had been children without a mother. We were now mothers without children. In the cards that were dealt to us, inexplicably, there always seemed to be a misdeal. Who was cheating us? Who was hiding in the shadows to make the hand go awry and force us always to lose? And yet, whether from brashness or unconcern, we ponied up the bet every time, playing double or nothing until the last of our coins was gone. Graves mounded up around us at the same cadence as baptismal certificates. Cécile had started talking into empty space, real conversations, with questions and commands, addressed to her passel of ghostly children. My delirium was of a different order: I composed little ballads that I cast like messages on the water to my friends still in the capital.

Judging that I was not strong enough to face the cliques and the cabals, I dared not return to Paris.

"It would be in your best interest," Délia advised me, "to let people forget you for a time. Disgrace, you'll find, is as short-lived as public favor."

I considered leaving for good and finding a town that was still free of any trace of my family's history. Starting with a blank slate. Was it possible? I was finding it hard, though, to overcome my dejection. Returning to acting was distasteful to me. But how else was I to climb out of the mud? After my pregnancy, my voice had grown weaker still. I would no longer be able to sing, that much was clear. What was I to become?

DÉLIA WROTE ME at this point: one of my ballads had been set to music and printed in Paris. Buoyed by this pitiful success, I resolved until further notice to tread the boards once more. Brussels was hiring, I had heard. Why not?

But when the time came to go, in the spring of 1807, I was no longer sure of wanting to leave Rouen and its collection of little caskets. I had met someone who made me want to cling frantically to the side of the living. A man. His name was Eugène Debonne.

## 11

E ARE GOING TO ROUEN," Prosper finally announces, after hesitating a long time.

Eighteen thirty-two. I shudder. We have been in Lyon for five years. I am just coming around to accepting it. Rouen, worse luck. Any city but that one! My life seems to go in circles like a convict taking his exercise, the same circuit over and over, shackled to a ball and chain, dogging the footsteps of the man in front. Like a sentence that will never be lifted. The irony of it is that Valmore has chosen Rouen for my sake, believing I would welcome the chance to see my sisters again. He is far from imagining that nothing could displease me more. As usual, he thinks he is doing right. Were I to display any reticence, he would make an angry show of his good faith, his best intentions, and take deep offense. I sometimes wish that he were less generous, that he would think less about my happiness. He is irreproachable in his magnanimity. His virtues exempt him from all blame and at times, I must confess, exasperate me. I must hold my peace and thank him. Handle him with kid gloves. In our fifteen years of marriage, I have made continual efforts to erase anything from my past that might cause him pain and have avoided a multitude of dark corners. As far as possible. Hard nonetheless to hide Félix's debasement and Cécile's degeneracy. Valmore, being a man of elementary principles, finds excuses for my sister, because she is a woman and a victim. But my brother he condemns beyond the reach of all appeal.

"He is a drunkard, grasping and dishonest. You have a short memory, Marceline, but he is always trying to make a profit from your name, your celebrity. He even sold the letters that you sent him!"

"He has suffered so! His life has been a martyrdom. The army, jail, and then the prison boats in Scotland . . . He is a broken man."

"A good-for-nothing."

Prosper has no tolerance for human failings. My tendency, on the contrary, is to glorify them.

Out of caution I polish, rub, and smooth away all the burred edges from my story and my family's. Valmore is unaware of what happened in Rouen, of Eugénie's romances, of my father's drinking bouts, of the babies birthed and forgotten. And me. I also lived there, and worse. Many people in Rouen will remember it all readily. The prospect makes me tremble like a leaf. I rail in secret against my husband's generous intentions.

I write to Eugénie. On no account must we have the slightest contact with the Debonne family. Prosper must know nothing. Ever. With our departure from Lyon only a few days off, I am knotted with anxiety. I am afraid of the mistakes one never stops paying for, the wounds that forever reopen.


AT A CERTAIN age, time starts to race. Looking at my children grow up, I don't see that I am becoming older. The years in any case stopped counting off for me one spring. One of the women I am will always be thirty-some years old and rush off in the afternoon toward the pont de la Tournelle or the rue des Saints-Pères, her lips reddened in anticipation of a surfeit of kisses, her skin as blue as taut parchment. That is the woman I am always writing and rewriting. But when I emerge from poetry, I am drawn toward the people around me, the causes that need defending, the hopes wanting nourishment. On this score, History has served me well in recent days. I have lived, as though they were so many passions, the July Revolution, the riots in Brussels, the Warsaw uprising, and the Lyon silkworkers' revolt. The poverty of the Warsaw insurgents filled me with indignation. For their sake, I dipped into the food stocks in our pantry and publicly came to their defense in the pages of the local opposition paper, for which I sometimes write.

I have always hated the Restoration. Henri's conversation has made me nostalgic for the extraordinary events of the Napoleonic era.

"Louis XVIII and Charles X were only the last incarnations of a line already in serious decline. They had none of the Emperor's greatness!"

"My dear, you are getting carried away," said Prosper. "The pack of them are worthless, and one is as bad as the other."

"You never believe in anything."

"Let's just say that I am more restrained than you are."

"In 1821, I cried at the news of Napoleon's death. It was something greater than us all, something poetic . . ."

"You also cried, I might remind you, when the tricolor flag was raised at the Hôtel de Ville in this very city, in July 1830."

Prosper loves to point out my contradictions and play devil's advocate. I fight back tooth and nail:

"I thought at the time that Louis-Philippe was offering a peaceful solution. I was tired of the violence. And the House of Orleans struck me as less degenerate than the Bourbons. Remember that freedom of the press was entirely abolished in June 1830. I was stunned at the incoherence of it. How could a people that supported revolutionary reforms tolerate measures like that?"

"How could a fervent Bonapartist accept a royal grant? Fortunately Louis-Philippe stopped your pension. You are free to boast that you owe nothing to the monarchy."

"We could hardly have survived on just your earnings from the theater . . ."

Discussions between Valmore and me regularly swerve toward arguments. Little settlings of account, tiny grudges. We incite each other to it. His cynicism annoys me, and I believe he often finds my irrationality insufferable. We quickly make up with each other. It is our way of starting from a blank slate, of sweeping away accumulated irritations. Every couple makes its own accommodations.

OCTOBER 1831. UNDER our windows, men are dying again.

"Everyone down on the ground!" says Prosper.

"Are we going to die? Maman, do you think we are going to die?" asks Hyacinthe feverishly.

I pull my children close to me. We are lying on the floor of our apartment. A river of blood, of horror, runs at our feet. A bullet passes through the glass of one of the windows in the drawing room. The silkworkers have invaded the streets of Lyon to blare out their misery. The brutal repression by Casimir-Perier revolts me. At night I am awoken by the lamentations of the widows. And for a long time I suffer from insomnia, believing that I see their terrified eyes turned toward me in mute supplication. "You look at us and say nothing, write nothing," they seem to say. And so I write, absolved for once of writing about myself. I join the company of all women who cry, knowing that I must sing for them all. I like to help the needy, the oppressed of every kind. I pay visits to streetwalkers, to prisoners. Over the years, it has become a true vocation. My good offices are well known. The downtrodden stand elbow to elbow at my door. But my poem on the silkworkers remains unpublished.

OUR LAST MONTHS in Lyon are difficult. Prosper is earning less, and an editor has swindled me. In the world of letters, now that Latouche no longer protects me, I am defenseless. It is no more than I asked for. Over the course of our correspondence I have gradually freed myself from Henri's literary influence. A question of pride. I owe him a great deal, as I well know. His advice, though apt, perpetuated a relationship between us of master and pupil. Today I believe that in the only bond that still unites us—epistolary, romantic, and poetic in nature—we must stand on an equal footing. Latouche is no longer part of my reality. He has entered my mythology. He is in fact at its center. To deal with current business, I have chosen another literary director. In any case Henri has found himself another little pearl from the provinces. "A country-woman of his," Pauline wrote to me, "a certain Madame Sandeau, whom he has renamed, nurtured, and edited, and to whose groping efforts with the pen he has given a lover's encouragement, or so they say. Latouche offered this George Sand a column in *Le Figaro*, his satirical gazette. But she has proved a poor journalist, and he is the only one to believe in her writing talent. She is mired in divorce proceedings. Some are muttering that your one-eyed man of letters, who just celebrated the successful publication of his novel *Fragoletta* and provoked a second *Hernani* with his play *The Queen of Spain*, is named in the lawsuit."

My own Henri inhabits a different sphere. I preserve his image in me as though it were a bronze medallion, fixed and inalterable.

Right until our departure from Lyon, the streets stay the color of the blood I saw spilled there at my helpless feet. Neither rain nor the tears of the widows and orphans manage to wash it away. This red watercourse through which we are forced to wade revolts me. Because of the cholera epidemic that is racing through the capital, I change my plans at the last minute and decide not to go to Paris. We have just come through a siege of scarlet fever, and my dread of illness is strong. Strong enough even to forgo Paris. That leaves me only Rouen and its plagues of another sort. In Valmore's presence, I pretend to rejoice at our move. Inside, though, I am trembling for Félix, my brother, who escaped from the asylum in Lyon where I had him interned for several months without Prosper's knowledge. As we prepare to leave, I have no indication of Félix's plans, or of his physical and mental state.

CHOLERA IS ALSO raging in Rouen. The inhabitants are wracked with cramps, diarrhea, vomiting. Arriving there bilious and exhausted on April 28, 1832, I reflect that there could have been no worse augury than this putrid welcome. Yet it has the merit of being frank. We do not hide our mutual aversion from each other, this city and I. But the epidemic passes quickly. Filled with dark foreboding, I spend the summer cloistered in the handsome apartment we have rented at no great distance from the theater. I am trying to be as discreet as possible, always clinging to my children and going out only to visit my sisters. I mostly see Eugénie, who has managed in her closeness with her husband and children to have her past forgotten. She conducts her life with measure, tact, and a modesty that borders on poverty. She provokes no one's envy, casts no one in shadow. As always, my sister is good and simple, but now she lives in honorable destitution. It is a different case with Cécile, who was long ago abandoned by the man she loved and her two sons. She talks to her flowers and her cats, lives from charity and hunks of bread, dribbling her life away hopelessly in the depths of her hovel. Only Eugénie ever enters it, once a week, carrying a basket of food and the laundry she has managed to clean with ash. I stay guiltily away, so that tongues will not wag and also because of Valmore. Cécile's destitution is more horrific even than Eugénie's letters have described it. Her decrepitude splashes onto me, stains my right to happiness and success. Next to her, glory is repugnant, vulgar. She hurts me. And she aggravates more than a few others.

I am not happy. I am afraid of everything and attend no performances. The past holds me by the throat, and the ghost of my little boy who died so long ago, before my marriage, pursues me. Prosper can't understand my attitude, senses that he doesn't know everything, and avoids asking questions. My children are my only happiness. I allow them to surround me like small thorny hedges.

"Hippolyte is twelve years old," Prosper said to me one day. "He is perfectly old enough to be sent to boarding school, where he will get a serious education."

"I don't agree. It's too soon. He is still a child. It would be very painful for me to be separated from him. And for him too. Look how much he needs me."

"Exactly. You are smothering him. He does nothing. Look at him. I'm afraid he'll never do anything. He is apathetic, soft. It's for his own good, Marceline, and you know it as well as I. In September he will leave for a school in Grenoble. The director is an old friend. As a favor, he will take Hippolyte on reasonable terms. Come, the matter is settled."

Prosper is probably not entirely wrong. My maternal instinct, struck down so many times, broods over my first living son too closely. Hippolyte is the nicest boy, but he shows no desire, no ambition other than to be at my side. This attitude drives Valmore to distraction. I must yield. But I arrange to accompany my son as far as Grenoble.

THE TRIP IS hard, harrowing. Yet I am not sorry to be leaving Normandy for a time and getting away. Rouen has started to prattle. Rumors are reaching Prosper's ears, though he does his best not to hear. I have watched in terror as the storm cloud rises toward his face, ready to burst. Questions, suspicions, and a deep-seated bitterness, I sense, knock against each other in his lovestruck and jealous heart. I pack Hippolyte's belongings hastily and we leave like thieves after a burglary. Travel agrees with me less and less. With age, long journeys have become unendurable. The smallest thing causes me injury. Soon indisposed, I require frequent stops. I stay in Grenoble nearly two months, unable to part with Hippolyte. Finally my son is torn from me. The moment is one I have dreaded so long that when it comes I am almost relieved. Now each minute brings me closer to seeing him again. But I am exhausted and in no hurry to return to Rouen, where Valmore has been reading over, with care and in a new light, the whole of my published poems.

At the poste restante in Lyon, where I stop on the way, a letter from Henri awaits me. "What's this?" he writes. "You shamelessly return to Rouen without making a detour to the capital?" He is tired, he confesses, of the tribal wars between the Romantics and the classicists. As he refuses to join any group at all, he is pilloried as a follower of Lamartine at one moment, and as a partisan of Chateaubriand the next. No one knows what to do with him.

*I have decided to retire to the country like a woman who has been pretty and who disappears from society out of coquettishness when she ages. I have a good reason for going there besides. I have managed at last to realize a dream that has been nagging me all these years and have bought the Hermitage of the Vallée aux Loups, the house that belonged, as you know, to my beloved Chénier and, more recently, to the author of* René. *It is there, in the days of his glory, that Chateaubriand received Madame Récamier . . . Which reminds me! She has been asking for you, and I have promised that I would bring you to the Abbaye aux Bois as soon as ever you might favor us with a visit to those parts. Almost blind and financially ruined, she is still remarkably fine-looking, with a nobility of spirit that has made her fiercely refuse to sell Benjamin Constant's letters, which every publisher is trying to pry from her. Royalists and liberals, they are all rodents. While they may differ in their literary and political opinions, they join together in greed. It is a calamity. If you are eclectic, the whole world turns against you . . . I know a bit about that, but then*

*I needn't belabor it to you. And you are not in that situation,*
*you who are a stranger to all trickery, all calculation, and*
*whom Paris loves unconditionally. If you were ever to show*
*yourself here, you would quickly observe how far you surpass us*
*all. Your presence might perhaps enliven my state of dejection,*
*despite the sandy soil, the purple hills, the tawny plains, and*
*the fruit trees of my astonishingly Tuscan retreat . . .*

Latouche needs me. It is certainly the first time. Citing literary business as a pretext, I send Prosper word that I will be
stopping for several days in the capital.

RUNNING TOWARD MY rendezvous with Henri in the Palais-
Royal's Galerie Montpensier, I feel the same emotions wash
over me as I felt at our first meetings. It's idiotic. We are both
of us ugly enough now, and tired. Five years ago Henri didn't
want to see me, but today he requests me. Just to spend a minute chatting, like brother and sister? Henri is not my brother,
and he never will be! I can't help it, my stomach is in knots, my
hands are moist with sweat and I keep rubbing them together.
I wonder whether my legs will carry me the whole way. My
body is so weakened that I can barely stand. A tambourine is
thumping in my chest. I am no more than an ageless body,
and I like it. Already I am imagining the nature of our meeting, so many years after that night of storm by the Seine, that
black-crepe April dawn when we parted. Yes, I can already see
Latouche sauntering at the far end of the arcade, a smile on his
lips to mask his emotion, his pleasure. Mist swathes the garden
in half light, hangs time motionless above our heads while the
world beside us turns its attention away. It is only a respite, I

well know, in this already lost race against time, but I savor it as a soldier savors a momentary cessation of hostilities. Love is in a way an armistice. And also a merciless guerrilla campaign in the hills of time. It's hard to make sense of it.

THE SILENCE SEEMS almost panicked. We have each of us tried to arrive a little late, so as not to be first and have to pace awkwardly the length of the Galerie Montpensier. In the end we arrive at the same time, he from the Théâtre-Français side and I from the rue du Beaujolais, as I am coming directly from Pauline's. I stroll up through the arcades, trying to take my time, amend my gait a little, afraid that it looks heavy and provincial. And to catch my breath more than anything. An anxious vanity eats at me. I am so old, so horrible-looking. Obviously it's absurd, as I have never had the grace of one of the truly great actresses, a Mademoiselle Mars or a Mademoiselle George. And it's not at the age of forty-six that I will suddenly acquire it. Henri loved me precisely because I resembled no one else. Yet I am overcome with anxiety. I spent the morning examining my face, blotting out this, accentuating that, calling myself a fool, amused, secretly happy, shrugging my shoulders, giving up the battle, then leaping to my feet again, inspired, to peer into the mirror once more. The hours passed slowly. The last were as interminable as our years apart. Ten years. More than ten years. The episode at the Opéra, which occurred five years ago, doesn't count. I've excised it from our legend. But today, in late November 1832, is it not a mistake to see each other when our letters have been our only mirror and our faces have developed so many wrinkles in the time apart? Lines of writing in which it would be wounding to find no mention of oneself, and equally wounding to find oneself mentioned too often. Would it not have been better to stop at writing letters? And what if everything collapses now, everything on which my life and my poetry depend?

But it is too late to turn back. I wanted this rendezvous, which is perhaps with myself. It has made me so deliciously dizzy that not for a second have I thought about my children. All my concern has been for myself, for my spinning head. At the far end of the arcade, behind a band of gawkers idling at an antiquarian's window, I have just recognized Henri's spectral silhouette.

## 12

UGÈNE DEBONNE WAS FORTY-FOUR. I was twenty-one. His sparse graying hair was slicked to one side in a provincial try at elegance. The skin of his face and neck was florid. The man quickly grew winded. Tired or perhaps discouraged, he always seemed to be catching his breath, and it was hard to see why life demanded such an effort on his part. His figure was far from having the nobility of the long-stemmed Louis Lacour. Instead it spoke of weariness and inactivity, but it was large and solidly built, imposing but at the same time reassuring. Fatherly, in a way. In my distress, this was obviously what attracted me. My father was stocky, bent, and drunk from noon on every day. In any case, he had lost all interest in me since I left the stage. He was barely aware that I had lost a child. It didn't concern him. He held a particular grudge against me.

"She betrayed me," he once said to Cécile.

For my part, I persisted in seeing him as the marvelous teller of tales of my childhood, the man who kissed me on the forehead every night at bedtime, rescued mutilated saints from churches, the dreamer with a thousand whimsical schemes. I struggled mightily not to identify him with his mass of lies, drinking sprees, and unforgivable mediocrity, and I cried hot tears because my father no longer loved me. Lying in his own piss and vomit, bitter, moaning, and filled with hate, he was still my father. The realization would come upon me with horror. I would have crawled at his feet if he would only have taken me on his knees and rocked me as he did in the time of my mother's *loées*. He used to sing ditties to me in a cracked voice, and the sound accompanied me to sleep. I closed my eyes reassured. The gentle refrain would stay with me until morning.

EUGÈNE DEBONNE'S VOICE sounded in some ways like my father's. It stood out from other voices in the way of a timid man who plies his elbows in a crowd and jumps up to get people's attention. Eugène was introduced to me by a friend of Cécile and Bigo. He struck me because of his gentle manner and kind eyes. I was not used to kindness. As my instinctive posture was one of defense, it put me off balance. I could not conceive that his behavior was natural. Suspicious, I put it down to calculation. Behind Eugène's clear eyes, I thought I saw the deceiving eyes of Louis Lacour. I had thought Louis different from other men and I had been wrong. Eugène genuinely was, but I refused to admit it. His heart was sincere, as mine was. With the passage of time, I recognized in his attitudes an echo of my own. Life had disillusioned him as well. He felt himself its victim and wanted only to slip away to a discreet and placid life, a stable existence next to a woman he would cherish in his strong arms and a child, his soft spot, his reward, after all the bleak years he had known. Very soon, Eugène spoke to me of marriage. It was too wonderful to be true. Yet I believed it, believed it with all my soul, because I thought it was time for a little luck to come my way. A hand reached out to me, and I longed to clasp it in mine.

But I needed to live. There was no question of remaining dependent on Bigo, who would take it out on my sister sooner or later during one of the abrupt changes of mood he was prone to. I did not want to be dependent on anyone. In April 1807 then, I left Rouen for Brussels, where I had been engaged by the Théâtre de la Monnaie. Eager and attentive, Eugène made a point of accompanying me, helping me settle into my new quarters. Unwilling to leave me alone in a strange city, he stayed on with me for a time. He was goodness personified. In the end, though, he left. His older brother needed him in Rouen. The Debonne family was rich and powerful. The two boys, orphaned at an early age, grew up squashing each other. Eugène was the one on the bottom. From an early age he had obeyed Jacques's orders, and Jacques ran the family business and the lives of those around him with an iron fist. His younger brother's liaison with a recently pregnant actress irritated him beyond measure. Eugène had been forced to invent a trip to Lille in order to accompany me to Brussels.

"In time, everything will work out for the best," he told me. "Jacques will come around. He'll have to accept the situation. He isn't completely heartless."

But for the moment, Eugène preferred not to stay away any longer and stole back to Rouen. His brother frowned on his absences.

On May 4, I made my first appearance at the Théâtre de la Monnaie. In spite of my fervent resolutions and my weak voice, I was once again acting in comic opera. With great success. Buoyed by Eugène's quiet love, by the long and sentimental letters he wrote me, I would find myself serenely dreaming of a balmy and respectable future far from the stage. The idea strengthened me, and I would dress in my costume and walk onstage with the secret knowledge that my days as an actress were numbered.

"It won't be much longer," I said to myself every night.

In Brussels I discovered my childhood friend from Douai, Albertine, now married and unhappy. Playing knucklebones on the town walls and in the church cemetery, we had been inseparable. We adored each other. Time and separation had made breaks in our life histories and worn creases at the corners of our eyes. We talked nonstop for hours. But once I had learned about her life and once I had told her the story of mine, our conversations gradually tapered off. Still, I loved feeling her calm and unquestioning gaze on me, her silent and unchanging friendship. Ageless. The past always brought us together. Together Albertine and I ran through the tombs of Notre-Dame.

I NEVER WOULD have thought so, but I missed Eugène. I had slid without much resistance into the insensibility of his love and was allowing torpor to overcome me. He invited me to return to Rouen. "You mustn't fret about material problems," he wrote. He would take care of everything. Meaning that I would be his mistress, kept by him in a plush and discreet apartment. An arrangement I had always refused whenever it was proposed to me, as to every actress. I relied only on myself. To turn myself over so completely to another frightened me. And made me ashamed. Pride and the need for action kept me from accepting his offer, which at the same time provoked an overwhelming desire in me for capitulation and submission. Was this a reflection of my true nature? "It is only a temporary solution while we wait for Jacques's authorization," said Eugène. "Madame Debonne," I said under my breath, climbing the rue Neuve to the place de la Monnaie, "Madame Marceline Debonne." Give or take a little, it was already my name, or very nearly.

And so after a triumphant season, to the stupefaction of the theater's director and all the company, and despite the grief it caused Albertine, I chose to break my engagement and forgo my comfortable wages for Eugène's gilded cage. I was wagering everything on his promise of marriage. There was no doubt an element of unreason in my decision—my father would certainly choke at the news—but I could not decently allow the opportunity to pass.

The pretty three-room apartment in which Eugène ensconced me in Rouen was on the rue de la Chaîne: I should have taken the omen at face value. And yet, when you ardently call on your happiness to attend you, you like to believe that it has heard. I wanted to see nothing in this address but a sunny portent, the first link in the legitimate bond I aspired to. It was a period in my life when everything delighted me. The horizon for the first time was clear of troubling signs. The storm, as if by enchantment, was dying down around me. People smiled at me, pampered me. I had hesitated for a long moment, but having made my choice I cast away all doubt. My will, steadfast and brash, brushed aside all regret. And I was not the only one to know a respite. My family also seemed to arrive at a measure of peace. Pregnant once more, our frivolous Eugénie had won the heart of a good man, Désiré Drapier, who heeded her request to wait until I was back in Rouen to celebrate their marriage.

Eugénie married! I was so moved that I cried all through the ceremony. My chest swelled with joy, and all the mud that had clung to us, the curse that seemed to dog my sisters and me, was swept away. Redemption was in fact possible. The poor girl had been allowed to expiate her misdeeds. Why not me? Cécile had just given birth to a fifth child, who was visibly in good health and oriented toward the realm of the living. My father, sickened by the nappies and the baby's crying, had decided to bolt to Paris, where he stayed at Constant's studio in the old Capuchin convent. In this spring of 1808, the air in Rouen had suddenly become pleasantly breathable. I felt well.

MY FIRST PRIORITY was to have my past as an actress forgotten. Now that my family no longer made me blush, I too needed to take my place among the acceptable members of society, so that society might finally throw open its doors to me—the front ones, not the back doors through which one passes with a lowered head, hunched shoulders, and a hasty step. I wanted the Debonne family to think well of me, by whatever means. Without special effort, I played to perfection the role of model wife and woman of culture. I sewed, mended, took lessons in harp and guitar, sat for my portrait, composed verses that were afterward read within my close circle, and welcomed a select group of friends into my home, from which the theater crowd, of course, was excluded. I avoided them like the plague, and if an acquaintance from the theater crossed my path I turned my back on him. It wasn't arrivism on my part. It was fear. But not everyone understood it this way. In hiding from the light, I was also attracting lightning.

As time passed and I shed my old identity, I became "Eugène Debonne's companion." We did not, of course, live under the same roof. Eugène went home to sleep at his brother's every night. Honor was maintained and appearances saved. Deeply in love, he spoiled me, gave me everything, and exposed himself more and more to his brother's wrath by openly appearing with me. I reveled in his adoration, drank it in greedily, so starved of love had I been that it seemed I could never get my fill of it. After a brief embrace, which cost him a good deal of effort and me a little imagination, he would fall asleep peacefully in my arms. Eugénie had taught me a few tricks. I therefore thought it was always like this. Nothing dazzling, but nothing rushed either. A straight and sober line, then the stertorous breathing of a tired man.

"CONSTANT HAS HAD a picture accepted, his first, in the Salon of 1808!" my father wrote from Paris. This was an important event. It meant recognition for an outcast, and a chance to thumb his nose at the skeptics and false judges. My father's letter had a triumphant tone, I felt. Only necessity could have made him sell his son and beg from his daughters. But what suffering it had caused, what heartache! Father! You loved us, then! I was prepared to forgive him everything. Eugène drove me to Paris to attend my uncle's opening and to see a few dear friends. Constant and he got along from the start. They both had a taste for solitary reflection, in a world they had built themselves beside the one in which they felt unable to hold their own. Constant at least painted. But aside from loving me, Eugène did nothing. Neither of them was sour or bitter, simply elsewhere. And in this elsewhere, they had quickly found each other.

My dream of getting married was starting to cloud over somewhat, but I still refused to admit it. All the more so because my father now shared the dream with me. Reconciled, we had gone strolling arm in arm along the rue Royale, not far from Constant's studio, which was at that time on the place Vendôme. We spoke little, but his free hand rested on mine.

"Eugène is a good man," he said.

"I'm glad you approve of my choice."

In truth, Eugène was probably not the man of my choice. But my father liked him. I was trying not to rile my father and to regain his love. At any price.

ON OUR RETURN from Rouen, Eugène, still intoxicated by the liveliness of the capital, Constant's friendship, and my father's tacit consent to our union, was bubbling over with enthusiasm.

"I want a child, Marceline. A little tyke all my own, to run between my legs and put his arms around my neck . . . I'd teach him to read, and all the things that fill my head uselessly because I have no one to pass them on to. My life makes little sense without a child."

Eugène dreamed of a child as if it were a toy. He could already see himself, far from the company of power-seeking adults, in that imaginary space where his son would leap into his lap and let out peals of laughter. Eugène would never have admitted it, but he was at bottom dying to play with dolls. I was only faintly swayed by his fervor. I would have preferred to be first done once and for all with clandestine love.

"A child will make my brother decide in our favor."

I wanted to believe that he was right. By the fall of 1809 I was pregnant.

WHEN MY CONDITION became too obvious, I was obliged to hide.

"There just isn't a good moment to tell Jacques about it," said Eugène. "I'm afraid that if I make the slightest misstep, all our hopes will be dashed."

Forcing myself to concentrate on the life that was gaining ground within me, I refused to be disappointed. Pregnancy exhausted me. I chafed at being forced into seclusion, when what I needed most was to stroll along the Seine on Eugène's arm or with my sister. Once again my condition was not a cause for rejoicing. Instead it was a sort of punishment that had to be borne as quietly as possible, a disgrace visited on the belly of a woman, as though it inseminated itself. An act of disobedience, of irreverence. When he learned of my pregnancy, Jacques Debonne took it as an open challenge to his authority, unsurprisingly. The effect was exactly the opposite of what Eugène had planned. The fault was all mine.

Saddened by the banishment quietly imposed on me, I chose not to deliver the baby in Rouen, where my presence was becoming more unwanted every day. Eugénie stoutly joined me in my Paris exile and stayed at my side the whole time. We told no one. My father and Constant only learned that I had had a child after the fact. Eugène, strictly forbidden to follow me, prudently bowed to his brother's will.

When I returned to Rouen several months later with little Marie-Eugène in my arms, he nonetheless recognized the boy as his own.

"It's only a question of time," he said. "Jacques is starting to soften toward us."

THREE YEARS SLIPPED by. At first my feelings toward the mewling creature were so confused that I was wracked with shame and grief, never managing to work out whether I wanted him to live or to die, whether I loved him or not—from fear, most likely, of becoming attached to him too soon and losing him overnight. I witnessed Eugène's effusions toward the child while taking no part in them myself. He was smitten with the boy to the point of idiocy. After the sad precedents of the past years and the death of my sisters' offspring and my own Louisa, I refused to turn my baby over to a wet nurse and decided to nurse him myself. Love came little by little. Life triumphed over all fears and doubts. Marie-Eugène was a wonder. By his presence alone he quelled my inner conflicts. I pushed away my skepticism to smile confidently at existence. There was an underlying logic to all this: preserving my faith in Eugène and the possibility of our marriage spared me temporarily from having to make any other decision. The battle that I was waging despite myself with the Debonne family had changed into a cold and sullen hostility, with never a confrontation. Marie-Eugène was a part of my life and I didn't want to hide it any longer. He was my pride and joy. I visited my sisters and appeared openly in public, my head unbowed. I knew that if I blushed at my own situation I would only invite general condemnation. That was out of the question.

During this period, I started going back to the theater, but as a spectator this time, enjoying the delicious and uncomfortable sensation of sitting with the censors, the honest citizens who had come to clap disdainfully at the traveling players' entertainment. One evening I even witnessed the acting debut of the boy who, in a fit of childhood bravado, had kissed me on the lips in Bordeaux: the son of the Valmores, young Prosper. But I avoided going backstage after the performance to greet the parents of this sublime creature, who was not quite yet a man. I had no wish to venture behind the curtains, in the wings, where my respectable consort would have fooled no one. I simply gazed at the boy's silhouette from a safe distance. His mother could well be proud of him. Prosper Valmore had lost his babyishness. He was handsome as the devil.

NOTHING WAS EVER going to change. One day I simply knew it in my heart of hearts. My blond boy was charging around nearby. Eugène was away on family business. I would never be his wife. It was as plain as plain could be. How could I ever have imagined anything different? We had allowed the situation to come to a standstill, to settle into this lovers' garret, Eugène from cowardice and I from patience. Yet my ambitions had not been immoderate. I hadn't dreamed of taking over a whole house, just one floor. But this attic paid for by Eugène had become insufferable to me. I had made up my mind. I would leave. With my son, against all opposition, I would make my way to Paris and take up my work in the theater again so as to earn enough for the two of us to live, in garret rooms, but without bars. Constant, who adored Eugène, would tell me I was mad. My sisters and my father would condemn my behavior, which they wouldn't understand and would attribute to my impulsive and unstable character. Eugène might possibly die of grief. Only my brother Félix, a prisoner somewhere in Scotland from whom I had recently received news after months of silence, would secretly envy my lot. I was escaping from the prison ship of complacency and buying my freedom at a price I could perhaps not afford. But I was buying it. And Félix, stagnating in a life he had not freely chosen, would have been prepared to pay it too, had it not been too late. Alas, he had already abandoned the struggle. As for me, nothing could hold me back.

In February 1813, clasping my son's hand firmly in mine, I left Rouen. My heart was full of rage at having hoped so long in vain. Two days later I had settled in Paris. I wanted to eat the capital whole. I didn't yet know how. Within a week, moving heaven and earth, I managed to get a two-year engagement at the Théâtre de l'Odéon.

I would brook no further opposition to my will.

## 13

THE YEARS HAVE SWOLLEN MY FEATURES, hacked at my cheeks unmercifully. They have flattened themselves against Henri's forehead and around his eyes, making his dead eye bulge more prominently than ever. With my hairnet, my graying locks, the arthritis that is already deforming my hands, I look more countrified even than before, while Latouche's air of slightly weary dandyism gives him the aspect of an aging Romeo. A couple that complement each other better could hardly be found: we are both as repulsive as we are grotesque.

Henri has not come to the Palais-Royal alone. I am horribly disappointed. The man accompanying him is David d'Angers, the sculptor.

"He so wants, dear Madame Valmore, to include you among his portrait medallions of famous contemporaries," says Latouche.

"Come, he must be thinking of another person. I would hardly put myself in this period, and I am certainly a closer contemporary to Beaumarchais than to your friend George Sand, who reportedly smokes cigars in public and appears at every turn with a new gallant on her arm."

The pick is well placed. Henri takes the blow impassively, though his lips tighten and he turns a shade paler.

"Your poetry, Madame Valmore, is ageless," David d'Angers offers.

"If only my profile, as modeled by your hands, might be equally so."

I laugh. They do too. The incident is closed, and my bitterness with it. I am happy to see Latouche again, am moved by his ugliness, his discomfort. Jealousy provides a ground for our complicity. Sand, his little protégée, has with his help just published a novel, *Indiana*, which people are talking about as much as her extravagant dress and her scandalous behavior.

"I would never have imagined," I say, "that tobacco could help sell books."

Latouche smiles openly, while I pretend to sigh.

"You have always given me such intelligent advice, Monsieur de Latouche, and you must be frank with me now: should I or should I not take up cigars?"

"A pipe, Madame Valmore, you must smoke a pipe."

FOR AN ENTIRE week, Henri drags me with him everywhere, waving me like a special permit or a shield.

"Nodier's salon has gone out of fashion," he tells me. "Now it all happens at Hugo's place, on the rue Notre-Dame-des-Champs. They all want to see you. The inner circle. That's where the battle for *Hernani* was mapped out. You'll meet Dumas there, and Mérimée, Sainte-Beuve, Nerval, also your old acquaintances Gautier and Vigny. I'll introduce you to Balzac as well, about whom I've made such high claims. You'll see that I was right."

"Weren't you on poor terms with some of them?"

"The thing of it, Marceline, is that in its early years the Romantic movement leaned toward the monarchy, and all these young whippersnappers who preached revolution in literature found themselves, paradoxically, to be royalists in politics. Whereas I, as you well know, am entirely liberal."

"And today? How do things stand?"

"Now they are liberal too. How could anyone support Louis-Philippe? But we are not members of the same generation. I don't have their energy, their faith. They have achieved glory before the age of thirty, and their arrogance will make you blush."

"Must we really go, Henri?"

"Your poetry is no longer selling, Marceline. Hugo has published *Les Orientales* and *Les Feuilles d'automne* in quick succession. The literary world is in crisis. You are either a part of it or you disappear."

"How terrifying."

"You needn't tell me!"

After a few days, I have to admit that Latouche is right. Editors are disinclined to talk to me, reject my poems. At the same time, I am being asked everywhere. All the popular actresses are sending me pressing invitations, which I decline on the pretext of poor health. Henri introduces me to Charpentier, a young editor who is much taken with my latest poems. He already imagines publishing them, he says, with a preface by Alexandre Dumas. Skeptical, I turn to Latouche:

"Would Dumas do that?"

"Absolutely," says Latouche.

"But you told me that he never reads poetry!"

"And he won't read yours either. But I can guarantee you as I stand here that the preface will be excellent."

I am shocked, I confess. Withdrawn inside my house, busy with my poems and my charities, I would never have imagined how books were being made in the capital.

"Monsieur de Latouche claims that you devote a large share of your time to prison inmates, that you go and visit them, along with the poor and disadvantaged of every ilk. Is it true, Madame Valmore?" asks Charpentier.

"Yes, but what connection does that have to my poems?"

"Have you chosen a title for the collection as a whole?"

"*Tears.*"

He scowls.

"Well, it's not bad, but *My Tears* would be better. More autobiographical. Stronger. We could suggest the idea of your laying yourself bare, of your utter devotion, of art as the only defense against distress—"

"Out of the question. I categorically refuse."

Henri comes to my rescue. He is fond of imposture, but not of lying and sordid manipulation.

"Madame Valmore is the only pure spirit of our age," he says. "Let us protect her from these vulgar calculations. Say yes to Dumas," he adds, speaking to me. "It won't cost you anything and you'll find it useful. For the rest, stay true to yourself and have nothing to do with these mercantile strategies. People cling to the legend that you live as a recluse in an attic with your brats and your strolling player of a husband. Let them say what they like. You cannot in any case go against it at this point."

"I see."

I write a letter to Prosper. "Paris is suffocating me. There is shouting and arm waving on all sides. I can't find my place here. People have already decided who and what I am. There is nothing to be done. The medallion of me by David d'Angers shows the state of things clearly enough: I have the sad face of a countrywoman advancing toward beatification. A kind of old provincial dame in wooden clogs, always asking for alms, stingy, pitiful." An adulterous and hypocritical woman putting on sanctimonious airs. But also a former actress of scant virtue, trailing a troubled past and numerous lovers. That's my image! And my poetry supports this view. My love for Henri is an open secret. Everyone thinks that our liaison was never broken off. I am not always here to defend myself, and Latouche, overtaken by events, is increasingly discounted and withdraws into a world where no one can reach him, not even I. People are starting to laugh at my tears. They say that they are forced and self-indulgent. I abhor my celebrity.

I LEAVE PARIS dismayed. On the return trip to Rouen, I cannot shake off my feelings of anxiety. In the future I will have to redouble my vigilance. My poems are prone to misinterpretation. They can give rise to harmful gossip and hasty conclusions. How will Prosper, who has recently reread them all, welcome me home?

Separation, and perhaps also the fear that I would not return at all, have on the contrary strengthened my husband's feelings.

"Your poems, as I now understand," he says, "reflect general, even universal feelings."

"I have always said that. I have taken much from my friends, borrowed from many women."

"Yes. In any case, I prefer to see nothing personal in it. Let's not talk of it anymore."

A lesson in absolute self-control. In fact Valmore is prey to devouring jealousy and suspicion. But believing the first to be stupid and the second undignified, he rises above his inner abysses so that we may not both be dragged down into them. He further allows me to turn freely to the preparation of my new collection. Meticulous, fearful, I am suspicious of every-thing. I find myself anticipating the reactions of my future readers and censor myself, which makes me testy. Prosper is unhappy, as am I. There is a rumbling within as well as without.

HOSTILITY TOWARD US is growing in Rouen, something we sense although it is not yet declared. The past is catching up with me. Comments are being made here and there. Unpleas-ant observations in the local newspapers. Envy and bitterness are the cankers of provincial life. Those who knew me here in my youth do not like the woman I have become. My status as a woman of letters, the intellectual respectability I have earned over the years, infuriate certain people such as Jacques Debonne, who has never stopped hating me and who is mounting a cabal against us with the aim of driving us out as soon as possible. My being in Rouen has always bothered him. In the days when his brother dreamed of marrying me, just as now when my small celebrity puts him in a bad light, I fill the role of chief trouble-maker. Will he never be rid of me?

At my urging, Valmore goes to Paris for a few days in the vain hope of getting an engagement there.

When he returns to perform in Rouen, there is a scene. Prosper can hardly set foot on the stage of the Théâtre des Arts. No one hears the start of his speech. Alarmed, he retreats backstage to the sound of jibes and catcalls. Half the audience is on its feet hurling insults at him. They heckle him mercilessly:

"What's the matter? Didn't they want you at the Théâtre-Français?"

"Did you come back here to weep and moan?"

My sixth sense had warned me of the impending massacre,

and I did not attend the performance. It was not Valmore they were aiming at, it was me.

Less than a week later we are packing our suitcases. Rouen, fickle and ashamed, honors us as best it can. Part of the public refused to go along with the Debonne faction. But the damage is done. My husband, stunned, still does not understand what happened. I know all too well and do not want to set foot in the town ever again. Not once did I see poor Eugène Debonne, whom I imagine shut up in his brother's house, helplessly bent double, his large and useless hands clapped over his ears.

And to think that I once loved this man.

I AM READY to do anything this time if it means returning to Paris. Between the small-mindedness of the provinces and the duplicity of the capital, I have made my choice. Even Valmore, though he would like to sign again with Lyon, bows to my insistence and is scouring the Paris theaters for a contract. Rage fills me with restless energy. I have been stung to the quick. All day I leap from editor to editor and from creditor to patron. At night, writing swallows up my hours of sleep. I try my hand at a novel, a form that is easier to publish, as I tell myself, and that provides greater returns than poetry. It may also be that I wish to establish a rivalry with George Sand, cast a slight shadow on her oppressive glory. Henri and she are no longer speaking.

"From romantic spite, you can be sure," says Balzac, whom I have come to know and who is also angry at Latouche.

In barely two years Balzac's genius, first noted by Henri, has blazed forth: *The Magic Skin*, *A Woman of Thirty*, *Gobseck*, and *Louis Lambert* have enthroned him as the greatest novelist of the age.

"Henri de Latouche, Madame Valmore, is all jealousy and resentment. He is a hack, and his misfortune is to be intelligent enough to know it."

"You seem to forget how much you owe him. Without Latouche, you would never have had your first success with *Les Chouans!*" my older daughter interjects, with all the haughtiness of a twelve-year-old.

"Hyacinthe!"

"No, let her speak. And she is right. But tell me, young lady, am I to remain in his debt for this all my life?"

The writer has hosted us in his apartment on the rue Cassini for two days running. He claims that his next stories will be set in Flanders, where he has no intention of setting foot, and about which he consequently presses me for information. Nothing pleases me more, nothing is easier than to push open the little gate at the end of the garden and enter the world of saints and gravestones, of lilacs, of honeysuckle and knucklebones, to smell the odor of *loées* and my father's pipe, of scorching hot chocolate, of the wood-fired stove, while outside the bells of Notre-Dame peal joyously. Telling him of my native north, I smooth the splintered edges of the past. It is also true that Balzac's company affords a somewhat tenuous but real link to Henri, to an alien and enigmatic part of Henri's life, which I can then inspect with only a slight sense of cowardice and disgust.

LOOKING FOR PROTECTORS, I lay out our dire circumstances, the unjust treatment we have received, to anyone who will listen. Am I selling myself? Am I attaching to my reputation as a provincial shrew that of an importunate beggar woman?

Mostly I want to surround myself with noise and voices. Not to hear Time consuming me. To outward appearances, I have no shame. In any case it is too late to change. I am the prisoner of my notoriety.

Out of pity for me, they have finally hired Valmore at the Porte Saint-Martin theater. His retainer is ridiculously small, and his roles are insubstantial. The poor man gamely swallows his humiliation, his frustrations, his contempt for the second-rate theatrics. Except for Hyacinthe, who keeps her own counsel, the children are all on my side. Prosper rages in silence, and his vexation is ready to leap from its cage, sometimes in spite of himself. Even at home, in our "den of Bonapartists," as he calls it, he feels alone.

"My admiration for you, Marceline, is the one thing that allows me to endure my abominable failure, my lack of talent, the pitiful showing I have made . . ."

Valmore's bitterness turns to despair. With all my might I hope it is a momentary prostration that will eventually pass. I am too busy writing and allowing the fever of Paris to enter me. One after the other, I manage to publish two novels, *A Mockery of Love* and *A Painter's Studio*. I feel a need for recognition. And money. My writing reflects this. The books are not very good and, with the veil of poetry removed, divulge the tattered fabric of my life. There is no distance. The tale of Ondine, the heroine of *A Painter's Studio*, is plainly the story of my meeting Henri at my uncle's Childeberte studio. With respect to Prosper, I have perhaps gone too far. I don't realize it.

DURING THIS SEASON in the capital, I see little of Latouche. My husband's presence weighs me down. Or rather, the simultaneous presence in the same city of the two men throws me into an

emotional turmoil I cannot master. Paris is like a mistress I refuse to share with both. Henri's Paris is not Prosper's, and vice
versa. At Latouche's side, I rejoiced every day in the city's body,
its curves, its clefts. To find myself before its nudity in Valmore's company, when he is oblivious to its beauty and, worse
still, execrates it, puts me in an intolerable position. There is
also another explanation. Caution, quite simply, dictates that I
keep Henri at arm's length from my home, from the children I
have kept hidden from him for many reasons. I don't want him
to see me as a mother, preferring our ties to be on a different
plane. And I must handle Valmore with care. The pretext of
having literary business can only serve me so often.

Latouche in any case goes into hiding at the Vallée aux
Loups more and more often. My obsession with him, of which
*A Painter's Studio* is a further horrifying example, no doubt is
as exasperating as it is flattering to him. Despite my protesta-
tions to the contrary, my eyes still gaze at him with loving admiration. He must sometimes find it hateful. His misanthropy
has grown stronger. The solitude into which he has retreated
makes him more and more prickly. I am afraid of his reactions.
And I am particularly afraid of certain demons. For this reason,
I start to call my daughter Hyacinthe by the name Ondine, like
the heroine of *A Painter's Studio*, claiming that she served me as
a model. Others follow my example. The girl finds it amusing
and says nothing. I breathe again. It seems to me that I have
erased the last trace of my misdeed.

AT PRESENT WE are living, after yet another move, on the rue
de Lancry, away from the city center, near the Gare de l'Est,
the two girls, my father-in-law, a servant, Valmore, and myself. My health is growing decidedly weaker. I maintain a busy

routine on the surface, visiting hospitals and prisons and writing like a drudge. My attacks of nerves are more frequent, my edemas numerous. I often lose my sight, sink into delirium. When Hippolyte returns for a few days' visit, he panics. Inès laughs. Ondine and Prosper can hardly contain their irritation. The elder Valmore, dying in a corner, is not always certain what is going on.

"It's Madame Marceline," the serving woman tells him. "She can't see a thing. So she cries out, her head back, her eyes staring into space. Maybe she is appealing to heaven. We don't know. It gives me such a fright to see her . . ."

Valmore rages, accusing Paris of every evil under the sun, and threatens to pack his bags for Lyon. The children are hysterical. A house full of demented people. In a trance I go back to my poetry, a combative, political, and anticlerical poetry. It feels to me as though I am unhinged. I feel an irrepressible urge to live, to inhale everything, say everything, as in a last nighttime ramble among all the things that might draw and keep me on the side of the living. With Dumas's preface in hand, I finally decide to publish *Tears*, a collection that I dedicate to Balzac. He shortly publishes his novel *The Quest of the Absolute*, set in Douai, or more exactly in my Douai, the one that I showed him by pushing open the doors of faceless houses where silent tragedies were being played out. In turn he dedicates a story to me inspired from a legend that I told him, *Christ in Flanders*. An exchange of polite gestures. We are two extremely well-bred individuals.


YET DESPITE ALL my efforts and Prosper's, our financial situation remains precarious. The fact is well known and draws visitors to look in on me, partly from concern, partly from curiosity. One day when I am expecting Dumas, there is a knock on the door. I run to open it. Madame Waldor! A captain's wife, she is a former and notorious mistress of Dumas's, on bitter terms with him since the publication of *Antony*, where he paints an unflattering portrait of her.

"Mélanie! Good Lord, do you know who I am expecting to arrive at any minute? Monsieur Dumas!"

Imperturbably, she directs herself to a chair, determined to weather any storm.

"I hope at least he won't be trailing that Krelsamer woman, the one who took my place in his heart."

Another knock at the door. It is Dumas himself with Charpentier in tow. Dumas, as tall as Achilles and kindness itself, bends over double to bring my hand to his lips. On peering under what he assumes to be my hat brim only to find Madame Waldor, pale as a sheet, he is paralyzed with astonishment in midbow. I put everyone at ease by prattling about this and that until the two have time to collect their wits.


As DISCREET IN death as he was in life, the elder Valmore now departs from us. I sense that nothing will now keep Prosper in Paris, where his pride is being bruised daily. I do everything in my power to get him into the Comédie-Française. I write him love poems. Heartfelt ones, too. Useless. After a year of small humiliations, of affronts suffered that I might be allowed to have my way, my husband makes a final bow toward the boulevards of Paris and sets off again for the Rhône Valley. I must follow him, having no other choice. My income is meager, my future more uncertain even than his. In March 1834,

I take the road to Lyon with my daughters. Prosper went ahead several days earlier, and Hippolyte has gone back to Grenoble.

I CAN HARDLY believe it. We are back on the place Terreaux, where we lived during our first stay in Lyon. Hardly have we settled into our fifth-floor apartment on the corner where the rue de Clermont enters the square than the April workers' riots break out, bloodier even than those of 1830. As if waiting for our arrival. Again everything happens under our very eyes. But worse. Bullets fly. We live in the back portions of each room, on hands and knees for the most part, frightened, under threat even in our home. The execution squads line up right below us. The violence of the royal army makes me ill.

"Both sides are at fault," says Prosper, more skeptical than I.

Still seething, I write my most virulent poem, "In the Street," which no one dares to publish:

> *Murder crowns itself king,*
> *The victor whistles and walks.*
> *Where is he going?*
> *To the Treasury, for his blood money.*

From my house at night I hear the prisoners singing. Fragile even before the massacres occurred, my health declines still further. I become moody in the extreme, suddenly praising Valmore to the skies, then despising him, finding him the best of men or the most tedious. Irascible, despairing, full of grudges, I heap curses on Lyon and on this life of wandering that is forever tearing me from Paris and from all I love to live over a powder keg. My face swells up again, my dizzy spells return.

I miss my Hippolyte, so gentle and submissive. Everything irritates me.

BECAUSE OF THE events, the theater must close temporarily. The show is happening in the streets, and we have unintentionally taken seats in the first tier of boxes. But with Prosper's salary cut off, the charming four-bedroom apartment where we have not yet hung our curtains proves beyond our means. We must climb to the story above, among servants living in attic rooms where my reputation has preceded me. The picture of my life as it is handed around in Parisian literary circles is surpassed by the reality. I'd laugh if I still could. But the effort is far beyond me. Horribly sad, I spend my days writing pages-long letters to one person or another. "We have come out alive, following all the horrors of this civil war that kept us prisoners indoors for six days . . . Living at the town hall, we saw everything . . . What blood! What courage everywhere! Death was on all sides, on the roofs, in the streets, it came in through the cellars, and exploded the houses, killing all their residents. For six nights and six and a half days, cannon, bullets, bells, fire . . ." I write everyone in search of reassurance, long-standing friends and recent acquaintances, because every hour brings me closer to the end, and I have still done nothing. Lived nothing. Not enough. What I dreamed of doing, of being, is all so far beyond me. I loved myself unconditionally, but with a hope that was frustrated and smashed to the ground. My life is not by any means the life I would have wanted—nor my writings, nor my loves.

Beyond the garret windows on which the rain is sheeting, the lives of all whom I will never know pass furiously. I drum against the pane.

I beat on the pane like a madwoman.

## 14

FTER A FIVE-YEAR HIATUS, I returned to the stage on April 29, 1813. I had been given the role of a young woman who, seduced and raising a child, must face public dishonor and the disapproval of society. By chance, Claudine was a character in my own mold. I cried so many real tears in that role and spoke in such sincere accents that I was an immediate popular success. In a trice, I was once again the most talked-of actress in Paris, the prodigal child. My banishment had lasted long enough that I was forgiven everything and my past was forgotten. Success did not heal my broken heart, but it allowed me to remain true to my resolve and unmoved by objections. I didn't have much to fear in any case. Eugène Debonne begged me to return, but only from a distance, being unwilling to defy his brother. He pointed to our son, hatefully, as his argument of last resort in a contest I refused to join. Marie-Eugène was my whole life, my one success. And I never forbade his father to come visit him. He might if he wished. But his fatherly love would first have to overcome his brotherly obedience. It was not within my power to bring that about and I no longer cared.

When he learned of my new circumstances, my father, who had meantime moved to Les Andelys to be with my sister Eugénie and her husband, now returned quickly to Paris to live under my roof. My sister and brother-in-law were in serious financial straits. Cécile and Bigo, who had just had their sixth child, were also going through troubled times thanks to the textile crisis. In short, and against all expectation, I was again the one managing best. I was the only one to write my poor brother, a sergeant in the Imperial Army who was still a prisoner of war in Scotland. Without having ever thought it possible, I—the youngest—was at present the head of this exploded family.

I was assuredly working too hard. I wanted my little boy to lack for nothing. I had to pay for my lodgings on the rue de l'Odéon and for the servant girl who looked after Marie-Eugène. In May, dropping to my knees during a tragic scene, I felt a stab of pain in my kneecap. Yet I had to continue, stay in that position until the curtain fell. Torture. Leaving the stage, howling with the pain I had miraculously stifled, I collapsed. I was carried to my apartment, where a Dr. Alibert came to visit me. He saved my knee and was beguiled by the bits of writing I was bold enough to show him. A lover of poetry, this doctor gathered at his home on the rue de Varenne a select group of literary figures. He encouraged me to continue writing and assumed in the most natural way the role of my adviser. He was a man of advanced years, but for all that not unseductive. He could at times seem frivolous, and he was thought a schemer by some. He certainly enjoyed the social whirl and was willing enough to resort to low tricks when it served him. But it was thanks to him that I did not limp for the rest of my life and that I began on a regular basis to publish pieces in those literary annuals known as keepsakes.

On some days, my decision to leave Rouen cost me dearly. I felt spent and alone. Had I made a mistake? Should I not have taken the easier course and stayed on as the spoiled mistress of Eugène Debonne? My future and my child's had been assured. But soon enough I would become convinced again that a different life awaited me. The accommodation had not been to my standards, even if it was sometimes nice to rest one's head against the solid support of a man's shoulder. The boredom in the long run would have worn me down. I would eventually have despised myself.

MY ADORED UNCLE violently disapproved of my course of action. Eugène had called on him for help and complained of my cruelty. Constant felt he was in the right. Twisting the facts, he made Debonne out to be the victim and I his executioner.

"You have torn a son away from his father. Poor Eugène, who loves you in spite of everything and suffers the torments of hell. He is writing me heart-rending letters. Your attitude, Marceline, is unconscionable."

"I am surprised and hurt, dear Uncle, that you who have always preached freedom and avoidance of compromise, should fail to defend me now, when I am struggling, not without regret, to fend off a demeaning servitude."

"Being an actress strikes you as nobler than maintaining a hearth? Eugène might well have married you in the end—"

"The decision was never going to be Eugène's to make, unfortunately . . ."

"Whatever are you holding out for? Nothing is going to come your way now! You are twenty-seven years old, Marceline! Success has gone to your head. Think of your son! I'm afraid you've inherited your mother's unstable character, which—"

"Uncle! That's quite enough. Let's leave my mother in peace, shall we? And me with her. I have certainly inherited her inability to stand for mediocrity."

I walked out on Constant, his hair in wild disarray, standing in the shambles of his studio, holding Eugène's letters in his hands like dripping paintbrushes. Anger drove me. It hurt me to consider how male solidarity trumped logic and the natural affinity that should have put my uncle unhesitatingly on my side. Eugène's life and mentality were so dissimilar to his own! Constant and I had so much in common. He was my spiritual father. I was the daughter he would never have. Yet despite his openness of mind, the only thing he heard in this business was the grief of a man abandoned by the woman he adored, probably triggering a memory of events he himself had experienced and couldn't stand to see reenacted. He patently saw himself in Eugène, and this led him to abandon his usual reticence in an unexpected way.

It was thus stupidly that silence established itself between Constant and me. My isolation was only made harder, and his own more bitter.

I ALLOWED MYSELF to be carried along by the whirlwind of success. Having known rejection and shame, I was not sorry to have attention lavished on me. The applause I received night after night quietly restored my self-confidence. I was still to some extent young, young enough at any rate to take my place in the waltz of pleasures, but no longer so young as to be deceived by what was futile. I remained quite different from the others, more mature, lucid as to reversals of fortune, and determined to enjoy for the time being the freedom I had bought so dearly. A discerning observer would have immediately picked me out from the group of actresses I easily melted into. The character I played was pure construction. The flounces, the coquettishness, the cliques, the romances—it all amused me without really meaning much. I had quickly assimilated the rules and was waiting for the chance to circumvent their laws. I thought myself stronger than they. Discreet and secretive, I composed my little ballads between rehearsals. Those who read them applauded their truth and simplicity, which they imagined to be the result of much work and artful planning. Dr. Alibert helped me publish them in keepsake books, gave me advice, and spurred on my clumsy literary efforts. I regularly joined his Sunday dinners that included writers and other actresses.

In the acting company I was reunited with Délia, who had grown even more beautiful and who took upon herself the mission of overseeing my romantic education. All Paris had lost its head over her lustrous skin, her voluptuous rump. I liked the contrast we two formed. We could not have been more different. Dark and impassioned, Délia had the insolence and confidence of women who are accustomed to being admired. Someone was always on hand to love her. She had only to raise one eyebrow a fraction for half of the Left Bank to come running. She played with this endlessly, sometimes cruelly. Now that I knew her better, I penetrated her worldly shell and understood how much her attitude was only a preemptive revenge for what her life would eventually become.

"As long as I am beautiful," she would say, winking a sumptuous eye, "I'll take advantage of it. I'm storing up memories."

Later, her protectors would scatter, unsurprisingly, and find new seductresses to stroke their mustaches. Délia knew this;

she was protecting herself. Which didn't keep her from having fun at the same time. She was too fond of the intoxication that came into men's eyes when they wanted her, at the moment they lost all modesty and submitted wholly to her will. Délia was the most irresistible of sluts.

When I was with her, I sometimes felt the call to lewdness, but I was too prudish. I dreamed as much of having Délia's carmine mouth as of having a bourgeois interior with a paunch-heavy husband and a clutch of yelping children. I no longer opened letters from Eugène. At first, I had hoped too hard for word of our impending marriage, which I was now no longer certain of actually wanting. The stultifying languor of home life. I had come close to disaster, to a repetition of my mother's misfortune. There are inheritances it is best not to accept. Even so, returning some nights after a debauched evening at Délia's, half ashamed and half confused, to huddle against my sleeping boy, I would have given anything for a clean-living man to marry me, just so that I might never feel again the awful conviction that I would end my days alone, always alone. Would I ever be loved again? Had I not committed the mistake of my life?

But love, I sensed, was different either from the feverish haste of Louis Lacour, whose marriage to a young woman of good family I learned of at this time, or from the breathless awkwardness of Eugène Debonne. There had to be another current, a different amplitude.

It was then that I met Olivier Audibert.

HIS NAME, IN point of fact, was not Olivier. It was a literary convention between us, partly a game and partly a matter of discretion, because I started to versify immediately about our romance. From the moment I felt love, I needed to be writing. It would have been inappropriate, as well as less poetic, to sing the public praises of Louis-François-Hilarion Audibert, his real name. A native of Marseille, he composed verse as I did, though more as an exercise than out of a devouring need to speak. I actually needed to write, to put myself in danger. He set his sights on the theater, drama in the noble style. Becoming a fashionable, an acclaimed author. Audibert was looking for glory at any price and snaked his way through the backstages of Paris looking for anyone who might lead him to it.

I had met him thanks to Délia, with whom he had been in love earlier, like many another, and whom he had continued to attend assiduously, on the principle that one should never shut doors behind one. At the very least, they can still serve as emergency exits. Audibert was a vile person on the whole. Naturally, his assertive personality won me to him. Even his ambition moved me. I saw it as the determination of a poor young man from the provinces to erase the slaps in the face he had received for years, the childhood stolen from him, the parents who hadn't loved him or been interested in him, because he had been the laughingstock of the neighborhood, the little fat boy. In his story I seemed to see the mirror of mine, a lust for victory, a desire to make one's name ring loud and clear. Unprepossessing physically, he made one forget his heavy features by his presence, his strong, deep voice, his grandiloquent gestures. It was fascinating at first and exasperating afterward. Audibert would most likely have made an excellent actor. He was constantly in performance, never forgetting the hypothetical spectator to whom he was always playing, even when alone, with a candle burning in his garret. That spectator was for the most part none other than himself.

.  .  .

OUR LIAISON CHANGED me utterly. I drank in Audibert's words as a child nurses at the breast. I had waited so long that I now bit at the brown nipple of love, squeezed it to the last drop, unsated, impatient. I thought of my mother, of being alienated from a man's smell, a man's hands. To be weaned was impossible. Everything was making my head turn—the audiences' acclamations, the publication of my poems, the revelation of the body's language. I was freed, it seemed to me, just as my brother had been freed with the fall of the Empire and had come from prison to live with me as my dependent. I was even happy about it, about supporting this one and that, son, father, brother, sisters. I had always asked myself why I escaped the yellow fever and the ocean storms. Now I had the explanation: I was responsible for a number of destinies. I had the strength for it. Love made me invulnerable. Audibert's sweet words clothed me in an armor that I believed was without chinks.

In fact, his intransigence was crushing me, though I didn't notice. His will made mine bend like a sapling. Délia had warned me, but I thought her words came from jealousy.

"He's using you, my sweet. Because you're the actress of the moment and can open doors for him to any theater he wants. The day your star dips, the man is gone."

I didn't listen to her, I was even angry at her for casting doubt on my beautiful love.

"You have nothing in common, Marceline, look at the facts, for dear God's sake! He is a royalist, and you swear by the Emperor. He is a conniver and fickle, while you have the purest and most loyal heart . . ."

Délia insisted, and I smiled back at her, my cheeks flaming. My skin had made the decision for me and I could do nothing about it. I had fallen under the sway of the first man to make me moan who also met my intellectual requirements. He might be just a consummate rascal. Too bad. I was flying and nothing could touch me. I wrote out my love, signed myself over to it, forgave my mother, and forgot in Audibert's arms the many responsibilities that fell to me. I felt acknowledged. Even if I was in fact the author, blinded to an extraordinary degree, of my own praises.

"COME," SAID DÉLIA one night, catching my arm after the performance. "I'd like to introduce you to someone who is in Paris for a few days."

Without waiting, she dragged me to her box. I resisted. After coming offstage, I little relished making a round of bows and curtsies, a kind of inevitable sixth act. I was somewhat tired at the time. My knee was still hurting and I was sleeping only fitfully because of my dependence on Audibert.

"Another journalist?" I asked Délia, who gripped me tightly.

Her pretty mouth twisted into a pout.

"Yes and no," she said.

"An author, then?"

A few meters from her box, which I sensed already was packed as full as an egg, Délia stopped.

"Henri de Latouche. Does the name ring any bells?" she asked.

"I don't think so."

"It's true that he dropped out of sight a few years ago. Like you. He is just back from Italy and on his way to the Berry, where he owns property. He had a play performed, some time ago now. Right here, at the Odéon. The truth is, he's a man of many talents, brilliant. Frighteningly seductive," Délia added, her glance full of meaning.

"You say that about all the men you've had," I observed.

"This one is truly different. You'll see. An exceptional case."

I gave little weight to Délia's words. She was plotting to pry me from Audibert's clutches, and going to great lengths to do it because of an old grudge. Resignedly, I followed her swaying haunches, and a chorus of applause greeted her return to her box. No one was especially waiting for me that night. Audibert was busy elsewhere, and I was in no hurry to get home, where I was likely to find Félix and my father already in their cups. My son, indifferent to the two drunks, would be asleep on his stomach, his hair tousled and his little mouth in the form of a heart. My angel. I would go and give him his goodnight kiss as soon as I had met this old lover of Délia's. Someone who would proffer the usual inanities, while I listened with half an ear and thought how pale a figure I cut beside dusky Délia. Was she using me as a foil? No. That was ungrateful. She loved me sincerely, her admiration for me was in no way feigned.

"I am so ignorant," she often said. "Will you teach me, Marceline, will you teach me all the things you know so much about?"


HENRI DE LATOUCHE looked nothing like what I had imagined. In the first place, he was so ugly that I almost fell over backward. He was a man of medium height, about my own age apparently, but already well filled out, corpulent, though of extreme elegance. His manner showed a grace and taste that were at odds with his slumped body. But what struck one disorientingly at first sight was his extraordinary face. It was framed by chestnut curls, the gay swirls and peaks of a child's ringlets, and elongated by side-whiskers that accentuated its unexpected refinement. His features were of astonishing purity: an aquiline nose, lips so delicate as almost to vanish, soft cheekbones, and small dimples that surfaced here and there, at the corners of his mouth, in the folds around his eyes. And then his eyes, which were an enigma. For Henri de Latouche was one-eyed. His gaze seemed to twist like a prisoner in a cage. His living eye moved in every direction while the other stayed fixed, a disquieting oddity that gave him the appearance at times of a statue, at others of a lunatic. The man was thoroughly unfathomable. He had an insufferably haughty manner, as though he soared high above the common run, but moments later his expression would be of such warmth and gentleness it might have melted a cannon.

One couldn't help but be fascinated or repulsed by the many impenetrable masks he clapped on his face. Not to speak of his voice. Warm and muffled in tone, vibrant, deep, easily piercing the fabric of one's clothes, penetrating through one's skin to the bone, and sinking into one's carcass to echo in one's innards. Henri de Latouche's voice was what stayed with one after leaving him. Like a bite.

"I have read your ballads, Mademoiselle Desbordes," he shot at me without preamble, cutting Délia off as she prepared to introduce us.

A surprising conversational opener. Usually people spoke of my acting, my diction, my tears, and all that I displayed onstage. Allusions to my discreet publications in keepsake volumes were rare. The comment caught me off balance.

"Truly, Monsieur? Then it was you?" I mumbled awkwardly.

He smiled. I smiled in turn. Something about this man already pleased me greatly. I had no idea what. And everything else about him was a mystery.

Henri de Latouche discussed the virtues and flaws of my poems with me. He then spoke of Italy, the sculptor Canova, the political situation, his sympathy for the Emperor, his passion for theater and for literature, his hatred of intriguers and mediocrities. After touching on his native Berry and my own province of Flanders, our conversation came around to our respective sons, both almost the same age. In a few hours, we told each other the story of our lives. His conversation had no equal. My bad mood dissipated quickly. At first intimidated, I chose my words carefully and refined my expressions. But naturalness soon took over. In his company, I was my unfeigned self. And I could view that self favorably.

Late that night, returning to my lodgings, I happily realized that I had spent my best evening in a long, long time, perhaps the best ever. I felt strong and proud. Henri de Latouche. A rare encounter.

Yet the next day I would slip into my theater costume again, and my life would once more resume its usual course under Audibert's shadow.

## 15

*I* AM GETTING MY STRENGTH BACK. In the spring of 1835, Hippolyte joined us in Lyon for the school holidays and his presence set me back on my feet almost instantly. My darling son is all mine, whereas my daughters, who started boarding school this year, are acquiring a measure of autonomy. Ondine in particular, so quick and sensitive, is putting distance between us. Even though she also wants to write, while Inès plans to be a musician, it is without the out-pourings, the spontaneous excess, that characterize me and that she finds execrable. Like Prosper, Ondine is very decisive. I, on the other hand, am all hesitation. And the school she at-tends in Lyon is exposing her to other influences. Recently, for instance, she elected to be baptized. Neither Valmore nor I were in a position to oppose her. While unsettling, her resolute personality also fills me with pride, I must admit. We do not always disagree. Ondine is persuasive. Since hearing her talk about Catholicism, I have even let myself drift back toward my former religion. Of course, I wouldn't breathe a word of this to Prosper.

The silkworkers' second rebellion was crushed and the Grand Théâtre reopened its doors after a forced closing of four months. My literary pension, though I don't know why or by whom, has been increased. We have therefore moved back down a floor and recovered our honor. I breathe again. Lyon, once more the sleepy city it remains between uprisings, has again become a necessary stop for travelers on their way to the south of France, Spain, and Italy. And among the monuments not to be missed is me, whom the isolation of the insurrection has made more needy. Inclined to open my doors to anyone, I have become the object of many pilgrimages, some of them strange, even bizarre. For all their silliness, they add spice to my daily life. Fortunately. Hippolyte had to return to Grenoble, and I couldn't help but accompany him back there a second time. I am not dwelling on his absence. Once back in Lyon, to kill time, I set to work on various translations, which have brought me no satisfaction. But it's the fashion. My editor, Charpentier, convinced me to take part in the four-handed adaptation of an English tale, though in the end I had very little to do with it. That my name appears at all on the cover of *Le Salon de Lady Betty*, published in March 1836, is a deception. Luckily its presence goes unnoticed. The book is bad and doesn't sell.

In the midst of my boredom and my deliberate efforts to convince myself that Prosper could make me happier than any other man, I am treated to the arrival in Lyon with a bang and a crash of the extraordinary Marie Dorval.


THE LOVELY ACTRESS, Alfred de Vigny's muse, is the acknowledged rival of the aging Mademoiselle Mars. She has come to Lyon to act in a production of *Chatterton* opposite Valmore. My husband is troubled.

"It's bothersome," he says to me. "Mademoiselle Mars has been our friend for a very long time. She has always helped us, and even now, whenever she can, she insists on having me play opposite her."

"I don't see how the fact that we entertain Marie Dorval can be interpreted as taking her side. She is after all going to be your partner on the stage. I am simply responding politely to her request. She wants to meet me. I can't just refuse to see her!"

"The problem is that is she isn't discreet. And she must have her own reasons for being so eager to meet you. In any case, I know you'll do as you see fit."

Prosper cannot get used to the court that gathers around me wherever I go. I, on the other hand, am not disturbed by it. And I have always had a weakness for pretty women, a secret envy perhaps, which only increases as the years pass and I grow more horribly ugly. Competition between us being at an end, I no longer fear having them in my entourage and being relegated by their presence to a different level—even in the eyes of my husband. I find delight in the contrast, playing the duenna in moth-eaten lace, poorly togged out, a nasty net holding my hair, my crooked fingers gripping their lovely arms. The day I realized that no part of my face could be salvaged, that only my eyes survived in the massacre around them, I abandoned forever my remaining traces of coquetry. I embrace my physical disgrace, more acceptable now with advancing age, assuming majestic airs, entering fully into my role as an old poetess from the provinces, a Pythian priestess whom travelers come from far and wide to consult. My oracles fly with startling speed to the capital, from whence they return to me distorted in the letters of my correspondents. It often makes me laugh out loud.

It is in this context, then, that the delicious Marie Dorval arrives and throws herself into my arms, relating her life to me in detail, her scandals, her loves, Vigny—from start to finish. Her sincerity and her distress, her difficult path, and her disillusions strike a deep chord in me, shifting a thousand things I thought firmly in place. Marie instills in me a joyful and exasperating chaos. At the same time, I feel keenly her frivolity and lack of elegance. How can so beautiful a woman, capable of playing the noblest heroines onstage, be so vulgar in life? I don't understand. Coarseness has always grated on me. Making a conscious effort, I am able to find extenuating circumstances for Marie. Her daughter, who is the same age as Inès, has moved in with us for the whole of her mother's stay in Lyon and is horrified at the city's unwholesomeness.

As soon as the two of us are alone together, Marie Dorval returns to her favorite theme: Vigny. Any pretext is sufficient. I know this kind of obsession well. She endlessly makes me describe the Nairacs' salon in Bordeaux, where I met and frequently saw—some thirteen years ago—her then unknown poet.

"Your little Inès has such a romantic profile," Marie exclaims more than once. "Her long hollow face, her enormous eyes— and her hair—that color . . . It is the spitting image of Vigny! Don't you think she looks like him?"

At first I find Marie's idée fixe enormously amusing, though it disturbs me. I see in it the signs of true mental alienation, of a woman's great love. She sees Vigny everywhere, brings everything back to him in the most inappropriate places, and would unabashedly befriend each of his former mistresses for the sole purpose of being able to speak always and forever of him. Then one day, catching Prosper's frowning examination of Inès, and surprised to read so much suspicion in it, I realize that Marie Dorval's comments are far more than a simple misapprehension. She is truly convinced that Vigny fathered my younger daughter, now twelve years old, born the fruit of our love in Bordeaux. And her certainty has finally infected Valmore, who was only waiting for a propitious moment to explode with jealousy. It's too much! The proposition is so harebrained that I am not sure at first whether to laugh or take offense. By a grotesque irony, the suspicion I have always been afraid my husband might feel, which wakes me suffocatingly in the night and can attack me at any hour of the day, the suspicion that for years has threatened the family equilibrium, which I have built with my own hands and defend like a tigress, the suspicion that could corrode all of our lives, has come to rest briefly where I expected it least. And where it has no business being. I wonder what to make of it, how to interpret it. Perhaps it is lucky. I want to see it as being lucky.


THE PERFORMANCE OF *Chatterton* astonishes me beyond anything I could have imagined. It is the great theater event of the Lyon stage. Marie Dorval is sublime. Though I belong to a different era, I am awestruck at the beauty of Romantic theater, the energy of these young authors, Vigny, Musset, Hugo, their arrogance and talent. If only I could be in Paris where it is all happening! Because once the scenery is folded away and the actors have moved on—with Marie in tears and having to be torn from my arms, to Prosper's great irritation—the Grand Théâtre relapses into its old torpor. The public in Lyon has no great appetite for the new works from the capital. Curiosity, and perhaps snobbery, drive them to attend Parisian imports, but they really only like opera and dance. Everyone knows this. The management decides to cut its costs. Valmore's contract will not be renewed and ends in April 1837. Though I am weary of trunks

and storage warehouses, and though I am proud at having finally managed, after three long stays, to win over the populace
of this strange town, I am not sorry to be leaving Lyon. A sad and
dangerous city, it frightens me. Its workers, starved by Louis-
Philippe, haunt the streets. The city reeks of death still, it attracts death. I could not stand a third rebellion. Perhaps it is time
to go back to Paris once and for all. Prosper is tempted to sign
a contract with the Marseille theater, but I angrily prevent him.
Once again, he would like the calm of a provincial town, while I
am drawn to the tumult of the capital.

"Give me a little time," I entreat him in early April. "While
you finish the season here, I will go to Paris with the girls, find
you a position, perhaps outside the theater. And why not? It's
time to start thinking about it. You've reached an age where it's
hard to get parts, too old for the leading man, too young for the
noble father. You won't have to do anything. I'll take care of it
all, including our lodgings and our household move."

"As you wish," Prosper groans.

A few days later, I am in Paris with Ondine and Inès, whom I
drag everywhere, intriguing left and right, hardening myself to
make tearful and unscrupulous requests. We have invaded Pauline's apartment. But at the end of three weeks, I have to face
the facts: in spite of all my efforts, I have found nothing, except
a position for Ondine as a reader for the duchesse d'Orléans.
This I turn down, after a period of hesitation, on the grounds
of political conscience. It is a luxury I can still afford. We are at
a dead end and Valmore is going to arrive at any moment.


FOR FIVE MONTHS we live on public charity. Our reserves are
scant, and I am capable of spending in an hour the money

intended to last several weeks. We stay at one house or another, waiting until we sense exasperation in our hosts, which tells us it is time to pack our bags and pitch camp elsewhere. Poor Prosper is in agony. Forced to accompany me in the frenzied dance of strategic maneuvers and favor currying, he sees himself forever mortified, viewed by others as a man permanently attached to his wife's apron strings, and welcomed only because of her urgent entreaties. Hate-filled, Valmore is a hair's breadth from madness. I, for my part, am seeing the last of my resources dry up. In my discouragement I start to lower my guard. Finally my obstinacy pays off. The news arrives as if by miracle: Prosper has been named manager and administrator of the Théâtre de l'Odéon, starting October 1.

With my husband's affairs back in order, the girls and Hippolyte once more in their respective schools, our clothes tucked away in the new bureaus of the apartment we are renting—at my insistence—on the rue Montpensier, I can finally turn to my own business and allow my thoughts to roam under the arcades of the galleries at the Palais-Royal. What a delight to live in this place! Our balcony looks out over the gardens. Having attained the goal of many long years—to be here, in these precincts freighted with my personal history—my mind, freed of its burdens, is subject to violent hallucinations, to visions where Henri's face appears lit up in glory. The perfect, absolute lover. A sort of grandiose statue or stele, an idol, which I will continue all my life to worship. I hear voices. At certain times of day, I can clearly make out a flame above the big fountain in the middle of the gardens, a flame that represents, as I know, the eternal sentiment that binds me to Latouche. Nothing, absolutely nothing, can extinguish it. My face becomes fixed, ecstatic. As though experiencing a revelation. I must dedicate myself to producing a body of work that will center on the cult of Henri and on our love, but purified, stripped of its sordid contingencies, of my skin creased like an old, worn sheet, and of the women through whom he maintains the meager certainty of being alive. The thought of this obsesses me. Fifteen years have passed, and my useless flesh still clamors. Jealousy churns my insides.

PROSPER—AND HE IS not alone—has started to have serious doubts about my sanity. Everything in me veers toward excess. I burst into a loud laugh, then break into tears. I work feverishly to help others, assist one poor woman in childbirth and another to find a domestic position, I write letters to this prisoner and that renegade, then think only of myself and tell everyone to go to the devil. Doing the rounds of jails and hospitals, I sometimes go into ecstasies over a flower, a tree, a public bench where I suddenly behold the indestructible couple that Latouche and I once formed in times immemorial, the two of us seated with our hands clasped, our souls joined. I don't hear the passersby murmuring, as they tug on the arms of their amused children: "Look at the crazy old lady, staring into nothingness with haggard eyes. She looks as if she's seeing ghosts."

I see ghosts.

With Ondine, but in secret from Valmore, who abhors anything to do with it, I have taken an interest in mesmerism, which is currently all the rage. We have surreptitiously attended and taken part in spiritualist séances. Pauline, too, finds it fascinating. Passionately caught up in it, I have been trying with the help of the occult sciences to find my dear departed ones, my mother, my father, my children, my beloved Albertine, and even my old friend Dr. Alibert, who is also deceased. Terribly confused, drifting through every period of my life, unable to separate the dead from the living, I even try to hold an impossible conversation with my son Hippolyte, whose absence from me I cannot bear. My dreams are haunted by the crowds of workmen who fell in the streets of Lyon, by stinking corpses thrown over the railing into the ocean from a brig that is carrying me away forever from those I love. I am possessed. Exhausted, I write several hours each day, each night. Valmore, whom I see relatively seldom, rests his troubled, disconcerted gaze on me from time to time, before setting off again to wage senseless administrative battles in which he is always bested. Only Ondine, whose influence over her younger sister and me constantly increases, sometimes shakes me by the shoulders and forces me out of my rapture. More inward looking, a brooder, Inès is terribly jealous of her. I often show a decided preference toward Ondine, whose natural gifts and precocity are unmistakable. I also have another reason.

I would die rather than confess my secret. It is a source of great and reinvigorating joy at times when I have to recognize that I lost Henri's love—lost it irretrievably—long ago. I am assailed all over again by doubt as to whether he ever loved me. Latouche took his revenge on me for all the women who made him suffer and stole even his aptitude for happiness. In truth I paid for the others. The unfairness of it, when I was so sincere. My train of thought destroys me. Devastates me. Suffocating, my eyes starting from my head, I fling wide the windows onto the frozen, leafless trees of late winter. But I have Ondine. Ondine! A living portrait, a kiss that Henri cannot take back from me.

Latouche. I see him now and again. Like separated parents patching things up, we walk through the Galerie Montpensier, chatting about theater and poetry. I actually enjoy this Henri's company. But I don't confuse him with the other Henri, the one who lives in the written word, where his body takes possession of mine and forces it, skirts flipped back and corset unlaced, to talk, to summon pain, to want his name carved on my slapped and kneaded skin. They are two different men. There is the one who drifts from bed to bed and mutters against the world at large, a solitary wolf, ensconced in his Hermitage. And there is the one who rises before me on my poetic journey, spitting in my face after kissing me with his teeth. That one is all mine.

ONE DAY, VALMORE explodes. An accumulation of rage, resentment, blame, and hurt. He even becomes insulting. I have never seen him in such a state.

"This has gone far enough! The Odéon is shutting its doors, my contract has not been renewed. Out of the question to stay in Paris any longer."

"Are we moving again?"

I wail. Prosper brushes all arguments aside.

"I have just been offered a tour through Italy, mainly Milan. I sign with the impresario tomorrow. It starts in July."

"But what about the girls?"

"They'll come with us."

"And Hippolyte?

After failing his baccalaureate, my son has recently come back to live with us. He had been missing me so much. The prospect of returning to Grenoble in the fall to study an extra year for his examination upsets him. And me. I am considering enrolling him in the School of Arts and Crafts here in Paris, to be nearby.

"That boy has no character, no ambition. He is incapable of breaking away from you, of deciding for himself what he wants to do in life," Prosper rages.

"It's normal for a boy to love his mother!"

I mumble a few further ineptitudes. My arguments, I have to confess, don't really hold water. The truth is that I want Hippolyte to stay by my side.

"He will not come to Milan but spend the summer in Paris studying to retake his baccalaureate. That is an order."

Valmore is in a state. His handsome face ripples with emotion. Rage becomes him. How seductive my husband is when he recovers his dignity and self-esteem! How admirable he is! I bow to his will and ready my belongings for the long journey ahead of us.

"But it's crazy," says Sainte-Beuve, who is my constant visitor.

At odds with Hugo ever since his liaison with the poet's wife, he has been trying in every way to win me to his side.

"Don't leave! Think of your health, Madame Valmore. A voyage like that! You have no idea!"

"Dear friend, I am afraid there is no wriggling out of this decision. My husband is bound and determined. One doesn't argue with him, you know."

I sigh, proud and untruthful.


IN THE END I convince myself that it is not so bad. We don't have an alternative, and it means, thank God, that we won't wind up again in Lyon! I am of course distraught at leaving my beautiful apartment on the rue Montpensier. But I remind myself that the girls, whose health at times seems fragile, will benefit from the Alpine air and from seeing a bit of country. They are actually looking forward to traveling for a few months with Mademoiselle Mars and several other well-known actors, their father among them. In some part of my mind, I tell myself that I will also benefit from this plan, leaving behind the hallucinations that have attacked me daily. A little mental rest will do me no harm. But at the same time I doubt it. For me, Italy is not the country of Michaelangelo and Canova. It is the place where Latouche lived for three years before we first met. I pack my votive candles and my offerings.

I feel as though I am setting forth on pilgrimage.

## 16

TILL SHORT OF MY THIRTIETH YEAR, I was no
longer, after all I had endured, in very good
health. There were nights at the Odéon when I simply couldn't
go onstage. My legs wouldn't carry me, my face was inflamed,
I suffered from allergies of every kind. When I succumbed to
fever, my father and brother cautiously took refuge in a far corner of the apartment, leaving me in the hands of Quinquin, the
serving woman, and Dr. Alibert. Or else it was Marie-Eugène
who fell ill. I couldn't bring myself to leave him, even for a
few hours and in the care of Félix, whom he adored. The up-
shot was that I often fell short of the terms of my engagement,
which the management of the Théâtre de l'Odéon found gall-
ing. I knew this. Perhaps I was trying to break off relations
without saying so explicitly. I held the theater in too low regard
to want always to be accountable to it and sacrifice myself to
its laws. I listened only to my body, which either overflowed
with energy or collapsed, inert. Weary, paralyzed, I would sink
deeper into the quicksand. I must have been afraid of happiness. I preferred to avoid it before it betrayed me, left my lips
dry and my arms empty.

FOR SOME TIME, probably sensing my imminent disgrace,
Audibert had been slowly edging away from me. I was unable

to read this kind of sign. I noticed only a certain change in his feelings, hard to define or even prove, yet painfully present to me despite his disclaimers. My stomachaches returned, sawing me in half as curtain time approached. Seeing perfectly well that Audibert was starting to love me less, I lost my animation, my combativeness. Did my well-being depend so much on others? Did I need to be under another's sway to be happy, to believe that I was happy? In moments of abandon, among the fantasies we deposit on the lips of the other and that taste of clay, I had imagined that we might marry. I did not believe that things were immutable, I was persuaded that others could be changed, that certain mechanisms could be disrupted, that love—once it took hold of two souls—could annihilate any obstacle, even abolish the past. How infinite was my capacity for blindness. And how compatible a field it found in poetry.

Reality was in the end so disappointing.

ONE NIGHT AT the end of March, after the performance, I saw Henri de Latouche again. A year had passed since our first meeting. I had hardly thought of him. To tell the truth, I had even forgotten somewhat who he was.

It was at the time of the Emperor's escape from Elba and his return to France. The news created a violent stir backstage. I was among the most fanatic. The atmosphere was one of confusion, hope, and fear. It was in this context that Latouche reappeared. Hostile to the reinstatement of the monarchy, he had withdrawn to his native Berry, where he had mounted a few playlets to pass the time. Napoleon's landing on French soil brought him abruptly out of isolation. On March 20 he was at the Tuileries for the great man's arrival, he told me in lively language, his bronze eye brimming with excitement.

"I was named secretary to Maréchal Brune and subprefect of Toulon. I leave tomorrow."

"And you decided that you could not decently leave Paris without going to hear Martelles one last time," I said teasingly.

Martelles was my designated male partner. For the past two years, we had been the most famous pair of actors in the capital. But Martelles was sixty years old. His appearance as the young leading man made many in the theater laugh outright. Including the public.

"Precisely," said Latouche, a smile on his lips.

And he smoothed his side-whiskers with a gesture I had noticed before and that seemed familiar to me.

"You wouldn't have believed me anyway had I told you that I came to the Odéon tonight just for the pleasure of chatting with you."

"Certainly not."

I was delighted to see him, and elated at the idea of enjoying his company for a few hours.

"Tell me about your boy Léonce. He would be about six years old now, no? I remember that he is a year older than my little Marie-Eugène."

"Precisely six years old. You can't imagine, dear young lady, how absolutely dazzled I am by the boy. I never would have thought it possible. In him I seem to see all that never blossomed in me."

In talking about his son, Henri de Latouche dropped his airs and abandoned his affectations. Though rather a rare thing for him, it all seemed natural to me.

I had led him away from the press of people around the boxes. Sitting on a bench, part of the scenery for a pastoral play, near the stage machinery, we started a discussion that carried us through the night. No one came to bother us. We had inadvertently built an unscalable wall around us.

THE NEXT DAY I was still dazed. We had talked until dawn, hardly pausing for breath. In the dark, deserted theater, dimly lit by a guttering candle, among a myriad of props and painted flats, we were alone. The last stagehands grew tired of waiting for us and left. As did everyone else. I was oblivious. Henri de Latouche had a way of cutting me off from everything around us. In his presence I saw only him, his fascinating face and the books that could be read there. Behind his mismatched eyes, I could sense a world beyond, as yet inaccessible, that powerfully aroused my curiosity and drew me toward its mystery. With his voice of copper and brass caressing me, I examined every crease in his skin, every corner of his face, trying to convince myself that he was ugly, that he had many faults, in a determined effort to resist his magnetism, which settled over me like a supernatural halo.

That punctured eye is disgusting, I kept telling myself, it looks like a moldy basin. How grotesque. And his yellow teeth, his skin that turns red at the slightest effort, as I saw earlier when he had to climb three steps. He is not even thirty and already he is spent. In a few years, it will be painful to look at him, a shame. And there's the disdain, the false unruffledness with which he looks at everything . . . it's unbearable. His seeming contempt for others is equaled only by his great regard for himself. He is aware of his superior intelligence, and stumbles in daily life, unable to walk normally with his steps of a giant, his stride of an enormous bird. He knows this, clearly. Lucidity is his best enemy. Some long-ago hurt keeps him from advancing, I am sure of it—the loss of a childhood garden, or of a vast house filled with the good smell of fruit tarts. Dispossession makes us all mad. It's also why he is so affecting, so likable: his feeling of dismay at himself, of not being the person he would have liked himself to be. How well I understand him, since I am the same. We are alike, he and I, both of us waking up in the morning and wondering when it was we made our mistake. Despite all our vigilance! How infuriating! He has told me many things, but what do I know about him in the end? Nothing. Or he about me? Less than nothing. How does he find me? What does he think of me? Is he drawn to me? What exactly is he looking for when we are together? What a secretive man he is! I would like him to take me in his arms, I think. Yes, I would like him to find me attractive. It would be flattering. I am probably trying to seduce him, without admitting it to myself. All the same, he is married, even if he no longer lives with his wife. And he's not the kind to divorce. What future could there be for us? None. I'll lose a few more feathers here, for certain. And then I have a little boy . . . But what does it matter? I don't find the man attractive! He's ugly. As if I weren't in deep enough trouble with Audibert already. I'd best sweep my doorstep clean before I do anything else. Anyway, he's leaving for the south of France. And the way things stand, I'm not likely to stay in Paris much longer. It's probably for the best . . .

I was surprised, though, in the following days, to find myself thinking often of Henri de Latouche.


AUDIBERT AND THE Odéon were both breaking off their associations with me. Detached, letting myself drift bottomward, I had stopped exerting any effort. This lack of reaction, which was hardly like me, this strange resignation mystified me. Pure indifference. At times, I didn't care a fig about either of them. Audibert or the stage. Fighting so as not to lose a thing is so much more tiring than fighting to win a thing. I was exhausted and wanted nothing more than to be free again. Even if it meant taking a fall.

True to my presentiment, things came to a head in April. My contract was not renewed, I was let go. This wasn't a surprise, yet I felt it as a heavy blow all the same. What would become of me? And of my child? To what life of wandering was I fating him? And what would become of my father and Félix? Distraught, I cried hot tears into Délia's lap. Audibert had fled without a word. It was over, I would never see him again.


THE ACTORS GATHERED to express their support for me to the management of the theater. Finding the door closed, they organized a benefit performance on my behalf. That was it. They could do nothing more. I was alone. I had to move out of my apartment on the rue de l'Odéon immediately to take less expensive lodgings on the rue Caumartin. These were small and dingy, and the five of us had to squeeze into them. Quinquin, the serving woman, looked after everything. Sniffling, sighing, dragging my feet, I was no use at all. Everybody had abandoned me. Except for one person. Eugène Debonne, loyal Eugène, the only one to remember me, to write me letters every day. I had stopped reading them long ago. But still. I started to write him back, perhaps because I was heartsick, terrified at being alone. I wanted to pierce an opening in my daily life, which was too trite, too disappointing. Give it spice, sprinkle it with a taste from elsewhere. Even from the past.

Eugène came running right to me. He never loved me more than when I was sick or in a weakened state. My independence, my victories disturbed him, stripped him of what little manly confidence he had, took his usefulness away. Eugène only felt himself fully a man when I was but the shadow of a woman. He was tender with me, gentle, patient, listened to my woes, my rants, picked me up when the news of Waterloo dashed me further, helped me to endure Paris under occupation. Finally, he gave me the energy to set off on the offensive once more and try to get work. But Paris was going through a period of uncertainty and anguish that was too close to my own black mood. The city and I were scowling back and forth at each other. I had every cause to turn my attention elsewhere. Brussels for example.

Promising to send them a regular cut of my wages, I bade my father and brother farewell. Eugène joined Quinquin, the boy, and me to make the trip to Belgium and help us settle in.

MY THOUGHTS WERE unfair, brooding. With its ornate boxes, its candlelit chandeliers, its 1,200 carmine-colored seats, the new Théâtre de la Monnaie, built by the Emperor on the same square across from the old one where I'd played before, easily rivaled the top theaters in Paris. The terms of my contract were unexpectedly favorable. The best in all my career. My fees had never been higher, and the terms, covering the next two years, were excellent. But it meant joining a royalist acting company. For a dedicated Bonapartist, this was an enormous concession. For me to be fastidious at this point, however, was out of the question. As I had done seven years before, I rented an apartment on the rue Neuve not far from the theater, but this one was much vaster and had great charm. It looked out onto the

Finistère Church, whose bells I heard at every hour of the day. I liked the sound of bells, which reminded me of my childhood, of games, of freedom from care.

Eugène left us at the end of August to return to Rouen, where his brother needed him. I had to work like a cart horse. The tradition at La Monnaie called for a triple opening, which I had to honor. I therefore appeared within the space of a week in the title role of three separate plays of different genres. The critics praised me to the skies. The public ratified their judgment. It was a sweet revenge on Paris, but far from a bed of roses. The pace of work increased to an unbearable rate. In October I appeared on stage no fewer than fifteen times, going from Beaumarchais to Molière to Marivaux to Destouches. Despite the friendly relations that existed within the company, I could not get used to the idea that I had become an "Actress Ordinary to His Majesty the King of the Low Countries." One night I even had to play before the king, who was hosting the emperor of Russia. Every time I would hear someone refer to Waterloo as the "victory of the Holy Alliance" I felt a kick to my stomach. I constantly accused myself of fraternizing with the enemy. The theater had always been a house of prostitution to me. Now I was not only selling my body but I had gone so far as to lose my soul. I was ashamed of myself.

My beloved Albertine still lived in Brussels, married now. My sweet friend had paled considerably. She was deathly sad. To think that I had envied her, that I had idealized her peaceful existence, her untroubled home, her sumptuous private house, the indestructible safety that surrounded her, a respected and respectable wife! But the poor girl's life was one of martyrdom. Her health, frailer than mine, was under attack even in the bosom of her home. Her husband cheated on her brazenly with her own sister. Albertine never voiced an objection. She endured this dual betrayal with the wide eyes of a little girl who wonders why the other children are cruel to her when she has done nothing and is even happy to lend them her toys. I seemed to be seeing her once more at the foot of the walls of Douai, her pupils huge and filled with doubt, asking me in consternation, "Why are they doing it, Marceline? Why? Explain it to me." Alas! In those blessed days I could play the protective older child, defending her against the worst ruffians and boxing the ears of those who hurt her. Now I could only fold her into my arms. Like two silly geese, we both cried about marriage. She for having experienced it, and I for waiting for it so long.

THE HECTIC PACE sometimes forced me to stop working altogether. My inflamed throat would emit no sound, despite my daily regimen of gargling and the folk remedies that all actors resort to. I had fainting spells, fevers. Brussels's endless winter was horrible. The days seemed inadequate, lasting only a few hours. The icy wind cut to the bone. The walk from the theater to my house was not a long one, but those few steps cost me dearly, especially at night after the performance. I felt that I was being assaulted, beaten violently by the cold. As soon as I arrived home, I went to stand in front of the fire that Quinquin carefully tended. I warmed my body and my hands before going to Marie-Eugène for a long hug. My darling angel was also having trouble adjusting to the harsh climate of Belgium. Prone to chilblains and frostbite, he seldom went outdoors and was growing feebler by the week. I had no idea what to do. The doctors, summoned by me at the slightest symptom, told me I was worrying needlessly.

"Let him get some air occasionally. The boy spends too much time indoors. Wood fires are bad for the lungs, the respiratory apparatus," they told me.

"But it's so cold outside! When he comes back in, he is trembling all over. It takes him hours to recover. It worries me to death. This child means everything to me, you know . . ."

I would break down in tears.

The doctors twitched their lips in embarrassment.

On March 2, 1816, Quinquin went to tell the management of La Monnaie that I couldn't perform in my role that night. Marie-Eugène had a high fever. His little body would shiver all over, then he would start to sweat. He called for me constantly, asked for his father, begged us to make the bells of Notre-Dame de Finistère stop ringing. The doctors bled him. They tried a thousand and one cures that twisted my insides and made me scream in silence, my head pressed against the window, my swollen eyes fixed on the church pediment, *laus tua in fines terrae*. For a month I didn't sleep. Sitting by my son's bed, I kept watch over his moments of quiet, of respite, over the terrifying fits of delirium that would suddenly come over him. I sponged him and gave him kisses. Albertine and Quinquin stayed by my side unflinchingly. I muttered psalms, furious at my inability to help my little sufferer, wanting to believe, accepting as though poured from a chalice the words of the doctors—of all the doctors, the specialists, apothecaries, and charlatans—who filed through the apartment. It was unthinkable that Marie-Eugène should not live, not grow up alongside me. What a beautiful boy he was going to be, with his blond hair and blue eyes! I could already imagine his face as a young man, my pride and joy, the deep voice in which he would say, "Mother, you've done enough, it's time for you to rest," and the envious looks that would follow me in the street as I walked on his arm.

But a strange hue had stolen over his face, greenish.

"Is it the croup, maybe?"

The doctors didn't know, argued amongst each other.

In a lull between moans, my son asked to see his father. I sent an urgent letter to Rouen. On the twenty-eighth of that month Debonne arrived, taking over from me at Marie-Eugène's bedside. The boy was dying, unable to understand why life, like an ebbing tide, was retreating from his body, aged five years, nine months, and a few days. How unfair it was, by God, to be an adult, a helpless adult confronted with this little sea of suffering! It was my fault, everything was my fault! The earth had given him to me, and the earth was taking him back. I would have given up everything to save my boy. Quinquin and Albertine ran constantly to the church across the way to light votive candles. The sorrowful actors came every day to ask for news. Eugène shouldered his part to the end, even managing to draw a few smiles from our patient with a buffoonery beyond my means. I could see a veil drawing over the boy and knew that nothing could tear it away.

On April 10, my son's heart stopped beating. And mine. There are no words. A mother without a child. Absurdity, unspeakable excess. I took to my bed, refusing to believe it. Two days later, I had to be carried to the burial service. I could not stand. In his fantastical chair with its floral designs, the priest ran through the ceremony in a few minutes. The bastard son of a foreign actress deserved no better. Horrid organ notes accompanied our exit. *Fines terrae . . . caudent ad sonitum organi.* A cold rain pelted the meager funeral procession. Little wooden slats, as for a sewing box. They lowered him into the earth, and the earth covered me over. Five years, nine months, and seven days.

Then it was night.

ummer 1838. We are traveling to Italy. The sunrise over the Alps is extraordinary. The light pins us to the summit. Ecstatic at the sight, my daughters and I cry out our bedazzlement, communing with a shared fervor at this outdoor High Mass. We race around the coaches, which, loaded down with costumes and scenery, proceed at a walk. The caravan that is taking us to Italy makes slow progress. It takes us four days to reach Lyon, three more to reach Chambéry, and they have just told us that we will not arrive in Turin for another forty-eight hours at least. From there, though, we have a straight run to Milan. Ondine and Inès have picked up my habit of collecting flowers, leaves, and just about anything that speaks of a place's character, so as to carry away, pressed between the pages of a book, a parcel of arrested time. My daughters have caught my passion for reliquaries. Although I am over fifty, I still feel the urge to collect, perhaps more strongly than ever. The herbariums and caskets in which one preserves locks of hair, pebbles, and seashells are no longer enough for me and haven't been for many years. I try to hold on to every step taken, every action made by me or those I love during the course of our daily lives. I hoard them for my own. Writing is a museum. Not a day passes that I do not visit it, that I do not fall into a reverie before familiar items. And I bring new ones. A bottomless collection that, with this journey, can expect considerable enrichment.

The mention of Italy in Paris society elicits a chorus of praise, but I hear the name differently. For me, Italy is Latouche. A young Latouche, who, in 1812, after years of living in a stale marriage, pacing like a caged lion in his office at the Tax Bureau, fled toward freedom and the south. The image of this rebellious Henri, in quest of something more, hungry for knowledge, has always haunted me. I had not yet met him then. Twenty-six years later, at loggerheads with everyone, Henri de Latouche lives in almost total solitude. Bitter, mean, disappointed at the vanity of men, the calculation of women, he grumbles about everyone and can hardly bear his own company. This image of him is painful to me. Which is why I like the idea of joining him on the roads of Italy, to ride *en croupe* behind him with the wind in my hair. Among its innumerable treasures, Italy chiefly possesses an unpublished portrait of Henri, markedly different from the old curmudgeon he has lately become.

IT IS RAINING in Milan. The company starts right in on rehearsals. We are staying in a shabby hotel not far from the Piazza del Duomo, on a narrow, grimy street. The girls, who have been given small parts, spend the best part of the day with Valmore, thus escaping my lugubrious watch. The Milanese rain drips into my veins. I find it absurd and stinging, like well-directed slaps in the face. It wounds me. I try to flee, ducking into churches so as not to taste its saltiness in my mouth. The Madonnas on every side resemble my mother, fixing me with their accusatory eyes. My mind wanders as I kneel on hassocks worn by centuries of kneeling. The idea of death assumes unexpected shapes. Even my sewing, which I have been carrying around with me everywhere, in the wings, the bedroom, the trattoria, the galleries, seems to speak of death. I sew to kill time, pierce it through the middle with my needle, and to give order to my manic actions. The next moment, a glimmer of hope penetrates the grayness around me. Perhaps all is not lost! I may eventually find meaning in all this, in this cavalcade that buzzes in my ears and gives me a relentless migraine headache. A horse's hooves galloping in the night. Young Henri, sporting a delicate mustache, laughs under the stars as he proposes sweet nothings to Madame Récamier. With his one eye, he looks a bit like a centaur. I am sure that he is still being talked about in the villages of Lombardy.

ACTUALLY, IT WAS in Rome that Latouche lived for three years. He only ever passed through Lombardy, probably on his way to visit the lake region. But I hardly dare dream about Rome. It is a fantasy quite out of keeping with our present program, and I would be taken for a madwoman if I suggested a visit, so I decide to hold my peace. I find, on attending the first performances of the French company, that they meet with general indifference, a discouraging presage for the rest of the tour.

The arrival in August of Mademoiselle Mars finally brings the desired success. The public listens in rapt and docile attention for several nights in a row. The company thinks it is saved, but after the last performance in Milan the impresario vanishes into the night. No one is paid. A swindle in the classic mold. The actors look high and low for a scapegoat, cursing the nation of thieves that has fleeced them so royally. Old resentments resurface and personal dislikes flare up. Valmore is attacked on all sides for having brought the company to Italy in the first place but defends himself without complaint. I avoid entering the fray, shutting my eyes so as not to see in this disastrous trip the story of my life.

"Perhaps we could take this opportunity to visit Rome?"

I had to make the attempt.

"How would we do that? And with what? We barely have enough to get back to Paris."

Mademoiselle Mars's fame makes it possible for us to organize a benefit for the French actors, who are the butt of ridicule all over Italy. The event will pay for our return journey at least. Its tail between its legs, our poor company returns to France, and no more is said of Milan, the Duomo, or the endless applause that echoes through La Scala after a triumphant performance.

LIFE RESUMES ITS course in Paris. I rave about my unhappiness to anyone who will listen. Valmore, humiliated and out of patience, chases a position. We are staying on rue La Bruyère, far from everything. Actually, our situation is not entirely desperate. After a round of begging, I have obtained additional support for my literary efforts. But this wheedling has become a habit with me. Perhaps because I am so afraid of poverty. Shortly after our return from Italy, I publish a new collection of poems, *Poor Flowers*. It is my most polished work. Most of the poems were inspired by memories of Henri. Paris is abuzz with rumors. Yet when compared to my earlier publications, there is a difference. Latouche, the lost lover who flees and is regretted, still haunts my new poetry, but Prosper also has a place in it as the permanent and reassuring lover. Pure calculation, say the cavilers, to flatter the injured husband. Who could ever understand my dual heart, which has led me to love them both in their own way for more than twenty years? I long thought I had to choose one or the other. Today I know this to be false. Valmore is the luminous side of Henri. Henri is the opaque verso of Prosper. I need both one and the other, these two opposite forms of love. I am myself these two extremes.

The literary world, obviously, doesn't see it this way and is once more titillating itself with the romance of the wrinkled Flemish crone and the acrid hermit of the Vallée aux Loups.

AND AS IT happens, our correspondence has picked up again intensely. Our letters nourish each of my days. One epistle necessarily calls for another, and another still. Writing Latouche is a ritual of my daily life. I perform it without fail. Some maintain themselves through prayer, people the emptiness of their existence with church meetings, and, so as not to hear the plaintive music inside, resort to transepts where swelling hosannas drown their discontent. I go to another confessional altogether. Between Henri and me, our writing is the vow we never exchanged, our correspondence the nave where we two meet at the appointed time. One sometimes waits longer than usual for the other. In his impatience that person may waver in his faith, retracing a thousand times his path through the archways, where he listens respectfully to the other's silence, knowing that it will be broken sooner or later. Our correspondence is our common religion.

Other than through letters, we rarely have contact. And since April 1821 when our bodies separated forever, we have seldom really seen one another. Since my return from Italy, however, things have changed. We are so old now. It is allowed. We have acquired the right to see each other without causing a scandal. We are beyond suspicion. In fact, it is Valmore who encourages me to reach out.

"Poor man, all alone in his Hermitage . . . After everything he has done for you," says Prosper, "you should go visit him. The girls will accompany you. It will be good for their health."

I have often wondered whether Prosper has ever suspected anything, in all this time. What does he know? After all these years and the letters we send back and forth, my ambiguous poems, has he convinced himself that Henri is simply an old literary mentor who has become a friend? I don't like my husband's pity toward Latouche. Or is it a trap? Is Valmore trying to catch me out? I am also afraid to have Henri meet Ondine. It would be playing with fire. But what excuse can I make to Prosper?

And so, as one travels far into the countryside to visit a family grave long abandoned to the mournful wind, I decide to go and see Latouche.

To REACH AULNAY, one takes the coach to Sceaux or Antony, then proceeds on foot along a small path, through fields and meadows bordered with apple and walnut trees. In this splendid setting with its tawny hues always in motion, one eventually comes to a tiny dwelling, a former presbytery. It consists of one room per floor, with an attic at the top connected by an outside wooden ladder. The girls fall in love with the house from the very first, especially the ladder, which they swarm up and down like children, laughing. The room on the second floor was André Chénier's retreat, then Condorcet's. Henri has made it his office. To general indifference, he has continued to publish a historical novel every year.

"I'll tell you something, dear Marceline, I've made more authors than I have books. And for what glory? Look at them,

Balzac, George Sand, what ingratitude . . . And you, who would have every right to hate me, you are here . . . Admirable turn of mind . . ."

"I owe you everything, Henri. If not for you, my writing—"

"It all came from you. I did nothing. Maybe I scratched your soil at the right place to reveal its riches—to your own eyes. It comes down to a question of gardening. Just think of the time spent in arriving at this truth. I've finally become, as they say in this part of the country, a real *peilleroux*, a peasant. And I'm proud of it."

The place is remarkably well tended, it is true. Latouche's natural meticulousness, his perfectionism and care for detail, are everywhere evident. The walls are buried in ivy. The garden, with its cloying violets and mignonettes, berry-bearing alders, strawberry trees, and privet, spills out to the evergreen trees of the dark surrounding forest. Still spry, Henri and I walk for hours, often visiting the big magnolia that marks the border with the neighboring property, which lies neglected. Over there is the Thessalian temple that once sheltered Chateaubriand and Madame Récamier. Tired and breathless, we collapse on the stone bench, where the girls come running to us with cool beverages. The hours fly by. Night arrives and we have not noticed the day passing. Bad luck, it is time to go home! Dragging our feet, we start back toward Paris vowing to return at the earliest opportunity.

INTIMIDATED AT FIRST, Ondine and Inès develop over time a mocking affection toward Latouche, whom they adopt as though he were a difficult baby. The old anchorite, for his part, allows himself to be cajoled, mewling with pleasure. I take good care to say nothing that might awaken his suspi-

cions about Ondine. The passage of the years protects us.
The boldness of it, too. Henri can hardly imagine that the
young lady I have set before him . . . No. At any rate the presence of these two pale and gracious girls in his garden melts
his defenses away. He is tender toward them to the point of
indulgence. He then gets hold of himself by clenching his jaw
and changing the subject.

"Art must be treated as seriously as political or religious belief," he says. "For an artist, it is his only business in life. You
will say that you have children and that you love them more
than your books . . . And you would be right . . . Alas! If only I
had children of my own!"

Henri forever mourns his darling son, who died at the same
age as my own. Our angels. If only we believed in heaven! His
eyes cloud briefly in the swamps of memory. The past sucks at
us like mud. We often wind up both of us in tears, he remembering Léonce and I my Marie-Eugène. I force myself to keep
Ondine's secret. Have I the right to let this man waste away
in grief when I possess the balm that could make him whole?
Is not my silence criminal? The question tortures me. But
Latouche's gaze quickly regains its virulent hue. My doubts
evaporate. I tell myself that it's too late. If I say anything, it
could kill Valmore. And damage the girl. And I will see a life-
time of effort trampled underfoot. No. It makes no difference
anymore. I am satisfied to note how Ondine and Henri hold
each other in mutual respect, recognize their kindred intelligence, and exert a fascination on each other. I even take a
slightly perfidious pleasure in it. I believe the danger is past.


Thus Latouche has gradually and naturally introduced
himself into our life. Our visits to the Hermitage assume a

routine and familial aspect. Prosper joins our party more and more often. I am dismayed to find that he and Henri find common ground and often spend hours at a stretch talking. I sense a crisis coming. Yet they spend most of their time denigrating Paris, spewing their bile over the press and the different circles that have wronged and jilted them. But the bond growing between them is a whip that lashes me at every moment. I read Henri's attitude as perverseness, while Valmore is simply being blind. One is depraved, the other stupid—these are the two men to whom I've forfeited my life and my reason! As the days pass, I begin to find the situation intolerable. And what if Prosper's attitude masks deliberate calculation? And Latouche's hides remorse? Talk! They certainly will end up talking! My fear is also bound up with possessiveness, a desire for exclusivity that I can't quite explain. I can shrug all I like and shake my head in convulsions of denial, but my reaction is clear enough: I am jealous. The people whom I love incompatibly are forging independent links between themselves: Henri and Prosper; Henri and Ondine. My dread of not being loved, of no longer being loved, is dispelling any shreds of good sense I might have left. My health is once more vacillating. Swollen patches are appearing on my face. I have sudden onsets of fever. In my delirium, I even wish one or another of them would die. Or fall prey to illness. Illness would be better, really, as it would restore me to a position of power, would make me necessary again. I am constantly on the edge of a nervous collapse.

Luckily for me, Valmore is finding rejection and discouragement at every turn. His spirits are in decline. Paris still wants no part of him, and he feels such aversion for the city that he decides to go to Lyon the following spring. The question is whether we will follow him there or not. Leave Paris! For several days I lie awake considering the prospect. Henri eventually manages to persuade Prosper to try his fortunes in Lyon alone this time.

"The girls and Madame Valmore are delicate. Moving in no way helps them. Besides, I am here to watch over them."

It is hardly believable. In April 1839, Prosper sets off for Lyon leaving the girls and me in Latouche's care.

HENRI TAKES HIS role seriously. Too seriously. He is obsessed with Ondine's education, everything that concerns her puts him into a state of agitation. And emboldened by the mandate Valmore has given him, he quickly oversteps his bounds. The authority he wields over me and the girls becomes unbearable within a few weeks. My lover occupies my husband's place, a vast place that the latter never totally filled. Too late. Nothing is worse than this grotesque confusion of periods and persons. I violently rebel at this illegitimate usurpation. Latouche and I gradually harden our opposition to each other. And what I have been dreading all along finally happens. Henri marshals his growing suspicions—fueled by a troubling gesture, a familiar expression, an equivocal look—and concludes that he is Ondine's father.

"I have examined the dates," he whispers in my ear one day, almost pulling my arm from its socket. "It is all perfectly clear to me now. Ondine is mine! What sort of a monster are you to have hidden it from me, when I am wasting away from grief and at night eating the dirt where my little one is buried? I can never forgive you for this!"

I deny it. I will always deny it. Before the Lord Himself I will maintain that Ondine is truly Valmore's daughter. I am barely lying. After so many years, and within my own world, I have managed to convince myself of it. Peace, the fruit of so much resignation, so many stifled sobs and unplanted kisses, must be preserved above all else. Unconditionally and at any cost. Latouche proves in the end to be my dearest enemy. Henceforth no holds are barred between us, and no tactics are off limits. As Medea sacrificed her own flesh to be joined in pain with the man she loved, I choose carnage. I will lose Henri forever, yet keep him in a corner of my hatred.

I write to Prosper, to Sainte-Beuve, to Balzac, to Pauline, mounting a scandal against the poet of the Vallée aux Loups, the man whose eyes well with tears at the stanzas of André Chénier, who speaks to titmice and, in his garden, knows how to lay seeds and cuttings patiently between layers of sand or soil.

I say that the old one-eyed devil has hideous designs on Ondine. Dishonest intentions. That the poor innocent girl is entirely unaware of this and sinks further into his clutches every day. That the horrible truth was revealed to me in time to save my daughter.

That I never in my life want to see this abject creature again. This traitor.

OUR INTRIGUE IS a bloody one. Henri de Latouche, already unwelcome in literary circles, already hated with or without reason by a large number of people, is placed in the pillory. A criminal execution. Wounded, roaring, he struggles for a time, tries to restart a dialogue with me that I angrily refuse, languishes beneath our windows, demands to see Ondine (further fueling the horrible rumors that I put out about him), loudly proclaims his innocence, then beats a retreat. Not once has he mentioned his likely paternity of the girl. He respects my honor to the end.

It's over. He made my career, and I have just annihilated his forever. Remorse convulses my nights, knots my throat and stomach. A part of my life, cleft in two, now lies at my feet. There is no going back, no sewing together what is irreparably torn. Roll memory into a ball and toss it into a corner, discard the image and idea of us as though it were a defunct identity, and try never, ever to think of him, alone in his Hermitage, his eyes fixed on the silence of the sky. The stars go out. Nothing exists anymore except tomorrow.

But I have my daughter! I still have my daughter!

And the tapestry of my life, that I weave according to my whim.

## 18

HAD LOST EVERYTHING. In April 1816, I believed that my days would never be divested of
their crepe. Brussels would always wear the color of mourning, black. A dull, extinguished city, deaf to my windedness,
my stupefaction. I had cried so much my stomach gave a hollow sound. A desiccated well, down which boys took pleasure
tossing stones that bounced against the walls, my raspy walls,
mold-ridden, where nothing took hold but rank grasses,
where spring never came, where everything died, the least
bud, the smallest shoot. I was filled with revulsion toward
myself, my useless belly, my sterile earth. My clayey soil, flat
and bitter, inspired nothing but disgust in me. I would soon
be thirty, and my life was a stony desert void of any mirage,
any prints in the sand. I didn't understand how I had arrived
there, whence I had come, or where I was going. Nothing
ahead, nothing behind. Among the stones, I encountered only
myself, waiting for me. And I didn't like myself. I was hoping
a cyclone might move through. Only a monstrous cataclysm
could save me, something that would knock everything down,
especially memory. But hurricanes were rare in Belgium,
where sorrows drown in drizzle. I hated drizzle.

At the end of the month in which I buried my child, I once
more appeared on stage at La Monnaie. The theater had

granted me a few days off for mourning. The time had expired. Officially the incident was closed.

After our son's death, Eugène Debonne remained for a few days at my side. His large hand, which he slipped into mine at night, kept away the visions that haunted me, a doll's casket, my little one sculpted in marble, cold and hard, lodged forever in a rotten corner of a foreign cemetery. My mother in the Antilles and my son in Belgium. Why? Why would I always be separated from those who were dearest to me? Because I had no intention of staying in sad Brussels. Even my son's grave could not keep me there. With Eugène having slavishly returned to Rouen and his brother, and all prospects of our marriage definitively shattered, I had only Albertine to turn to, but she was sinking every day deeper into the abyss. The poor woman no longer asked anything of life and wanted only to merge with everlasting sleep. She was already dead. During Marie-Eugène's agony, she had made a superhuman effort to anchor herself somewhat in the world of the living, out of love for me. Since then, nothing held her any longer. She was present only intermittently, her mind already errant. When I saw Albertine, I sometimes had the impression that I was looking through her.


How I DON'T know, but I survived. Unwillingly, I even renewed my contract with La Monnaie at the end of the year. I would have given anything to leave Brussels, where an unbearable odor of incense seemed to linger in the air. Even its name hurt me horribly to hear. But the theater made much of me. The terms of my new contract were again excellent. And I really didn't have the choice. I was still responsible for my brother, and for my father, who was gradually declining and had gone back to Douai, like an animal dragging itself at the hour of its death back to its birthplace. If I was not to go into decline myself, it was best that I remain active. Playacting seemed rather appropriate, all in all. Pretending, always pretending.

I took refuge in letters. Debonne wrote me, though less and less, as did my sisters regularly, and Félix and my father. They were rustic letters, crude sometimes, but signs of life all the same, a pulse, palpitations that linked me to something. To a handful of people, I still mattered. My existence was more than an encumbering presence. After Marie-Eugène's death, any tendered branch might pluck me from the void, even a rotten limb. And it was my brother, my drunken old brother, who understood this and shared my suffering most intensely. I wasn't surprised. I knew what was gnawing at Félix, deep in his heart, under all that wine. My sisters had perhaps lost too many children to register my misfortune as more than the usual village burial—the knelling of the church bell, and the sound of clogs dragging over an empty road on a leaden morning. They had walled themselves in behind their rigidified babies. Solid constructions. I was all cracks and fissures. This my father perceived, to my great surprise. The loss of my darling boy brought us together. As soon as my schedule allowed me, I went to visit him in Douai. I would walk kilometers for a caress, to feel his trembling hand in my hair. When I arrived, it was often to raise him from the vomit in which he sprawled unconscious, to change and feed him. I came to diaper my father. If I could have, I would have nursed him.

A YEAR AFTER my son's death, I was playing on the stage of La Monnaie to more acclaim than ever. I was a thoroughly broken-in engine, the machinery well oiled, tears delivered on command, the pathos more nuanced, less brutal. The whole repertory went through the mill. In my state of general indifference, I sometimes felt moments of calm, sudden small indefinite sensations that lifted me for a time out of my torpor. I no longer had anything but that. At my age, and with my looks, I told myself, there was no question of my flesh still palpitating. I had put aside love. Even if I had never experienced it. But it was too late. The theater, as I believed, was my convent.

In late April 1817, La Monnaie decided to make a great sensation. So as to compete with the major theaters of Europe, the management hired the French actor who was most in vogue at that moment. It turned out to be the boy with extraordinary looks whom I had met when he was still a child in Bordeaux and later in Rouen. It was said that he was turning the heads of respectable ladies and cutting a wide swath for himself. He was an inconstant man, whose career on the stage had been made possible by his parents, André and Anne-Justine Valmore, and who had been helped along by the special favor of certain aging actresses. A resplendent sun, appearing before me in the role of Hippolytus, with a narrow waist, straight limbs, erect carriage, flaring nostrils, arched eyebrows, broad forehead, brown curls, stentorian voice, high buskins, and a red-plumed helmet. A light of sorts. Prosper Valmore sprang into my forlorn and blackened Belgium without warning and tore down all my funeral drapes.

Our *Phèdre* opened on May 20. Despite being seven years older, I played the part of Aricie, Hippolytus's mistress. At every speech, the young actor's supplicating eyes would bore further into my defensive walls. It had to be acting, I told myself all through the performance, a show of energy, of arrogance, the son of Theseus addressing the woman he loves. "When you are near, I run from you; when you are absent, I find you; In the depths of the forest your image pursues me . . ." For a long time I had paid no attention to the words recited at my feet, I hardly heard my own lines, which seemed like foreign sounds, vocal exercises. My intonations, shadings, hesitations—all of it was memorized. But that night I seemed to hear Racine for the first time. "Tonight I seek myself and am nowhere to be found . . ." How was it possible? This chasm, this strangeness . . . The boy was drinking me in with his eyes. Though several steps away, I felt his breath mix with mine, his saliva already in my mouth, his tongue thrust into my cheeks. His lips consumed mine, sucked at them impatiently. "Perhaps the telling of so savage a love / Makes you, hearing of it, blush."

Madwoman, old goat, get yourself in hand. What cruel bet has this impudent boy made with himself? How far will his perversity extend? He is as handsome as the day, and I am already sunset. He can have all the soubrettes he wants. Jealousy rises in me, and a sense of my powerlessness. By what bizarre force is he driven toward my sour face and empty mother's body? No, no. This ardor I see is a lie. I knew him as a child. He is still only a boy. I am beyond dalliances. He must have heard of my misadventures, my past dishonor. Under my theater dress, I am a bruised and shriveled woman. The kind one no longer marries and only takes to bed for lack of a better. He has plenty of choices. I am like Aricie only in that I wear her costume. He is pure. What game is he playing? I no longer want to hear him. "Emerge from the slavery to which you've been reduced, / Dare follow me, dare flee with me, dare be seduced . . ."

At the end of the performance I ran home. Youth is fierce! The desire glowing in Prosper Valmore's eyes had undone me. Here I was blushing in front of a twenty-three-year-old actor!

I felt so ridiculous that I very nearly slapped myself in the face. He take a fancy to me? I must be delirious.

Two nights later, however, there could be no shadow of a doubt: Prosper Valmore was desperately in love with me. We had removed our tragedians' costumes to play a pair of love-birds in one of those low comedies imported from England that the public was then keen on. The play was called *Tom Jones à Londres*. The two main parts, Tom and Sophie, fit us to perfection. Everyone around us was aware of it. There were smiles behind our backs, knowing looks. But solicitude as well. The other actors were going out of their way to be kind to me. They are all accomplices, I thought. It's a general conspiracy. What do they want from me anyway? I was fearful, paralyzed at the thought of being hurt again, mocked, betrayed. This had to be nothing more than trifling raillery, a frivolous affair. Attraction sometimes exceeds any reasonable measure. The young man was taken with a passing predilection for a pretty skirt.

But the truth was far different. Valmore truly loved me. I didn't believe it and repulsed his advances. Not for my honor's sake. I could have been his mistress. What did I have to lose by it? To the contrary, in my bleak desert he was an unexpected oasis. But I was afraid of his body, of growing attached to him and being thrown over in mid-ocean. I was afraid of love, which had taken everything from me. I resisted. "Leave me, I beg of you," I wrote him. "Sad as I am, I am not made to love. Nor can I ever be loved. I don't believe in happiness . . ." But Prosper was determined not to listen to me. And then the unimaginable happened. Everything stopped. In June 1817, a month after we met in Brussels on the stage of the Théâtre de la Monnaie, Prosper Valmore asked for my hand in marriage. At the same moment, in Douai, my father was dying, alone, half comatose, drunk, ignorant of why he had lived and how he was dying. By the time a courier reached me with the news, he was already underground.

I SHED FEW tears over my father's passing. I forbade myself to. I was interested only in Prosper, slipping him little notes between acts, clinging to happiness, to the silly play by Desforges that had brought me back into the world. There would be no black on my wedding dress. I had worn enough mourning as it was. I was starting a new life. I felt like one of those orphans who are so eager to be loved and who, after years of beatings, small acts of nastiness, surreptitious violence, finally finds a family to take her in. I cleared the decks, sweeping away parts of my past that might have put furrows in my future husband's handsome brow. I rearranged the events in my life as I pleased. I was my own best biographer. But it pained me to cast Marie-Eugène into the well of silence. It was as if I watched him die a second time. And Prosper, who arrived in Brussels a few months after my little one's death, could hardly have been unaware of him. He never spoke to me about him, though, and avoided the subject. So as not to hurt him I understood that I would have to resorb the pain and bury it deep inside myself. How could it be otherwise? It was inevitable. I could not ask Valmore to share with me the memory of my dead son. Across the board, I wanted to obliterate everything I had been before meeting my husband. Arrive intact under his body, that he might baptize me anew, provide me an identity along with a genealogy, ancestors, roots in some soil. Forget that my adulterous mother sold me into the theater as a girl, that my sisters had opened their thighs to armies of the unwashed, that my brother's youth had been hacked to pieces, and that my father had just died pathetically in the public hospital in Douai in a puddle of piss and vomit. Yes, I would have liked to erase all that. Be nothing but a fountain, a spring, virginal, wholly devoted to my man.

WE WERE MARRIED on September 4, 1817. A little furtive ceremony under a pale sun. I had no interest in showing my joy, my all-too-new and fragile joy, to the envious crowd. Our unlikely pairing caused enough talk, sheltered though we were from the strongest blasts. All the pretty faces wondered about Valmore's lack of common sense, the flaws in his character, and the likely machinations that had precipitated this odd marriage. Was there not sorcery behind it? Anne-Justine, my mother-in-law, barely hid her disappointment. Only André, her husband, seemed genuinely pleased to see us joined. His affection made me soft and foolish. It smoothed away the jealousy that had sprung up around me. Someone loved me, that was enough. I could see nothing else.

I was crazy about my young husband, his vigorous embraces, his tireless sensuality, his inexplicable adoration of me. Thinking back to the clumsy pawing of Louis Lacour, the wheezing efforts of Eugène Debonne, the carnivorous struggles of Audibert to wring a moan from me, I realized I had never known nudity before, or intimacy. I had perhaps truly given myself before, I had always offered myself without reserve, but I did not have in front of me these lips flushed pink with desire, want, and promise, these eyes that solemnly swore to love me always, to protect me, to build with me a bridge linking my soil to his. It was artless and without surprises, but how I had dreamed of this feeling of peace! For the first time with Prosper it seemed to me that I wasn't waiting for anything else. Reaching this long-anticipated state of rest between two fevers, which before had been only a convalescence—I was still stunned by it. Brussels itself smiled brightly at us. The couple that Valmore and I formed had the sturdiness of rock. The greatest actresses of the day wanted us on the stage with them, and Belgium, no longer to be ignored because of us, witnessed the progress from Paris of Mademoiselle George and Mademoiselle Mars, eager to play across from us. We performed without respite, barely waited until we were in the wings to kiss like raw youths. I constantly needed to touch Prosper, to convince myself of his reality, to set him against the shadow of my departed son, who haunted me.

In January 1818, I noted with joy that I was pregnant.

I WAS REBORN, I blessed even the vomiting that convulsed me in the mornings. I was alive, fecund! Despite the tiredness resulting from my condition, I displayed an energy that astonished Prosper, and frightened him. With encouragement from André, his father, whom I respected, I started to write again, in a style not unconscious of the rhetoric of our eighteenth century, which he favored. Several journals had already published poems of mine, and I was pressed to produce more. I started to have friends. There were a number of French exiles in Brussels at that point, strong opponents of the Restoration, whom I sought out particularly—often alone, as Valmore, acting from caution and lack of interest, preferred to steer clear of politics. I was also taking English classes. It was at this time that I undertook to bring assistance to those in misery as well: prostitutes, the ill, poor devils whom I pressed to my bosom with mystic devotion. But nothing made me forget that I once had had a little boy as blond as a field of wheat, and that he had been brutally cut down. My greatest satisfactions were thus always kept within bounds. This memory prevented me from ever being fully happy.

Nonetheless, the shadows around me were losing ground. The success I was having on the stage was unmistakable, despite my exhausting pregnancy, which I hid as well as I could. The wardrobe mistress showed considerable ingenuity. And she needed all she had to give a woman of my age, and on the point of giving birth, the appearance of a young girl. It was thus that I kept the role of Junie in *Britannicus* until I came to full term.

ON JULY 22, 1818, in the middle of the third act of Racine's play, in a scene where I played opposite Prosper, who was sublimely arrayed as an emperor's son, I felt the first pains. I intoned my next lines with an uncomfortable smile:

> *Your image constantly is in my sight:*
> *Nothing can banish it.*

> *I understand you, madam:*
> *What you wish can be achieved through my flight . . .*

Lord but I was in pain! How was I to manage? How hold out until the end? We were only halfway through the performance! And there was Valmore looking at me with total incomprehension!

They were definitely contractions. I easily recognized the beginnings of labor. A nightmare. Draped in the flowing folds of an absurd Roman gown, I was standing in front of a thousand people, opening wide my frightened eyes as a signal to my husband.

> *. . . I believed my love vainly shuttered in my breast;*
> *Never to have loved would by far have been best . . .*

At the end of the scene, I collapsed backstage into the arms of Mademoiselle George, who was dressed as Agrippina.

"We must stop the play," said Prosper, panicking.

"Out of the question. I don't appear at all in the fourth act. I'll have some time to recover."

"It's too dangerous!"

Mademoiselle George soothed Valmore.

"It takes a good deal more than an hour for a child to arrive, my friend," she said. "We have time. And your wife won't be the first actress to begin delivery on the boards."

Prosper let himself be persuaded. The performance resumed, at a somewhat faster tempo. All the actors hurried so that I might be free to leave a little sooner. The last act was torture for me. Finally the punishment was lifted and I was able to quit the stage. Valmore, whose performance ended before mine, was waiting for me in the wings. The pain was horrible. I thought I was dying. They carried me home, where a midwife called in by Anne-Justine waited with her tools at hand. Less than an hour later, with Valmore beside me still in Roman costume, I brought a baby girl into the world. On the instant she was named Junie. The other actors, most of whom had not bothered to change their clothes either, were also present. The room was full of togas and buskins. It was at once ridiculous and poignant. His eyes full of tears, Nero embraced Britannicus. In the heat of the moment, he had even forgotten to take off his plumed helmet.

. . .

THREE WEEKS LATER my lovely little girl, in the care of a local wet nurse, expired suddenly. I was in despair, to the point of mute prostration, lasting several days. Prosper, trying clumsily to console me, only made my grief worse.

"We'll have others," he kept saying.

If he had known that two already had been taken from me! My mother-in-law, who hated my autonomy and my theatrical success that overshadowed her son's, but who had been somewhat appeased by the birth of the baby, now gave her hatred free rein.

"I have my doubts as to whether you are capable of bearing a healthy child," she said, "and I have my reasons. You do not lead a healthy life."

"What do you mean?"

"There is your correspondence with that Dr. Alibert. An ordinary friend? I quite doubt it. Oh yes, I've searched through your things. And what if I have? In the cause of my son's happiness any means are justified."

I protested, but Prosper looked at me differently from that day on. There was sometimes a tinge of hostility in his eyes, or sadness. His mother's words had hit the bull's-eye, and my grief, which he couldn't understand, revived his suspicions. I was crushed. A chill silence settled between us.

I recovered from my confinement as well as I could. A month later I was once more on the stage, though playing more and more seldom opposite Valmore, who was failing to win over the Brussels audience. He was starting to grow jealous, and on more than one front. His mother had convinced him that I was unfaithful to him, that I didn't love him, that I had married him for social advantage. And to crown it all, my first book of poems,

*Élégies, Marie et Romances,* was published in Paris at the end of 1818. Under my maiden name. Prosper was offended, taking it as a personal affront. Why was the book not published under my married name? Was I ashamed of him? It was ridiculous. The chill turned to ice. Was our beautiful love already over? I could hardly credit it. Were we henceforth to have only each other's presence, an accumulation of small resentments, a daily contact fed by habit more than desire, by fear of change more than the need to stay together, by resignation more than quiet joy? When would my rebellion start to rumble? My mother had refused to live a "why not?"existence, and it had been her undoing. Would I be able to stand it? And for how long?

RESIGNATION WAS NOT in my nature. I chose to act, and quickly. Rejecting the tempting offer of a renewal from the Théâtre de la Monnaie, I arranged to have Valmore hired by the Odéon in Paris. For my part, I no longer wanted to act. Despite my popularity and the brief pleasures it occasionally provided me, the theater was still more hateful to me than ever. A number of people had convinced me that I should devote myself exclusively to writing. This was just what I had been longing to hear. Dizzy from the success of my first book of verse, I believed them.

WHEN IN SPRING 1819 the Brussels public learned of my planned departure, it booed me harshly. It couldn't have mattered less to me. After an agony of many weeks, my friend Albertine had just died.

And there was nothing, absolutely nothing, to keep me in Belgium any longer.

## 19

ENRI AND I ARE AT WAR. January 1840: I destroy all his letters. Nothing must be left of the feelings that bound us together, no trace. Our love is dead, and in what better company than with hatred to mark its passing? He sends me back my portrait, Uncle Constant's pencil drawing of me that I gave him twenty years ago at our parting, on the back of which a long lock of hair has been glued. My face today has little to do with the one in the drawing. As though my life has been a long process of growing uglier. I put it in the back of a wardrobe. It is over.

"NOTHING THAT LATOUCHE says makes any sense," I say to one and all. "His wits have quite obviously gone astray. He was seen screaming with laughter recently at a burial. He rants wildly, and will try any stratagem to talk with Ondine. He even slipped a note for her to Sainte-Beuve, who was incensed and immediately turned it over to me. To end up like this! And he was such a brilliant man . . ."

I send my daughter to Lyon to live with Valmore. Aggrieved, Henri refuses to return my letters. Next he publishes a novel, *Léo*, full of nasty allusions to me. I manage to steer his mistress of the moment toward Balzac's bed and encourage the latter to

savage Henri's book in the press. We detest each other posses-
sively. And give no quarter. Gradually, though, silence reestab-
lishes itself between us, limpid and unbridgeable. By autumn,
I no longer speak his name. Latouche abandons the struggle
also and buries himself again in the Vallée aux Loups. Nineteen years exactly after our last kiss, we finally manage—or so I
believe—to end our relations.

The consequences are horrendous. Our love had kept us,
Henri and me, in suspended time. Within it, a part of us had
stayed immobile, ageless and without wrinkles, refusing to go
with the current. But now that the dike is breached, nature has
reclaimed its authority, all the more severely for having long
been thwarted. And now the years will rush by with nothing to
stop them, with their horrible freight of the dying and the dead.

CONDEMNED TO THE stage, Prosper shuttles back and forth
between Lyon and Brussels for several seasons, stopping off
in Paris from time to time for an unsuccessful performance.
I am now in the capital permanently, though my poetry is no
longer selling or even being published. Sainte-Beuve, who is
politely courting Ondine, has tried right and left to get my
poems published, but without success. I have gone out of
fashion. The current has petered out. With Henri gone, have
I said all I had to say? My *Bouquets and Prayers* appears in
1843, a resounding failure. I resign myself to writing for the
magazines and for myself, fitfully, as a vice. It provides me an
outlet. Our life at home is one of constant agitation, thanks
entirely to me. I am abusive and tyrannical. Because of me,
Inès seethes with jealousy toward Ondine, and Ondine toward Hippolyte. I cannot leave my children to breathe freely
outside of my control.

After two tries, and because I have obliging friends, Hippolyte finally passes his baccalaureate at the age of twenty-six. And though he drew a low number he avoids going into the army thanks to my maneuvering. I couldn't bear it if he went away. I have lost too many children, and my daughters, who regularly cough up blood, are liable to leave me at any moment, for all that I reject the thought. My son is my only sure possession. At one point he considers marrying a young lady. A momentary mistake. I squash this attempt at insubordination *in ovo*. It is to be the only one. Hippolyte takes painting classes but abandons them before long to care for me. I manage, after a lengthy siege of the Ministry of Public Education, to get him hired there. A civil servant now, my son takes his place permanently at my side.

Ondine is not so easily managed. Influenced by Latouche during the weeks when he acted as her tutor, her character has become more willful, tormented, and rebellious. Serious, self-controlled, often melancholy, she tries in every way possible to break free from me, to disappear as soon as possible from the madhouse of home, where, according to her, we entertain too much and where poor Inès, who is always sick, is wasting away, corroded by envy for her sister. Ondine is brilliant, precocious, and shows talent on all fronts. I am proud of her. But something vague in her, something evasive and undefinable, disturbs me and makes me prefer Hippolyte, who is more docile. Ondine is studying music theory, drawing, voice, and piano. She would like to teach. Her taste for education and autonomy is hardly to my liking. My daughter's cultural sophistication makes me distinctly uncomfortable. At the age of sixty, still blushing at the gaps in my knowledge, I devour the classics that I missed in my youth. I loathe to hear my verses praised for their simplicity. It is my shame. Ondine has studied the Romans and the Greeks, and she wants to enter a profession. I would rather she married, be a good wife in the next street over. But every match that I make on her behalf falls through. Most she refuses herself. Other suitors, like Sainte-Beuve, shy away at the last minute. Perhaps they find Ondine too independent, too demanding. Or else they hear in her fits of coughing an alarming sound that I have no wish to notice.

I DO CONCEDE that her health is fragile enough to require special care, and in the summer of 1841 I resign myself to letting her go to London for three months, where Dr. Paul Curie reportedly is working miracles in homeopathy. This new discipline is revolutionizing medicine and causing great excitement. In the letters she sends me from Brook Street, Ondine mainly writes about diets and passes along recommendations for Inès with a seriousness that is both touching and irritating. For a time, I go along with the general enthusiasm. I am ready to believe in any sort of panacea. At home, poor Inès grows steadily weaker, torn between adoration and aversion for her absent sister. Sometimes she is kept doubled up with vomiting for hours at a time. I feel my powerlessness to do anything for my sick child. Inès feels it too and distances herself more every day, full of rancor for the mother who no longer protects her. She grows capricious, insists suddenly that we move the furniture from the parlor into her bedroom. Ondine too is drawing away from me. Her letters become scarcer. She is very busy, she claims, attending on Mrs. Curie and her companion. The two women have developed a fondness for her and insist that she stay longer in England.

I start to have doubts about homeopathy.

Something doesn't ring true and unsettles me profoundly. Worse, I don't like the idea of these clutching women around my daughter. What do these Sapphic harpies want with her? Are they not trying to steal my child away from me? I am in a terrible state of nerves. Prosper finds me ridiculous, believing that I am making too much of it as usual.

"It appears that you constantly need something to be anxious about," he says. "Nothing is ever fine as it is. Something always has to be worrying you, shattering the peace you've managed to attain. As a last resort," he adds, "and if it really strikes you as the best thing to do, just write a letter to London asking that Ondine be sent home. Pure and simple."

I write immediately. The answer takes some time to arrive, but confirms my fears and distresses me horribly. Mrs. Curie writes to inform me of the extreme delicacy of my daughter's health. "To make her return to France," she writes, "would be to lead her straight to the slaughterhouse. Her meager chances of survival rest with us. As a concerned mother, you will undoubtedly listen to reason . . ."

"It's a contrivance! Blackmail! Ondine is not on the point of death. What a horrid lie! How could anyone torture me in this way?"

Mrs. Curie's letter sends me to bed for three days with a horrendous fever. I am in such a state of nerves that I have every visitor shown unceremoniously to the door. Best not to come visiting us at this time.

"What if it were true," says Valmore gently.

"Not a chance. They are holding her prisoner. I'll go alone if I have to and bring my daughter back from England!"

"I am going to ask you for one sacrifice, Marceline. Let us give them the benefit of the doubt and grant them a little time,"

Prosper cut in. "If Ondine's health does not improve in a month or two, we'll insist that she be returned to us willy-nilly."

I GIVE IN. To my great fury, Ondine remains a prisoner of Mrs. Curie and her mistress—because I am quite certain that that is the nature of their relationship—for two whole years. Two years of angry exchanges, letters of exasperation or supplication, which reduce my already sensitive nerves to a jelly. Finally, at the end of my patience, one morning in August 1843, I take the coach as far as Boulogne, then the boat to the English coast. Exhausted but resolute, I reach London the next day in a rattletrap coach. Around Grosvenor Square, where the Curies live, the little bricks making up the houses are very dark, almost black, in keeping with the sky. It is like entering a mine. Handel and Talleyrand lived on Brook Street at one time. It's as much as I remember about it. After a violent catfight, yielding a quantity of broken china, I snatch Ondine from the claws of the two witches, who give way before my determination. We set out immediately for Paris. My daughter, who is no better than she was, looks at me with guarded hostility. I no longer believe in homeopathy at all.

TWO YEARS LATER, Ondine becomes a teacher in a school in Chaillot. She has done what she set out to do: become independent, earn her keep, and live as far from us as possible. Since her involuntary return from London, our relations have grown tense. More than anything, because she prides herself on her writing, my poems disturb her. What flights of language for a happily married woman! She speculates a great deal. What of the business with Latouche? What really happened? She doesn't understand, suspects something terrible and ignominious. Besides, my constant importuning of others is loathsome to her, as are my devotion to fallen women, my generosity toward my sisters, who still live in poverty, and my indulgent attitude toward my brother. There are some subjects on which Ondine is as intransigent as Prosper, and she has not a shred of pity for Félix.

"There is a difference," she says, "between mercy and foolishness. Félix was hardly out of prison, where he'd landed for the thousandth time on charges of vagabondage, when he started selling your letters again. How can you forgive him? He shamefully uses your fame to make a profit and spends his life trying to extort money from you. He's a braggart and a drunk!"

"He's just a poor wretch. He's finished. For sixty years he's been finished. I'm the only one he can turn to."

"Kindness will be the death of you," says Ondine.

I lower my head and say nothing, in the humble attitude of a martyr.

The disapproval of my husband and my daughter notwithstanding, I do everything I can to place Félix in an asylum in Douai. My visit to him revolts my senses. The rot pervading my brother attacks my very flesh. I seem to see gangrene appearing on my skin. I kiss his pitted face without disgust and hastily leave my native Flanders. I will not return there.

STARTING IN 1844, Inès has to take to her bed. My little Andalusian, as I call her because of her jet black hair, long features, brown skin, and flashing eyes, is coughing blood and sometimes losing her voice for several days at a time. She is short of breath, has stitches in her side, and loses her appetite. The doctors are flummoxed, prescribe one treatment after another. Ondine, who still believes in homeopathy, makes her follow a diet of roasted meats, boiled vegetables, and fresh fish simply prepared. No coffee, salad, raw fruit, cheese, spices, or pork, she insists. Dress warmly and avoid large gatherings. Go to bed early. Drink only water. I go along with these injunctions. I agree to anything. One doctor has diagnosed a phthisis and ordered a footbath for Inès every night with four ounces of mustard, a handful of salt, and a half glass of vinegar. Another has her bled. A third applies cupping glasses to her back. A fourth orders hot baths to draw the blood away from her chest.

Inès is growing worse daily.


IN THE SPRING of 1846, her health becomes precarious. Her inflamed ganglions keep her from eating or sleeping. She has atrocious pains in her stomach. She feels cramps, heaviness, an insurmountable fatigue. Valmore is working in Brussels this year. Ondine is in Chaillot. Hippolyte cannot make a decision without me. I, too, am having nervous crises, sudden fevers, aches all over, rapid alternations between dejection and exaltation. At times I can neither write nor receive visitors nor go visiting myself. Everything seems tiresome, boring. I sleep badly. During my hours of sleeplessness, I gather my courage and sit with my sewing by Inès's bedside. I also write. The poem "Intermittent Dream of a Sad Night" is composed then. Poetry is the only religion left me. As I look at this little body by candlelight, advancing inexorably toward silence, I think back to my

first son, Marie-Eugène, to my mother, my life, my loves. I cry
in the semidarkness.

INÈS IS GOING to die. It is only a question of days. On her
twenty-first birthday, she wants to gather around her all the
people she loves. We carry her bed into the middle of the drawing room. Ondine makes tea, I prepare *loées*. There is music
and singing, someone sits down at the piano. Inès, racked by
coughs, manages to laugh, to applaud. It is a horrible masquerade for everyone involved.

"This way I will have attended my own wake," she says.

She believes that she is unloved, that I always favored her
sister and brother over her. I no longer have the strength to
continue the debate. For two years our apartment on the bou-
levard Bonne-Nouvelle has been pervaded with the smell of
drugs and bile. The poor girl angrily shouts insults and accusa-
tions, then breaks down in tears. Valmore, fulfilling his contract at La Monnaie, is unable to come home. Inès asks for him.

"Father! I want my father!" she wheezes.

She goes to sleep. Exhausted, I too drop off. Hippolyte
rouses me from my slumber by taking my hand.

"It's over, Mother. Inès has stopped suffering."

It is December 4, 1846.

IN PROSPER'S ABSENCE, Hippolyte makes all the decisions and
organizes the funeral proceedings. With Ondine's help, he
finds us a new apartment on the rue de Richelieu, so that we
can escape the Porte de Saint-Denis and Inès's ghost. I cannot
do anything except cry, riddled with guilt at outliving my child,

my children, not being able to prevent their deaths. At the last moment, weak, I decide not to attend my daughter's obsequies. Life has dealt me so many blows. I don't understand why.

Grief fells me for several months and curls me in on myself. Then I turn toward others again. Alarmed by my sister Eugénie's plaintive letters, I travel to Rouen. Her husband and she have become ruined over the years. Only two of their children are still alive. Not knowing what to do, they are considering moving to Algeria. Eugénie is tired, ill. I give them some money and use my influence to find work for my brother-in-law. Then I turn toward Cécile. She still talks to her cats, her geraniums. To her four dead children. To the man who abandoned her. To her two sons who no longer visit. My oldest sister looks like my mother, whose hair barely had time to turn white. Her face is smiling, absent, timeless.

Eugène Debonne has just died, someone informs me. My past is riddled with bottomless holes. But if there is a heaven, my darling son, who died one morning in Brussels, will finally have been reunited with his father.


IN 1848 THE barricades of the February Revolution appear under our windows, rousing me from my dejection. With Ondine and Hippolyte on either side, I take part in the insurrections. When calm returns, Ondine is named "Inspector of Schools and Pensions for Young Ladies in the Department of the Seine," though for reasons of health she seldom performs in her new position. The new regime soon disappoints her. She doesn't share my enthusiasm. We are often on opposite sides. All the same, Inès's death brings us closer. The fear of losing each other is stronger than any other feeling. My daughter is sad, she no doubt foresees the imminence of her own death, her solitary life without a man or children. I chide her regularly about finding a husband.

"It's too late," she says quietly.

But when Jacques Langlais, a lawyer and widower, the father of two children, comes at my request to pay court to her, I urge her not to refuse this last chance. My sister Eugénie has just died. Madame Récamier went next. The death knell is sounding all around me. Langlais, who is perceptive, doubtless knows that marrying Ondine will only relieve his widowerhood temporarily. But he is a good and generous man. My daughter might still give birth once. Deep inside, though aware that a pregnancy would kill her, she is keen to have a child. Langlais proposes to her. She accepts.

WE CELEBRATE CHRISTMAS of 1850 and Ondine's wedding together. Prosper recovers his spirits somewhat. Alone in Belgium after Inès's death, he considered suicide. Only my letters kept him in this world. Back in Paris again, not working, he lives in brooding silence, pacing the apartment in every direction, sighing, muttering. He is bored, asks himself why I married such a useless man, and flees at the first sign of a visitor, overcome by his long-standing sense of inferiority toward me. Yet I love my husband. During the course of our married life, it's true, there were times when I had to force myself to. But love is perhaps not a natural, spontaneous feeling. Today I can see how attached I am to this man who has shared my daily life for thirty-three years, my brilliance as well as my ugliness, who smiles at my rumpled face each morning, and who gave me children, a roof, and his name. All his life, this man wore himself out playing the clown in front of indifferent or hostile crowds so that we could live, so that I could write and publish. I owe him my freedom. I love Prosper Valmore as a piece of myself that nothing could amputate. Our love has known periods of astonishing revival, rising from habit and staleness, a sometimes painful rekindling of flame. In the end, we have never let daily life grind us down. The theater kept us from this. With Valmore traipsing from one stage to another, we were always in a state of frustration. We often lived apart. Nothing suits love better. Although the years have gone by, my husband is still jealous. Scrutinizing some of my old poems, he sometimes feels his old demons rise in him.

One day, out of honesty, he admits that he deceived me with other actresses and asks me to forgive him his petty infidelities. I plant a kiss on his wrinkled brow. We are once more on a broad and tranquil plain.

FEBRUARY 28, 1851. Sainte-Beuve comes to visit.

"Henri de Latouche died today in the Vallée aux Loups. Would you be willing to write a portrait of him, to eulogize him?"

I don't know if I can, if I will manage. For eleven years, entrenched in my anger and a prisoner to my lies, I have forced myself not to think of him. Henri is dead. A hail of bullets strikes me in the chest. I wouldn't have thought it. Who was Latouche? A mystery I never managed to fathom, one that both dazzled and frightened me. Henri . . . Everything comes up to the surface in me now, nothing remains of the paltry dikes I erected against the past. And the poetry that I dammed up gushes out. All the silenced pain. Henceforth, my song will know no obstacles. It belongs to me fully. Writing this love is my only possession, I who have been stripped of everything. I have struggled against it, but I relent today again. It is the direction in which my life has tended. It is perhaps there that the meaning of everything resides. At sixty-five, I feel how much I have lived and loved. The emotion survives intact. I have found Henri again.

I write.

And from beyond the grave, his bronze fingers close around the nape of my neck in a familiar gesture. I let him do it, bare my neck to his teeth.

My beloved torment, my invincible love.

## 20

ON THAT DAY I know that I will end up belonging to him. Sooner or later. It is only a question of time, of patience on his side, of resistance on mine. Everything might be against us, the very idea of our becoming lovers could seem absurd and improbable, yet it is inevitable. I understand it the moment I see him enter my uncle Constant's studio and walk with determination toward me. Unquestionably I am going to love this one-eyed and weary cynic to the point of insanity and endanger everything I have worked so hard to build. I have just married the best man in the world and I am pregnant. But it changes nothing. There are no explanations. Happiness may not be what I am looking for. Happiness, that static torpor, that semideath. For a long time I thought I wanted it. I was mistaken, though, about my own desires. By letting others make decisions for me, I came to take their wishes for my own. In any case, I have a great deal of trouble following myself. I move so fast that I sometimes feel I am chasing myself breathlessly. Looking at Henri de Latouche, I suddenly see myself squeezed into a life that no longer suits me. My figure has changed. And so have my tastes. But I want to ignore it and maintain it isn't so, like a woman of mature years who, bulging from a dress that she wore as a girl, convinces herself she is unchanged. Yet there has been a fracture inside me, the quiet but persistent sound of timbers working.

The summer of 1819 was cold and sunless. After Brussels, though, the light of Paris is dazzling, even in gray weather. In Constant's studio, triply exposed, light comes from every direction, hurtling against the easels, caroming off the palettes. Sitting in a corner with my notebook in my lap, I let the light carry me, my senses awakened and almost unbearably acute. I sense the slightest vibration. My body seems unable to hold this flux of emotions. At every pregnancy I have felt the same sensation, wanting to cry and exult at the same time, walk into the light and retreat into darkness. This time it is worse.

I am writing, I am fine. My uncle comes and goes, dragging his feet among his gouaches. My little boy's death and then my father's put an end to our estrangement. Our reconciliation took place standing over graves. And probably because we know its value, our love has been stronger than ever since my return to Paris.

"Go on, cry, my little *tiote*, don't hold back," says Constant, sensing that memories of Marie-Eugène are flooding through me.

In his studio, now located on the rue Childebert, I can be sad, I can be myself and grieve for my departed son. In the presence of my young husband and his mother, I have to play the part of the fulfilled wife, happy in her household and preparing herself to give birth. But between the walls of the Childeberte's second floor, I can loosen the knot in my throat, my mother's tragedy, my dead children, the downhill slide of my close family, my extorted childhood, the latest troubles of my brother Félix, who has just been demoted for drunkenness. The disappointment of my marriage. And it all comes out.

It has to come out.

"A reviewer for the Salon is supposed to visit me this afternoon," says my uncle. "An odd man, intelligent, disturbing, imperious, impenetrable. Rather worrisome all in all. He had two plays performed last year at the Odéon. And he publishes a stream of facile, careless books. Strange, in a man who is otherwise so exacting, so capable of both the best and the worst. A jack-of-all-trades. He reports on trials in the daily papers, publishes travel guides, novels. But his real triumph, a very recent one, is to have exhumed the poetry of André Chénier, which was all but forgotten."

His hair rumpled, his eyes looking inward, Constant pauses.

"He swears by Canova and David," he goes on. "This year, his review of the Salon was the most perceptive by far . . . He is afraid of nothing, and consequently has enemies everywhere . . . Latouche, Henri de Latouche. Do you know him?"

"Our paths have crossed, twice."

Not necessarily met. There was no collision, though we perhaps bumped together a bit, but both times in a theater setting. Papier mâché, false noses, wigs. Emptiness, fakery, and me on my guard, an actress. Till now, Henri de Latouche had been only a fleeting figure on my path, so that I have almost doubted his reality. I invent so many lives for myself, have known so many metamorphoses. Did I dream up what I read in his strange face? Probably. I have too much imagination. All the same, I am sorry that I am wearing this dress that makes me look more pregnant than I am. I have circles under my eyes, my hair is in disarray. At the Childeberte I don't care how I look and resume my provincial ways, far from the makeup of the stage. In my true ugliness, unfalsified, I find myself acceptable. This sudden concern with making myself attractive intrigues me. Is it my secret design to have this man like me? That's grotesque. He is repulsive, short. I don't like the pinkish tinge of his skin. Nothing about him attracts me. Maybe his hands. His voice . . . But I am a married woman.

"Marceline! Watch where you're walking!" says Constant. "You've tromped all over my paints! Dear girl, are you away with the fairies?"

The book of my life has turned a new leaf. With a little luck, I will never have to step onto a stage again, I'll live from my writing. Nobly. I won't have to sell myself anymore. The life I aspired to during my times of miserable loneliness is finally mine. Peace. To be preserved at whatever cost. Others are welcome to commotion.

"Madame Valmore?"

"Yes?"

Stocky and of medium height, with a strong jaw and fashionable side-whiskers, Henri de Latouche stands before me.


THE AFTERNOON DOES not last long enough. Four years have passed since our last conversation. I have lost Marie-Eugène, and he no longer has his son, Léonce. Darkness is gathering at the church of Saint-Germain-des-Prés. We are struggling to part ways, while people pass around us invisibly. He is going toward the rue des Saints-Pères, where he has lived since separating from his wife. I am bound in the opposite direction, toward the Hôtel du Paon to find Prosper and his mother. Stunned, dazzled, I take issue with my beating heart. Something has happened, I feel it palpably. I don't understand. Another world, never imagined, has allowed itself to be glimpsed. In all its horror and fascination. Shutting my eyes, I start to say the first thing that passes through my mind.

"My grandmother often said that April was the month of madmen, that people born in that month—"

"Good-bye. Take care," Henri interrupts me gently.

Turning his back on me, he rapidly disappears.

"Otherwise I would have kissed you," he later confessed to me.

I am troubled, intrigued. A disruption in my daily life. A daily life that, as I thought, contented me. Perhaps I deluded myself. Would it not be dangerous to see this man again? I have a great deal to lose. And to win? I don't like gambling. Though he does, unmistakably. He is so elegant. I am ashamed of my rags. From now on, I'll make sure to dress more carefully. In the bottom of a trunk somewhere I have a cashmere turban and an ermine-trimmed wrap. I walk toward the rue du Paon-Saint-Germain with a light step, despite being five months along in my pregnancy. No, I won't give in to a vulgar adulterer.

I have just declared war on myself.

OVER TIME, OUR meetings no longer come about by chance. A hidden logic directs us. Our love is in motion. I try to brake my fall as much as possible, but I can feel myself inexorably pulled toward him, falling pleasurably, painfully toward this other place whose breath I have felt. At first, without ever arranging a rendezvous, we meet as though naturally at Constant's studio. We speak for hours. My uncle is delighted by our budding friendship, which he heartily encourages.

"Go take a walk around," he urges us. "Only hermits of my stripe take pleasure in sticking to their caves. How many years has it been since I looked at the river . . ."

Through the streets of the capital we walk side by side. The city hides us. We never meet anyone we know. Our feet always take us toward the Seine. Almost despite ourselves, we always cross to the île Saint-Louis, the buttressed side of

Notre-Dame, the weeping willow that reaches down into a hidden hollow. There we push off from shore to glide along on a current of words, drifting far from everything. Released. At day's end, we are still standing on the pont de la Tournelle, with time suspended over our conversational silences. It is not the real world, we well know, it is an unreal place, though perfectly present, a place filled with the wonderful discovery of the other, one that cannot stay a haven long, though we make every effort to preserve it. It is there that Henri takes my hand for the first time and there that I hurriedly snatch it away. It is also there that he takes hold of it a second time a few minutes later. I don't move.

THERE ARE IN me, as it were, two women who understand each other very well. The first matter-of-factly ties a little apron around her swollen belly every day, shells peas, washes laundry, smiles sweetly to her husband, her mother-in-law, and at night slips delightedly into the conjugal bed. The second unties everything, apron, dress, petticoat, sets herself free in the afternoon from a routine that weighs on her, despite what she may say, to live dangerously and at full speed, in the urgency of her need to cast off lies. I discover with astonishment how much this splitting in two fulfills me. My two lives seem to complete each other, the first tempering the second, the second giving direction to the first. Two lives have been granted me, what riches! But I will sooner or later have to betray Prosper, and the very idea revolts me. I am not made that way. I believe sincerely in the commitment I have made to him and dread hurting him, for which I will only feel contempt for myself. The flesh is not what worries me, because the flesh is not what draws me to Latouche. The threat is much greater. But what exactly is it? I wouldn't put my marriage in danger, Valmore's trust in me, his love, for a simple sexual encounter. For what then? For the thrill of running away in the afternoon from old age and death, my feet barely held to the ground, feverish and resolute. Henri's eyes shoot daggers at me, his grip has not yet closed around me. There are many stabbing words and sentences between us, while there are others that hold their peace and bide their time. It is not yet too late. I have little to reproach myself. Latouche has only held my hand. But the alarm has sounded. Henri inhabits me already, soon he will possess me entirely. Time, hanging in suspension, will fall to earth and shatter. The moment I take my leave of Latouche, reality assails me. Reason recovers some of its lost ground. It is pure suicide. A monstrous mistake. Henri has nothing to offer me in any case. How can I play with fire this way? I don't know, don't understand. Of the two women that I am, which will win out?

I AM GOING to give birth. Nature seems to have made the decision for me. Drawing on an unassailable argument, I impose a pact of renunciation on Henri.

"What is more beautiful than a love that abstains?" I say without conviction.

In any case, we have no choice.

I am forced by exhaustion to take to my bed long weeks before my confinement. Truly irksome. Not to see Latouche, not to talk to him. Stuck in our cramped lodgings in the rue du Paon-Saint-Germain with my mother-in-law as a bedside sitter, I kill time by writing poems and stories about the Antilles. "Beware of your great facility for writing, which sometimes bloats your poems. You overdo it, as though you were trying at all costs to show that you are a good student." I miss Henri's advice, just as I miss his disjunct eyes. Unable to stand it any longer, I take literature as a pretext to have him come to me.

"Would you have any objection to a visit from Monsieur de Latouche one of these days?" I ask Prosper. "He is a friend of Constant's and has been very helpful to me . . . Besides, you may get a chance to act in one of his plays. You'll like him, I'm sure of it."

I am entirely unscrupulous. Seeing Henri takes precedence over everything else. "Come as a friend," I write him. Impossible to do otherwise. In my imagination he will stand there, by my bed, over my enormous stomach, making small talk with Prosper and Anne-Justine. All the things we have to say to each other will remain unsaid. Prosper will make an effort to appear up to the discussion. But Henri will be tactful with him. Perhaps he will even feel a pang at seeing my husband's superb figure, his perfect face. He will then most likely come to doubt his own power over me. There is a chance, all things considered, that the two men will feel a kind of rivalry. And in my bed, a supine queen, I will direct the joust.

I blush at my cruelty.


HENRI PLAYS HIS part to perfection and then withdraws, discreet, calculating. On the point of giving birth, my wolfish instinct draws me back sensibly toward the father of my child. It is to Valmore that I owe being a mother. A renewed feeling of tenderness, of gratitude to him, floods through me. My life with him is not unhappy. I sink back into cozy contentment, which my meeting with Latouche jarred. A passing fancy. But I belong to Prosper. An exceptional man, my husband, with unique virtues. Did I lose my mind to tremble in front of a man whose path is strewn with mistresses and failures, a man who sinks each day a little farther into himself? Was I to be his prey, one among many? I let myself be carried away like a little girl. It's high time to take myself in hand. My baby's arrival diminishes the one-eyed man's influence.

I GIVE BIRTH to Hippolyte with my sister Eugénie at my side. In the joy of having a boy, a beautiful, plump, healthy baby, I forget writing for a time and even the very existence of Henri de Latouche. I am crazy about my son, adoring him and the sturdy man who gave him to me. I finally have a child, a child who will live and survive me, I have the sure conviction of it. I balk a little at placing him with a wet nurse. The poor girls often lie, pretend to have enough milk, and three weeks later the child is dead. I know something about it. Eugénie insists that I put Hippolyte in her hands. She knows a woman in Dreux, right next to her house. She will go and visit my son every day and watch over his health closely. Prosper, enjoying respectable success in his first season at the Odéon, is constantly occupied with rehearsals. As he is away most of the time, he urges me to accept Eugénie's proposal. That way I will be able to devote myself more serenely to preparing my next book of verses. The editor is pressing me. I need all my energy. I give my baby to my sister and once more start going to Constant's studio. There is no question of remaining for hours at a time in the company of my mother-in-law.

By returning to the Childeberte, I know what I am walking toward. What kind of assignation, of love story. I feel its keen importance and don't want for it to pass me by, while I stand and watch. Cost what may.

• • •

ALONG WITH POETRY, Henri de Latouche returns to my life. Our conversations, our perambulations resume. Nightfall often finds us on the pont de la Tournelle, the wind drying our lips, which are not yet touching. But time is not standing still, time commands us to return to shore. Inside me is dissension. My two lives are no longer in harmony. Valmore's presence irritates me, seems like an obstacle to the impulse that carries me toward Henri. My husband's adoration, particularly since becoming subliminally aware of my withdrawal, raises my hackles, as does his utter blindness. I am bored of his company. What is happening? I was so happy. Prosper is so good. It would be monstrous to betray him. And for whom? Latouche. He haunts me. I see only him. Everything that is not him exasperates me. I am growing irritable and unpleasant, reproaching Valmore unfairly for every small thing. The hours I spend with Henri seem too short. I am so dependent on him that I live only to see him or read his words. We have started writing each other. Our letters quickly enter a daily rhythm. In writing them, the restraint that I force on myself when only centimeters from Henri's hands dissolves. I give myself entirely in them. Though he shows more modesty, Latouche also reveals himself in his letters. My violence, my power, my beauty, my vices—everything emerges in the pages I address to Henri. My writing changes day by day as a result of my contact with him. My poems reflect it. When *Poésies* appears, Latouche's influence is perceptible. Bolder, less naive, at last free.

THE WEEKS GO by. The two women in me no longer spare each other. Their discord consumes me. I no longer sleep, I experience moments of utter dejection and exaggerated rapture. I am Henri's prisoner, unable to escape. I must break it off, I tell myself over and over, it is the only solution, not to see him, not to hear him, not to write him. Not to live our love story? Give up this splendor, this communion? His love sucks my blood. How can we keep our bodies from joining? So I'll give myself to him, there is no other way! Only then, maybe, can I loosen his hold. Once desire has been satisfied, I will likely recover my reason, my natural caution. But there is Prosper, his gentle face, his tenderness. And here I am preparing to walk in my mother's footsteps. Like a curse long since cast. Yet I had sworn to do the opposite. When will I ever make decisions for myself? Have I measured the repercussions of what I am about to do? To give myself body and soul to Henri means to pass to the other side of things, to know a love that will make love for Valmore impossible, and that will prevent me from turning back, from finding married peace again. The risk is unavoidable. I am dying to do it.

"I will come to you tomorrow at lunch time." I have made my decision. Time for action. Tomorrow I will betray the man who gave me his trust, his respect and esteem. Tomorrow my body, which for three years has belonged only to my husband, will yield to another man's bite. My fingers, accustomed to Prosper's skin, will be clumsy, tentative. Latouche will undress me, see me naked and shy. And tomorrow night I will kiss Valmore as I serve him his supper, another man's smell on my skin.

What tranquillity, now. Every doubt has vanished. I struggled for weeks, months, but now I am sure of myself. I want to live.

There will be tears, and ugly patches.

But tomorrow I will think of nothing but beauty. I'll forget my little dead ones and all my life's bereavements. A short time before lunch, I will check my clothes one last time, my corset, my hair, my breath, mention that I am going to Constant's, and set off, my heart thumping, terrified, running, flying to my rendezvous with Henri, ashamed of myself, proud of myself.

FÉLIX DESBORDES died in 1851.

A year after her marriage in 1852, ONDINE VALMORE gave birth to a boy who lived only three weeks. Tuberculosis carried her off a few months later, as it already had her sister Inès.

CÉCILE DESBORDES passed away in 1854.

Struck by uterine cancer, MARCELINE DESBORDES-VALMORE spent the last two years of her life in bed in her apartment on the rue de Rivoli in Paris. Until her death in 1859, she wrote love poems, which were published posthumously.

PROSPER VALMORE outlived his wife by twenty-two years. With his son Hippolyte, he devoted himself exclusively to the memory of his wife and to her writings.

HIPPOLYTE VALMORE tried to censor several of his mother's unpublished poems as well as her correspondence. The originals have fortunately been found. He never married and died childless in 1892.

ACKNOWLEDGMENTS

AT THE PARIS OPÉRA on that April night in 1827, the bill carried no mention of *La Muette de Portici*. The first performance of Auber's work in fact would have to wait until February 29, 1828. Nor was the Seine visible from the windows of Henri de Latouche's two-room apartment at 69, rue des Saints-Pères, a step or two from the rue de Grenelle, which is to say at the far end of the street from the river . . . Just two examples, picked from a multitude of others. This novel distorts historical reality throughout. The actual life of Marceline Desbordes-Valmore, French woman of letters (b. Douai, 1786; d. Paris, 1859), was likely quite different from the one recounted here. And Marceline Desbordes-Valmore would not have told her story as I have. She would not have told it at all.

Biographers have performed the task for her. From the moment of her death, the presses have poured forth books about her—some of them serious, some entirely crackbrained. The authoritative work on her life was published only in 1987, Francis Ambrière's *Le Siècle des Valmore*. Representing thirty years' labor, it exposed all the previously written inanities for what they were. No strictly biographical study of Desbordes-Valmore could afterward escape being redundant. Fiction was the only alternative.

This novel has its own truth and its own sources. Delving for the Marceline who would become my narrator—in

Ambrière's two-volume work, mentioned above, and many other biographical essays; in the poet's preserved letters; in the streets and institutions of the towns where she lived; in her poetry and fiction, to which I returned many times—I was able to find only the warp of the tapestry. The weft would come from my own back pages. After months of research, I realized that I was drawing away from Marceline and closer to myself: to the self I might have been had I been her. I was ready to start weaving.

SELECTED POEMS BY
Marceline Desbordes-Valmore

TRANSLATED BY LOUIS SIMPSON
WITH WILLARD WOOD

ELEGY

You who took back everything,
Even the pleasure of waiting,
You left me all the same
Food for a tender heart:
Love! and memory, that keeps love
Living, and the past at hand,
Almost like having you back!
In memory you hear me, in memory
I worship you. There once more
I show myself unproudly.
My life is in that dream
Where you never turn from me.
Your voice is there: your own beloved voice!
In memory I can commiserate.
So many wounds and blasted glories
Marked your heart, always more generous
To others than to me.
I've heard you groan, I wept with you.

Who will feel sympathy for you,
In your seclusion,
When the news of my death
Intrudes? You'll wake to find
A milling crowd, the friends of an hour
Dispersing. Gone the kindred soul

## ÉLÉGIE

Toi qui m'as tout repris jusqu'au bonheur d'attendre,
Tu m'as laissé pourtant l'aliment d'un cœur tendre,
L'amour! et ma mémoire où se nourrit l'amour:
Je lui dois le passé; c'est presque ton retour!
C'est là que tu m'entends, c'est là que je t'adore;
C'est là que sans fierté je me révèle encore.
Ma vie est dans ce rêve où tu ne fuis jamais:
Il a ta voix; ta voix! tu sais si je l'aimais!
C'est là que je te plains; car plus d'une blessure,
Plus d'une gloire éteinte a troublé, j'en suis sûre,
Ton cœur si généreux pour d'autres que pour moi:
Je t'ai senti gémir; je pleurais avec toi!

Qui donc saura te plaindre au fond de ta retraite,
Quand le cri de ma mort ira frapper ton sein?
Tu t'éveilleras seul dans la foule distraite,
Où des amis d'un jour s'entr'égare l'essaim;
Tu n'y sentiras plus une âme palpitante
Au bruit de tes malheurs, de tes moindres revers;
Ta vie, après ma mort, sera moins éclatante;
Une part de toi-même aura fui l'univers.
Il est doux d'être aimé! Cette croyance intime
Donne à tout on ne sait quel air d'enchantement;
L'infidèle est content des pleurs de sa victime;
Et, fier, aux pieds d'une autre il en est plus charmant.

That pulsed at your hurts. Your life,
After my death,
Will be dimmer. Part of you
Will have left the whole.
How nice to be loved!
The intimate awareness of it
Casts a bright, embracing beam;
The faithless lover,
Happy at provoking tears,
Hot with the pride of it, pursues
All the more winningly
Another's heart.

Have you said as much? Yes, cruel one, yes.
All is forgiven, be happy, all is well.
The gods put you on earth
To make me feel
But gave me in return
No charms. And so I fly
Your feasts
Where you forge vows
Like wedges between us.
Distance! Sorry blessing,
But it drops a curtain over
Your conquests,
Muffles the shrilled names of
Your changing flames. I know them all!
Who turned my vows to ashes!
At least I am no longer choked
With uncertainty.
We'll die apart, it's what you want!

L'as-tu dit? . . . Oui, cruel, oui, je crois tout possible;
Je te pardonne tout, sois heureux, tout est bien:
Le ciel qui t'avait fait pour me rendre sensible,
Oublia que pour plaire il ne me donnait rien.
Et je fuis; je t'échappe au milieu de tes fêtes,
   Où tant de vœux ont divisé nos pas!
   L'éloignement, triste bienfait, hélas!
   Semble un rideau jeté sur tes conquêtes.
Je n'entends plus ces déchirantes voix,
Qui vont chercher des pleurs jusques au fond des âmes;
Ces mots inachevés, qui m'ont dit tant de fois
   Les noms changeants de tes errantes flammes:
   Je les sais tous! ils ont brisé mes vœux;
Mais je n'étouffe plus dans mon incertitude:
Nous mourrons désunis, n'est-ce pas? tu le veux!
Pour t'oublier, viens voir! . . . qu'ai-je dit? Vaine étude,
Où la nature apprend à surmonter ses cris:
Pour déguiser mon cœur, que m'avez-vous appris?
La vérité s'élance à mes lèvres sincères;
Sincère, elle t'appelle, et tu ne l'entends pas!
Ah! sans t'avoir troublé qu'elle meure tout bas!
Je ne sais point m'armer de froideurs mensongères;
Je sais fuir; en fuyant on cache sa douleur,
   Et la fatigue endort jusqu'au malheur.
Oui, plus que toi l'absence est douce aux cœurs fidèles:
Du temps qui nous effeuille elle amortit les ailes;
Son voile a protégé l'ingrat qu'on veut chérir:
On ose aimer encore; on ne veut plus mourir.

So to forget you . . . No, I'll never learn
To still my heart. You taught me well,
And now truth springs
To my lips. Truth calls to you,
But you don't hear.
Then let it die away, let it
Leave you undisturbed.
I've never mastered
Feigned frigidity.
What I know is
To flee. In flight
You hide your suffering,
Weary even your grief.

Sweeter to the true heart
Even than you
Is absence,
Which blunts Time,
Protects the ingrate that we dote on.
Absence makes love possible,
Life even.

## If He Had Known

If he had known what soul he hurt,
Heart's tears, if he had seen you,
Ah! If that swollen heart
Could still have managed utterance
He'd not have changed as he did,
Proud of arousing the hope he dashed,
To so much love he'd not have been unfeeling,
      If he had known.

If he had known all one can expect
Of a simple soul, burning and direct,
He'd have wanted mine, inspired by his,
To understand him. He'd have known love.
I kept my eyes lowered, veiling the flame.
Did he read nothing in my shyness?
A secret worth his soul,
      If he had known.

If I myself had known the power
One submits to looking in his eyes,
Blithely, as though taking in the air one breathes,
I would have passed my days under other skies.
It is too late to start my life again,
My life that was a sweet hope overthrown.
Would you not say, you who took it from me,
      If I had known!

## S'IL L'AVAIT SU

S'il avait su quelle âme il a blessée,
Larmes du cœur, s'il avait pu vous voir,
Ah! si ce cœur, trop plein de sa pensée,
De l'exprimer eût gardé le pouvoir,
Changer ainsi n'eût pas été possible;
Fier de nourrir l'espoir qu'il a déçu:
A tant d'amour il eût été sensible,
      S'il avait su.

S'il avait su tout ce qu'on peut attendre
D'une âme simple, ardente et sans détour,
Il eût voulu la mienne pour l'entendre,
Comme il l'inspire, il eût connu l'amour.
Mes yeux baissés recelaient cette flamme;
Dans leur pudeur n'a-t-il rien aperçu?
Un tel secret valait toute son âme,
      S'il l'avait su.

Si j'avais su, moi-même, à quel empire
On s'abandonne en regardant ses yeux,
Sans le chercher comme l'air qu'on respire,
J'aurais porté mes jours sous d'autres cieux.
Il est trop tard pour renouer ma vie,
Ma vie était un doux espoir déçu.
Diras-tu pas, toi qui me l'as ravie,
      Si j'avais su!

## No Longer

What made me so angry I no longer know
He spoke . . . and his offenses all vanished.
His eyes pleaded, his mouth wished to please.
Where did you go, my timid anger?
      I no longer know.

I no longer want to look at what I love.
The moment he smiles all my tears are gone.
In vain, by force or sweetness,
Love and he would have me love again.
      I no longer want to.

I can no longer flee him now he is gone,
All my sworn vows have become superfluous.
Without betraying myself I braved his presence.
But, without dying, to support his absence,
      I no longer know how!

## JE NE SAIS PLUS, JE NE VEUX PLUS

Je ne sais plus d'où naissait ma colère;
Il a parlé . . . ses torts sont disparus;
Ses yeux priaient, sa bouche voulait plaire:
Où fuyais-tu, ma timide colère?
        Je ne sais plus.

Je ne veux plus regarder ce que j'aime;
Dès qu'il sourit tous mes pleurs sont perdus;
En vain, par force ou par douceur suprême,
L'amour et lui veulent encor que j'aime;
        Je ne veux plus.

Je ne sais plus le fuir en son absence,
Tous mes serments alors sont superflus.
Sans me trahir, j'ai bravé sa présence;
Mais sans mourir supporter son absence,
        Je ne sais plus!

## The Last Rendezvous

My only love, kiss me.
If death takes me first,
Blessing on God, for you have loved me!
Our tryst had few moments,
As flowers have only one spring,
And the rose dies fragrant.
But when you come to visit me, dear,
Coffined beneath your feet,
Are you afraid I will not hear?

I shall hear you, my love!
Sad in my last resting place
Only if you lose courage.
Then at night, without a summons,
I'll go to you and scold you gently,
Saying, "God forgives us!"
And in a soft voice from beyond, dear,
I shall paint the heavens for you:
Are you afraid you will not hear?

I shall go alone, on leaving your sight,
To await you at the gates of heaven,
And pray for your deliverance.
Oh! even if I must wait a long time

## LE DERNIER RENDEZ-VOUS

Mon seul amour! embrasse-moi.
Si la mort me veut avant toi,
Je bénis Dieu; tu m'as aimée!
Ce doux hymen eut peu d'instants:
Tu vois; les fleurs n'ont qu'un printemps,
Et la rose meurt embaumée.
Mais quand, sous tes pieds renfermée,
Tu viendras me parler tout bas,
Crains-tu que je n'entende pas?

Je t'entendrai, mon seul amour!
Triste dans mon dernier séjour,
Si le courage t'abandonne;
Et la nuit, sans te commander,
J'irai doucement te gronder,
Puis te dire: "Dieu nous pardonne!"
Et, d'une voix que le ciel donne,
Je te peindrai les cieux tout bas:
Crains-tu de ne m'entendre pas?

J'irai seule, en quittant tes yeux,
T'attendre à la porte des Cieux,
Et prier pour ta délivrance.
Oh! dussé-je y rester longtemps,

I want to eke out my moments
Easing some part of your suffering.
And one day, bearing Hope, sweet one,
I'll arrive to lead you along the path;
Are you afraid that I won't come?

I'll come, because you must die
Still unwearied of loving me.
Like faithful turtledoves
Separated by dark days
We'll join our wings together
And climb to a place beyond time!
There our hours will be ever renewed.
After God quietly promised us that
How could I not hold him to it?

Je veux y couler mes instants
A t'adoucir quelque souffrance;
Puis un jour, avec l'Espérance,
Je viendrai délier tes pas;
Crains-tu que je ne vienne pas?

Je viendrai, car tu dois mourir,
Sans être las de me chérir;
Et comme deux ramiers fidèles,
Séparés par de sombres jours,
Pour monter où l'on vit toujours,
Nous entrelacerons nos ailes!
Là, nos heures sont éternelles:
Quand Dieu nous l'a promis tout bas,
Crois-tu que je n'écoutais pas?

## APART

Do not write. I am sad, and want my lights put out.
Summers in your absence are as dark as a room.
I have closed my arms again. They must do without.
To knock at my heart is like knocking at a tomb.
       Do not write!

Do not write. Let us learn to die as best we may.
Did I love you? Ask God. Ask yourself. Do you know?
To hear that you love me when you are far away,
Is like hearing from heaven and never to go.
       Do not write!

Do not write. I fear you. I fear to remember,
For memory holds the voice I have often heard.
To the one who cannot drink, do not show water,
The beloved one's picture in the handwritten word.
       Do not write!

Do not write those gentle words that I dare not see,
It seems that your voice is spreading them on my heart,
Across your smile, on fire, they appear to me,
It seems that a kiss is printing them on my heart.
       Do not write!

## LES SÉPARÉS

N'écris pas. Je suis triste, et je voudrais m'éteindre.
Les beaux étés sans toi, c'est la nuit sans flambeau.
J'ai refermé mes bras qui ne peuvent t'atteindre,
Et frapper à mon cœur, c'est frapper au tombeau.
      N'écris pas!

N'écris pas. N'apprenons qu'à mourir à nous-mêmes.
Ne demande qu'à Dieu . . . qu'à toi, si je t'aimais!
Au fond de ton absence écouter que tu m'aimes,
C'est entendre le ciel sans y monter jamais.
      N'écris pas!

N'écris pas. Je te crains; j'ai peur de ma mémoire;
Elle a gardé ta voix qui m'appelle souvent.
Ne montre pas l'eau vive à qui ne peut la boire.
Une chère écriture est un portrait vivant.
      N'écris pas!

N'écris pas ces doux mots que je n'ose plus lire:
Il semble que ta voix les répand sur mon cœur;
Que je les vois brûler à travers ton sourire;
Il semble qu'un baiser les empreint sur mon cœur.
      N'écris pas!

## WAITING

When I can't see you time is unbearable,
A weight somehow too great to lift.
My heart is sluggish and wants to leave me,
My head droops, I suffer and I cry.

When your strong voice enters my mind,
I shudder, I listen . . . and I hope,
As if God touched a wilting reed,
And I . . . all of me cries out, "God, make him come!"

When my mind turns to your engaging features
All my traits are stamped with fear and happiness.
My hair feels cold, my life oppressive,
And your name suddenly escapes from my heart.

Then when it is finally you! when my waiting is over,
Trembling, I run away, holding out my arms.
I dare not speak to you and I'm afraid to listen,
But you, seeking my soul, alone will obtain it!

Am I a sister, your wish at long last granted?
Are you the shadow promised to my fearful steps?
But I am trembling. I your sister. What an idea!
You, my brother! . . . Oh terror! Say that you are not!

## L'ATTENTE

Quand je ne te vois pas, le temps m'accable, et l'heure
A je ne sais quel poids impossible à porter:
Je sens languir mon cœur, qui cherche à me quitter;
Et ma tête se penche, et je souffre et je pleure.

Quand ta voix saisissante atteint mon souvenir,
Je tressaille, j'écoute ... et j'espère immobile;
Et l'on dirait que Dieu touche un roseau débile;
Et moi, tout moi répond: Dieu! faites-le venir!

Quand sur tes traits charmants j'arrête ma pensée,
Tous mes traits sont empreints de crainte et de bonheur;
J'ai froid dans mes cheveux; ma vie est oppressée,
Et ton nom, tout à coup, s'échappe de mon cœur.

Quand c'est toi-même, enfin! quand j'ai cessé d'attendre,
Tremblante, je me sauve en te tendant les bras;
Je n'ose te parler, et j'ai peur de t'entendre;
Mais tu cherches mon âme, et toi seul l'obtiendras!

Suis-je une sœur tardive à tes vœux accordée?
Es-tu l'ombre promise à mes timides pas?
Mais je me sens frémir. Moi, ta sœur! quelle idée!
Toi, mon frère! ... ô terreur! Dis que tu ne l'es pas!

## Are You Asleep?

Are you asleep on this beautiful night?
The water reaching in and moving away,
As when I offer you my rebel heart?
Are you asleep, my life, dreaming of me?

Are you untangling in your troubled heart
The sweet secrets that burn between us?
The long secrets that love appoints us,
Are you breaking them, in dream at my knee?

Have you joined your vibrant voice
To the chorus shaking the flowers?
No! It's just night's tuneless hum,
And my eyes will glisten for hours!

However painful, you must keep command
Over this love that threatens to betray us,
But also keep its hurt, that has me like a hand:
The hurt is sweet, though it will slay us!

## DORS-TU?

Et toi! dors-tu quand la nuit est si belle,
Quand l'eau me cherche et me fuit comme toi;
Quand je te donne un cœur longtemps rebelle?
Dors-tu, ma vie! ou rêves-tu de moi?

Démêles-tu, dans ton âme confuse,
Les doux secrets qui brûlent entre nous?
Ces longs secrets dont l'amour nous accuse,
Viens-tu les rompre en songe à mes genoux?

As-tu livré ta voix tendre et hardie
Aux fraîches voix qui font trembler les fleurs?
Non! c'est du soir la vague mélodie;
Ton souffle encor n'a pas séché mes pleurs!

Garde toujours ce douloureux empire
Sur notre amour qui cherche à nous trahir:
Mais garde aussi son mal dont je soupire;
Son mal est doux, bien qu'il fasse mourir!

## The Sincere Woman

*Ah! Finally I see you,*
*At last I hear the voice that I love best.*
*Why must I spend my days so far from you?*
*When I need you so much to blot out all the rest!*

— VICTOR HUGO

Do you want to buy it?
My heart is on the block.
Do you want to buy it,
Without further talk?

God made it of lodestone,
You will make it tender.
God made it of lodestone
For an only lover!

I've set the price.
Would you like to hear?
I've set the price,
Not terribly dear.

Is your heart all your own?
Give it! And truly I'll be thine.
Is your heart all your own
To pay for mine?

## La sincère

*Ah! c'est vous que je vois*
*Enfin! Et cette voix qui parle est votre voix!*
*Pourquoi le sort mit-il mes jours si loin des vôtres?*
*J'ai tant besoin de vous pour oublier les autres!*

—VICTOR HUGO

Veux-tu l'acheter?
Mon cœur est à vendre.
Veux-tu l'acheter,
Sans nous disputer?

Dieu l'a fait d'aimant;
Tu le feras tendre;
Dieu l'a fait d'aimant
Pour un seul amant!

Moi, j'en fais le prix;
Veux-tu le connaître?
Moi, j'en fais le prix;
N'en sois pas surpris.

As-tu tout le tien?
Donne! et sois mon maître.
As-tu tout le tien,
Pour payer le mien?

If it is yours no longer,
I want just one thing.
If it is yours no longer,
Let the bells ring.

Mine will be sliding,
Closed up in a wad.
Mine will be sliding,
Meant for none but God.

For, as our loves go
Life goes by fast.
For, as our loves go
Life is soon past.

The soul has to run
Like water under the sky.
The soul has to run:
To love! and then to die!

S'il n'est plus à toi,
Je n'ai qu'une envie;
S'il n'est plus à toi,
Tout est dit pour moi.

Le mien glissera,
Fermé dans la vie;
Le mien glissera,
Et Dieu seul l'aura!

Car, pour nos amours,
La vie est rapide;
Car, pour nos amours,
Elle a peu de jours.

L'âme doit courir
Comme une eau limpide;
L'âme doit courir,
Aimer! et mourir.

## Go in Peace

Go in peace, dear torment,
You have alarmed me enough,
Moved me enough, charmed me enough.
Go far away, my torment,
Alas! my invisible lodestone!

Your name alone will suffice
To keep me enslaved.
It is wrapped around my life
Like a burning bond.
In your absence your name will suffice.

Ah! I believe that unwittingly
I made a mess on earth,
And you, my unintended judge,
Came to me, then,
As an unwitting punishment?

First it was music and fire,
Children's laughter, dreams.
Then tears came,
And fear, the fiery nights . . .
Good-bye dances, music, and play!

## ALLEZ EN PAIX

Allez en paix, mon cher tourment,
Vous m'avez assez alarmée,
Assez émue, assez charmée . . .
Allez au loin, mon cher tourment,
Hélas! mon invisible aimant!

Votre nom seul suffira bien
Pour me retenir asservie;
Il est alentour de ma vie
Roulé comme un ardent lien:
Ce nom vous remplacera bien.

Ah! je crois que sans le savoir
J'ai fait un malheur sur la terre;
Et vous, mon juge involontaire,
Vous êtes donc venu me voir
Pour me punir, sans le savoir?

D'abord ce fut musique et feu,
Rires d'enfants, danses rêvées;
Puis les larmes sont arrivées
Avec les peurs, les nuits de feu . . .
Adieu danses, musique et jeu!

Make your escape along the fine road
Where the happy swallow flies,
The bird of amorous poetry.
So as not to lose it along the way
Leave your hand off from my heart.

Into your whispered prayer
At night let my tears enter,
Powerless to harm you.
In conversation, never speak of them,
But before God remember.

JUNE 6, 1857

Sauvez-vous par le beau chemin
Où plane l'hirondelle heureuse:
C'est la poésie amoureuse:
Pour ne pas la perdre en chemin
De mon cœur ôtez votre main.

Dans votre prière tout bas,
Le soir, laissez entrer mes larmes;
Contre vous elles n'ont point d'armes.
Dans vos discours n'en parlez pas!
Devant Dieu pensez-y tout bas.

6 JUIN 1857

## The Roses of Saadi

I wanted to bring you roses this morning.
There were so many I wanted to bring,
The knots at my waist could not hold so many.

The knots burst. All the roses took wing,
The air was filled with roses flying,
Carried by the wind into the sea.

The waves were red, as though they were burning.
My dress still has the scent of the morning,
Remembering roses. Smell them on me.

## LES ROSES DE SAADI

J'ai voulu ce matin te rapporter des roses;
Mais j'en avais tant pris dans mes ceintures closes
Que les nœuds trop serrés n'ont pu les contenir.

Les nœuds ont éclaté. Les roses envolées
Dans le vent, à la mer s'en sont toutes allées.
Elles ont suivi l'eau pour ne plus revenir.

La vague en a paru rouge et comme enflammée.
Ce soir, ma robe encore en est tout embaumée ...
Respires-en sur moi l'odorant souvenir.

## Intermittent Dream of a Sad Night

Land of our fathers where at eventide
Across the fields like waves young women glide!

Where fresh pasture and a limpid spring
Make the goat bound and the lake reeds sing!

O native land, my soul is greatly moved
To hear your name that I have always loved;

My soul without an effort turns to song,
Also weeping, for my love is strong!

Love was my life, so I was often sad,
But love was mingled with the grief I had;

That is why I have longed for death in vain,
And though it be suffering, I love again.

My cradle, enchanted hillside where I ranged,
Whose velvety dress I often disarranged,

That is why, toward your distant sky,
Skimming the golden waves of grain I fly.

## Rêve intermittent d'une nuit triste

Ô champs paternels hérissés de charmilles
Où glissent le soir des flots de jeunes filles!

Ô frais pâturage où de limpides eaux
Font bondir la chèvre et chanter les roseaux!

Ô terre natale! à votre nom que j'aime,
Mon âme s'en va toute hors d'elle-même;

Mon âme se prend à chanter sans effort;
À pleurer aussi, tant mon amour est fort!

J'ai vécu d'aimer, j'ai donc vécu de larmes;
Et voilà pourquoi mes pleurs eurent leurs charmes;

Voilà, mon pays, n'en ayant pu mourir,
Pourquoi j'aime encore au risque de souffrir;

· Voilà, mon berceau, ma colline enchantée
Dont j'ai tant foulé la robe veloutée,

Pourquoi je m'envole à vos bleus horizons,
Rasant les flots d'or des pliantes moissons.

The cow is lowing on the slope. She has
Fragrant moss to eat, and so much grass,

And follows with a moist, caressing eye,
Calling him to rest, the passerby.

Shepherds whose sheep have wandered from the fold
Will nowhere find such springs as your fields hold.

An infant when I crawled there, pale and weak,
The air breathed from your woods reddened my cheek.

The sunburned laborers would set me down
Among the new corn that my breath fed on.

Albertine, sister of butterflies, also
Pursued the flowers that grew in the same row.

For liberty is laughing in the field
As in the sky, with neither sword nor shield,

Without fear, sternness, or audacity,
Saying, "I am liberty, love me!

"I am the pardon that makes anger disappear,
I give man a voice that is just and clear.

"I am the cross exhaling a great breath:
'Father, they are slaying me, I have faith!'

"The hangman grasps me. I love him! And the more
For he is my brother, father whom I adore!

La vache mugit sur votre pente douce,
Tant elle a d'herbage et d'odorante mousse,

Et comme au repos appelant le passant,
Le suit d'un regard humide et caressant.

Jamais les bergers pour leurs brebis errantes
N'ont trouvé tant d'eau qu'à vos sources courantes.

J'y rampai débile en mes plus jeunes mois,
Et je devins rose au souffle de vos bois.

Les bruns laboureurs m'asseyaient dans la plaine
Où les blés nouveaux nourrissaient mon haleine.

Albertine aussi, sœur des blancs papillons,
Poursuivait les fleurs dans les mêmes sillons;

Car la liberté toute riante et mûre
Est là, comme aux cieux, sans glaive, sans armure,

Sans peur, sans audace et sans austérité,
Disant: "Aimez-moi, je suis la liberté!

"Je suis le pardon qui dissout la colère,
Et je donne à l'homme une voix juste et claire.

"Je suis le grand souffle exhalé sur la croix
Où j'ai dit: 'Mon père! on m'immole, et je crois!'

"Le bourreau m'étreint: je l'aime! et l'aime encore,
Car il est mon frère, ô père que j'adore!

"My blind brother, who throws himself on me,
Whom my love will bring back to your mercy."

O absent fatherland! My fertile country
Where fervent dreams took form and stayed;

Old walnut trees, true masters of the land,
Shading so well our fathers' resting places;

My father's voice that echoed when he sang:
"Hope" and "Hope" and "Hope" again it rang,

The song of men who burned with piety
And yearned to sow the cross beneath our sky,

And many steeples filled with resonant bronze
That still recalls them in its carillons . . .

I am sending you my child, the quick and fair,
Who laughs when wind is playing in her hair.

Of all the children you have fed at breast
This one is more enchanting than the rest.

An old man said once, looking in her eyes,
"Her mother must have dreamed her in the skies!"

And often as I lifted her I thought,
My hands beneath her arms, I felt wings sprout!

This fruit of my soul that so gently grew,
If I must yield her it is only to you.

"Mon frère aveuglé qui s'est jeté sur moi,
Et que mon amour ramènera vers toi!"

Ô patrie absente! ô fécondes campagnes,
Où vinrent s'asseoir les ferventes Espagnes!

Antiques noyers, vrais maîtres de ces lieux,
Qui versez tant d'ombre où dorment nos aïeux!

Échos tout vibrants de la voix de mon père
Qui chantait pour tous: "Espère! espère! espère!"

Ce chant apporté par des soldats pieux
Ardents à planter tant de croix sous nos cieux,

Tant de hauts clochers remplis d'airain sonore
Dont les carillons les rappellent encore:

Je vous enverrai ma vive et blonde enfant
Qui rit quand elle a ses longs cheveux au vent.

Parmi les enfants nés à votre mamelle,
Vous n'en avez pas qui soit si charmant qu'elle!

Un vieillard a dit en regardant ses yeux:
"Il faut que sa mère ait vu ce rêve aux cieux!"

En la soulevant par ses blanches aisselles
J'ai cru bien souvent que j'y sentais des ailes!

Ce fruit de mon âme, à cultiver si doux,
S'il faut le céder, ce ne sera qu'à vous!

With our milk that comes from a holy fountain
Fill the pure heart of this frail undine.

Mine ran sad and dry, but your milk springs
From virgin soil and happy harvestings.

To veil her forehead that a flame rings round
Open your cornflowers, so gaily crowned:

Such little feet do not crush the flowers,
And her innocence has all their colors.

One evening women blessed her, standing by
Water, and my heart gave a deep sigh.

In that young heart, bent upon things to be,
Your name rang, prophetic memory,

And with all my voice I gave an answer
To the fragrance of your wandering air.

Then let her go where nests sing in the sky,
For children know that they are born to fly.

Already her spirit has a taste for silence
And rises up to where the skylarks dance,

And, isolated, swims beneath the azure,
And comes back down, her throat filled with pure air.

May the gray bird's hymn, so high and pious,
Forever make her soul harmonious!

Du lait qui vous vient d'une source divine
Gonflez le cœur pur de cette frêle ondine.

Le lait jaillissant d'un sol vierge et fleuri
Lui paiera le mien qui fut triste et tari.

Pour voiler son front qu'une flamme environne
Ouvrez vos bluets en signe de couronne:

Des pieds si petits n'écrasent pas les fleurs,
Et son innocence a toutes leurs couleurs.

Un soir, près de l'eau, des femmes l'ont bénie,
Et mon cœur profond soupira d'harmonie.

Dans ce cœur penché vers son jeune avenir
Votre nom tinta, prophète souvenir,

Et j'ai répondu de ma voix toute pleine
Au souffle embaumé de votre errante haleine.

Vers vos nids chanteurs laissez-la donc aller;
L'enfant sait déjà qu'ils naissent pour voler.

Déjà son esprit, prenant goût au silence,
Monte où sans appui l'alouette s'élance,

Et s'isole et nage au fond du lac d'azur
Et puis redescend le gosier plein d'air pur.

Que de l'oiseau gris l'hymne haute et pieuse
Rende à tout jamais son âme harmonieuse! . . .

May your clear streams whose music spoke to me
Moisten her throat with pearls of melody!

Before she goes to her bed of fern at night
Let her go running, curious and light,

To the wood where the moon shines on a tree
In a sheet of tears and trembling quietly,

So she may sleep beneath green images
And they will cover all her infant graces.

The depth of those chaste curtains as they stir
Will keep the air around her heart still pure,

And if she does not have, to play with her,
An Albertine, her faithful follower,

She will face the flowers and dance with them,
But never take the flower from the stem,

Thinking that flowers have their mothers too
And know how to cry as children do.

Not stinging her forehead, your bees down there
Will teach her dreamy head to step with care,

For the insect has a muffled cymbal
That makes the caesura in one's musings equal.

So she will go, calm, free, and at peace,
A thread of living water, to happiness,

Que vos ruisseaux clairs, dont les bruits m'ont parlé,
Humectent sa voix d'un long rythme perlé!

Avant de gagner sa couche de fougère,
Laissez-la courir, curieuse et légère,

Au bois où la lune épanche ses lueurs
Dans l'arbre qui tremble inondé de ses pleurs,

Afin qu'en dormant sous vos images vertes
Ses grâces d'enfant en soient toutes couvertes.

Des rideaux mouvants la chaste profondeur
Maintiendra l'air pur alentour de son cœur,

Et, s'il n'est plus là, pour jouer avec elle,
De jeune Albertine à sa trace fidèle,

Vis-à-vis les fleurs qu'un rien fait tressaillir
Elle ira danser, sans jamais les cueillir,

Croyant que les fleurs ont aussi leurs familles
Et savent pleurer comme les jeunes filles.

Sans piquer son front, vos abeilles là-bas
L'instruiront, rêveuse, à mesurer ses pas;

Car l'insecte armé d'une sourde cymbale
Donne à la pensée une césure égale.

Ainsi s'en ira, calme et libre et content,
Ce filet d'eau vive au bonheur qui l'attend;

And the Madonna in the hollow tree
Will see her on the grass with bended knee.

Her sweet weight on my lap, all I would do,
My songs, my kisses, everything spoke of you,

Land of our fathers where at eventide
Across the fields like waves young women glide.

May my daughter climb on your green breast,
Sweet spot in the Universe, and be blessed!

Et d'un chêne creux la Madone oubliée
La regardera dans l'herbe agenouillée.

Quand je la berçais, doux poids de mes genoux,
Mon chant, mes baisers, tout lui parlait de vous,

Ô champs paternels, hérissés de charmilles
Où glissent le soir des flots de jeunes filles.

Que ma fille monte à vos flancs ronds et verts,
Et soyez béni, doux point de l'Univers!